A DREAM OF STONE

AND OTHER GHOST STORIES

Edited by
Díre McCain
&
D M Mitchell

APOPHENIA

A DREAM OF STONE AND OTHER GHOST STORIES
All stories Copyright © 2011 the respective authors. All rights reserved.

This edition published in 2013 by Apophenia

First published in 2011 by Paraphilia Books

ISBN: 978-0615814599

CONTENTS

INTRODUCTION

The haunted world.

By the 19th Century it was commonly believed that science and reason had effectively banished superstition, and done away with the belief in primitive ideas such as magic, witchcraft, vampires, werewolves, and spirits. Yet here we find ourselves in the second decade of the 21st century, where it's become almost impossible to deny the existence of ghosts. Daily, nightly, at the flip of a switch, we're able listen to the voices of people long gone, and watch flickering images of the departed. We can, at will, haunt ourselves with visions of historical battles, massacres, and atrocities.

Their name is legion and they stalk among us. Daily tabloids are replete with pages of phone numbers where, for a fee, we can talk with nameless incubi/succubae. Alternatively, we can venture into the twilight world of the internet, and converse with people who may or may not exist – the technological equivalent of a planchette and Ouija board. Who knows what's really on the other end, fastening onto our insecurities, desires, and fears?

The haunted head.

We should also consider the psychological perspective, the presumption that it's all imaginary.

1

The same could be said about the reality map, filters, and directive coded into the neurons and chemical transmitters that form the human personality, which is developed over time, but somehow regarded as innate or fundamental.

So who or what are these spooks that have taken up lodging in our heads?

Psychoanalysts from Freud onwards have suggested, even obligingly demonstrated, the limited nature of the free will we ascribe to ourselves. How a good deal of identity and behaviour is actually unfinished business, parental complexes, deep seated neuroses, and frustrated desires, how that which is regarded as objective value in the external world is, in fact, a projection and sublimation of internal chaos. Hungry ghosts; our ancestors ride on our bones.

The haunted word.

Words in motion, uprooted from the bedrock of post-enlightenment solidity, the flux of post-certainty and afterwards. Speech without a mouth, thoughts without a head, leading us to questions that have no answers. The possibility that what we feel and think and express may precede not only the acts of feeling, thinking, and expression, but the existence of the subject itself. Perhaps we exist simply because feelings, thought, and expression require a vehicle through which to manifest.

And so we find ourselves here, together, sharing thoughts that are not ours to share – about the world and people and how it all flows into the future and extends into the past, and how there's no real difference between one and the other. The ghosts are always with us, have always been here, and will remain after we're gone.

And the stories; they'll always be here as well.

THE SHADOW ON THE WALL
Matt Leyshon

Charlie watched from behind the counter as an elderly couple in woollen coats, bespectacled and musty looking, quickly hid their thermometer as the waitress approached with their order. He knew amateur ghost hunters when he saw them because the only reason that any new customers came to his coffee shop nowadays was because they thought that it was haunted.

It wasn't haunted of course, Charlie was pretty sure of that. These days he spent all of his time there and he had never seen a ghost. It was a spectre free zone. Nonetheless, tourists still stopped in Leddenton in the hope of being spooked.

Leddenton was a small town in southern England where the buildings preserved their drabness with the stubborn tenacity of the pebbles on Chesil Beach; it was the sort of town that drivers passed through without noticing, a remarkably plain place in which Charlie's coffee shop fitted perfectly.

He observed the waitress remove two teacakes from the grill and then take them to a familiar couple seated near the door. They had ordered in local accents but now they stared absently out of the window in silence, taking occasional sips from their cups of tea. Behind them on the wall in a glass clip frame was a print that recalled the pastoral landscape before the arrival of the train lines and the local brick industry in Leddenton. The man lit a pipe and then, returning his cup to its saucer, began to puff away as he did everyday with Charlie watching unnoticed from the counter, the no smoking sign visible behind him.

Everything in Charlie's coffee shop, aside from the shadow on the wall, was an inoffensive shade of brown. From the window frames, to the table and chairs, and even the handles on the cutlery, everything was brown; not the enchanting shades of an autumnal English wood but the Formica beiges of dated worktops and tawny wood chip wallpaper. The influence of Italian cafes and American chains could not be more remote; here the only choice to be made when ordering a coffee was whether to have one sugar or two. Against these pale tones the shadow was most conspicuous to Charlie in its darkness, and as the years passed it had become even more so.

The shadow was still slowly growing each day, and it made him increasingly afraid. Time failed to bring a comfortable familiarity to their relationship. And yet as the shadow on the wall grew larger he found himself becoming increasingly and inexplicably drawn towards it. It was there like a giant Rorschach inkblot but the only person whose psyche it seemed to disturb was Charlie's.

He turned his attention to a group of children stood outside his shop daring each other to go inside. It made him think of his own childhood...

The shadow had been much smaller then and the current seating area in the coffee shop had been the family living room. Where he stood now by the counter there had been the family's cumbersome transistor radio by the fireplace on a polished table of cheap wood.

Charlie had been a sickly child and his studying had all been done at home. His evenings and holidays were spent reading in what was now the dining area, his books spread across an old wooden desk that tipped to the side when he leaned upon it, and the shadow ever present at the periphery of his vision like a dust mote in his eye.

"Mum, can we move my desk?" Charlie had begged many times.

"Just do your school work, Charlie. The sooner you finish, the sooner you can go upstairs out of my way."

He had never been able to read for long before his eyes would roam and settle upon the shadow. Back then it had been like a little patch of mildew, except he had always known that it was something else. It was so impossibly dark at the centre, yet at the edges it was lighter in colour, blending perfectly with the brown papered walls. He had tried to scrub it off with spit on his sleeve, but the shadow would not shift.

Thinking back, he reckoned he had learned as much from the shadow as he had from his books. Gazing into its abstract gloom he would daydream of vampires and demons, of cosmic lurkers and witch houses. He had willed his wild imaginings into the shadow, perhaps thinking that it would deliver his macabre daydreams to a writer of weird tales in some foreign land and the writer, suddenly assailed by such strange and bleak fantasies, would wonder from where in the cosmos such terrible ideas might have come.

As a boy, Charlie would on occasion pluck up the courage to touch the shadow with his finger and he could recall now that it had felt like raw meat, cold, moist and pliant. It had smelled of wet metal. When he had pressed his index finger into its middle there had been a certain amount of give, as if he were pressing into cold dough. He would then sink his finger in up to the first knuckle before recoiling, shaking with fear.

Charlie had never told his mother about the shadow and he had felt sure that she could not see it, just as the customers seemed oblivious to it now. His mother had cleaned the home obsessively and he had been certain that if she had come across a discoloured patch of wall then she would surely have attempted to scrub it off with soapy water. Nobody had ever mentioned the shadow on the wall, not least of all Charlie.

Although the shadow had scared him then it had also thrilled him and, in a strange way, made him feel special. Of all the people in the world that the mysterious shadow could have appeared to, it had revealed itself to him, upon a wall in his home. And when Charlie had gotten older, he had also gotten braver. By the time he was a teenager he was frequently up to his elbow in shadow. The further his hand sank inside, the lesser the resistance became and his fingertips had wiggled quite freely in an icy void of cold air. Most peculiar was that if Charlie bent his elbow and brought his hand up and back towards his shoulder, his fingers never met with the other side of the wall. He had read in fantastic stories of portals to other worlds, and he had imagined that perhaps this shadow was one such doorway.

One day, when he had been a little older still, he had held his ear against the shadow and heard a peculiar sound of strange sibilance that sounded like dry leaves swirling in gusts of wind. The noise that he had heard became for a time altogether more frightening than the shadow itself. It sounded something like, "Ishakshar"; a word of dread repeated over and over in an otherworldly chant that seemed to never end. In time the sound became clearer and more resembled a voice, a rasping insect utterance. Whenever he was near the shadow he had heard it. Nowadays he could hear the monotonous drone of Ishakshar from wherever he was in the building, hissing like an old record.

Charlie broke from his reminiscences to continue watching the bravest of the children lead the others giggling nervously into his coffee shop. The children sat on a table right beneath the shadow, seemingly quite unaware of its presence and the horrible noises that it emitted. He watched the waitress take their order. The boy who had led them inside tapped a girl on the shoulder as she ordered a cola, and when she jumped the others all laughed.

Charlie thought back to when he had pushed a broom handle right inside the shadow. He had held the head and eased the shaft all the way inside. He had let go and stepped back to observe how the broom head seemed to levitate in the air against the shadow. Then he went into the kitchen. In the doorway he could see that the wall was around six inches thick and so the broom handle should have been protruding out into the kitchen on the other side of the shadow. To Charlie's horror, there had been no sign of it.

He remembered how he had often been tempted as a youngster to force his head into the shadow to see what was on the other side, to dive boldly into its monstrous, pitch exuberance. Why he was so unnaturally drawn to such terrifying thing like a moth seeking the darkness behind a flame, he did not know; but drawn to it he always was.

He felt it now as he observed his customers; the ever present and mysterious pull of the shadow, as irresistible as gravity, as if he were an ocean and the shadow was the moon. He stepped from behind the counter and navigated the tables, he passed the amateur ghost hunters and behind the local regulars, he shimmied past the table of children, and then stood before the shadow on the wall like a reluctant pilgrim.

Ishakshar. Ishakshar. Ishakshar. It sounded like the creaking complaints of a barn door swinging in a storm.

"It's gone cold in here," he heard the girl say.

10

"Don't be stupid. I'm not cold. It's nice and warm in here," replied one of the boys.

"I suddenly felt cold, alright," the girl snapped as she rubbed her shoulders.

"I think I saw a figure beside you actually, it looked like a cloud of mist," said the other boy seriously.

"Really?" said the girl, her eyes wide.

"Got you! Fished in!" laughed the boy.

The shadow was definitely much bigger now, thought Charlie as he stood and scrutinised its form. It reached right up to the ceiling and almost covered the entire wall. In places the surface looked like charcoal whilst in others, especially around the centre, it looked like a soggy sponge soaked in ink. He took a deep breath and reached out to touch it. His hand passed through as if he had prodded a big black soap bubble. He was tempted again to follow his outstretched hand and walk right into the shadow, but he resisted the urge.

Charlie had walked into the shadow once before. He was forty-seven at the time and had been diagnosed with intestinal cancer and was in great pain almost constantly. One night, in a moment of weakness and seeking distraction from his internal agonies, he had given in to the shadow's calling. He had pushed a table against its murky abstraction, mounted the wooden surface, and crawled boldly forwards, head first into the darkness.

Inside there was an imposing and tangible atmosphere that threatened him with an eternity of

11

gloom. It had pressed against his head like a snugly fitted death mask. He had felt as though he were in deep space, cocooned in antimatter, except there were no stars and no luminescent clouds of astral dust. At first he had thought that this awful and cavernous blackness was alive with an organic heart, but then he realised that the beating sound was his own blood coursing through his veins, throbbing at his temples, pounding at his eardrums. Inside it was actually silent; even the word of dread, Ishakshar, was nowhere to be heard.

He had felt around himself and established that he was quite precariously balanced upon a narrow walkway of cold, smooth stone, smooth but for rude annotations, queer marks and scratches upon it. As he felt them he had at first assumed the engravings to be quite random, but as he progressed he established that the marks were grouped into patterns of design that he found himself counting as he made his way forwards.

When he had outstretched his hands either side of the platform he was able to reach the edges. He had trembled at how impossibly thin his support had felt. As he crept forwards he had kept one hand outstretched before him in cautious anticipation of his walkway suddenly reaching an end. His fingers had traced the lines of the mysterious marks and searched for meaning in those awful lines.

Once the shock of his new environment had subsided a little he had become aware that the deep pain in his guts had subsided, and so he had continued crawling on. Deep inside the shadow such absolute blackness had made it impossible for Charlie to calculate in his mind how long he had been crawling for or for how far he had travelled. His knees had not hurt and nor had he been out of breath, and this had indicated to him that he had surely not crawled as far as he perhaps imagined. When he had counted fifty-nine of the marks carved upon the walkway he had become overwhelmed by some odd sense that touching the next one would somehow signify a terrible portent. And so he had stopped his advance into the shadow, turned around, and began the journey back to the coffee shop.

The return journey had had a very different effect upon his physicality. The stabbing pains of cancer began to return deep inside him and he felt as though he were attempting to scramble free from the brink of a giant abyss, like a spider trying to escape the nozzle of a vacuum cleaner. It had made for a difficult journey but Charlie had pushed himself forwards despite the pain, denying the unspeakable force that attempted to pull him back. So great was the effort required that he had considered more than once giving up and staying for eternity inside the bleak forbidding of the shadow, but he had continued on staunchly, and eventually emerged, tired and out of breath, inside the coffee shop.

The table had been moved and so he had dropped weakly to the ground like a baby bird falling from its nest. Thankfully the customers were too polite to turn and stare and carried on with their coffee and cake. Charlie had felt glad that people knew how little he liked a fuss. He recalled noticing how he had thought the customers were all dressed strangely, but he had known no more about fashion then than he did now and he had been more concerned with establishing how long he had been inside the shadow. He had seen through the shop window that it was daylight, and as he had gone inside during the night, he had figured that he must have been inside the shadow for hours at least, even though it had only seemed like minutes.

The lure of the shadow on the wall had not ceased in the years after his passage inside, even though, apart from a brief reprieve in the pain from his stomach, he could think of no good reason to go back in there. But he felt its calling more strongly every day and its darkness sought to tempt him even now as he watched the children trying to frighten each other.

Since venturing inside he had developed a compulsive obsession with going through to the kitchen to check the other side of the wall, to confirm that an endless world of darkness within his coffee shop was simply impossible. Whenever he saw the width of the wall and the untainted wallpaper on the other side, he knew that his voyage into the darkness must have been a dream, a medicated imagining.

With this in mind he moved carefully past the table of children towards the kitchen. One of the boys shrieked, pretending a ghoul had brushed against his arm. Then Charlie drifted silently through the door, like smoke from the old man's pipe escaping through the window, to check the walls again.

HOPE'S END
James Miller

I had received news from my esteemed colleague, Professor Cameron, concerning an archaeological discovery in North Dakota of considerable importance and as I am an expert on Neolithic American cultures, I decided to assist in the excavations. It was the summer and my teaching duties were finished for the year so I thought it might be amenable to drive from Cornell to the site with my lover, Jessica Bray. As an Englishman and an expatriate I was curious to see more of the United States than that afforded by the pleasant confines of my campus town. Stimulated by the prospect of a road trip, I hoped the change of scene might help to revive my relationship with Jessica which, due to the pressures of my research and her own anxieties concerning completion of her thesis on Mayan Harvest rituals, was floundering.

We were three days into our trip. I had purposefully sought to avoid major cities and had taken us on a somewhat circumspect route, cutting through upstate Pennsylvania and into Ohio, traversing the lakes before turning south through Indiana, Illinois and into Iowa. From Iowa, the plan was to take Highway 29 into the Dakotas and the site, approximately one hundred miles north of Fargo. So far I'd been somewhat dismayed by what I'd seen, the American sublime soiled by sloughs of deplorable suburban sprawl, dismal drive-thrus, vulgar Wal-Marts and ghastly retail parks built with the apparent intention of offending any aesthetic sense. Determined to find a more authentic, rustic America I had taken us on ever more obtuse routes, choosing ill-trodden back roads through nameless little hamlets and slumbering burgs. Jessica had grown increasingly sullen, complaining of car sickness and, being a vegetarian, bemoaning the poor quality food found in highway dining areas. Jessica is a rather contrary young lady, a native Californian with an encyclopaedic knowledge of eating disorders and food allergies. Our little jaunt was, alas, beginning to have an effect antithetical to my original hopes and I found myself beginning to question our entire liaison. I was, after all, more than thirty years older than her with a vengeful ex-wife somewhere back in England and enough hang-ups and neurosis of my own to keep the campus psychotherapist amply entertained. The charms of Jessica's youth couldn't hide the fact that she is a rather plain girl and despite her adherence to all sorts of outré diets, rather tubby. It wasn't her weight (about two stone more than she should have been) that I minded, after all, with my scraggy grey mane and saggy gut I'm more a shaggy dog than a silver fox. No, it was her chronically low self-esteem that really bored me, the tedium of having to micro-manage the pangs of doubt that assailed her on a daily basis concerning everything from her research to her appearance.

Anyway, I digress. At present, we were somewhere in west Iowa, driving through a flat terrain of fields neatly divided by perfectly straight roads. The weather had turned very hot and Jessica was paying no attention whatsoever to my disposition on the significance of the grid in the spatial configuration of the American mindset. The point, as I tried to explain, was that the grid eliminated mystery, it removed the possibility of a wrong turn and so, whereas Europe was configured by the mazy twists and turns of a complex history, the remorseless organisation of the American mid-west represented the conquest of reason over space and, in turn, the domination of space over time.

"You're only saying that because we're lost," she chided, her brown eyes scowling at me behind her glasses.

We passed through a melancholy settlement, a forlorn outpost of abandoned silos and warehouses, the gaunt structures stranded in an overgrown field. Off the main road we glimpsed a few small houses – trailers mostly – squat under lush trees. Aside from a single tattered Stars and Stripes and a couple of pick-up trucks pulled up outside one of the shacks, the whole place appeared almost entirely abandoned. I'd been rather charmed by the sight, the nearest one could hope to find – so I said to Jessica – to a ruined castle or medieval fort although she didn't seem particularly taken by the comparison. Of course, there was still the question of the discoveries in Dakota and I'd been thrilled by the pictures sent to me by Professor Cameron of a great hole descending deep into the earth, but in lieu of such a marvel I concluded that we would have to make do with more mundane remnants of the industrial age.

"We're not lost," I chided, reaching over to pat her leg. Much to my surprise, Jessica grabbed my wrist and pressed my hand against her thigh. Due to the hot weather she was only wearing a short skirt (she has a complex about her legs, which she considers fat, although I find them very soft and rather loveable) and no tights. She was looking at me with a most peculiar intensity and so holding fast to my wrist she moved my hand upwards into the nebulous, fuzzy warmth of her crotch.

"What are you doing?" I exclaimed, "I'm driving for heaven's sake!"

"What do you think I'm doing," she countered.

"Well..."

"Pull over goddamit and fuck me."

"Jessica!" I must admit, I was shocked. This was most unlike her. Jessica has always been rather prudish and when it came to putting my "thingy" in her "fu-fu" as she called it, we tended not to talk, doing it in the bedroom, lying down with the lights out.

"Just fuck me you old fart!" she snarled, pulling my hand harder so that my fingers slipped under her panties. She was very wet. Before I knew it, I'd stopped by the side of the road.

"What if someone comes," I protested.

"Who cares?" She hiked up her skirt and clambered on top of me. "We haven't seen another car for ages anyway."

Great heavens! Before I recount the following, I should say that this is most unlike me. I'm a books sort of man, not much of a sexual adventurer, if truth be told. I've never felt very at ease with all that naked shoving and grinding and what not. Naturally, in my time I've had a modest share of rumpy-pumpy although my ex-wife said I was "boring" as a lover and there have been plenty of occasions when the old "thingy" has just not been up to the job, either never really getting started or else shooting far too soon. "Terribly sorry" is a phrase I find myself saying all too often in bed. Sliding into the middle of middle age, I've concluded sex is one of those things best avoided if possible and I had thought that Jessica, with her chubby tummy, plump thighs and boring complex of body related issues might be the perfect partner, undemanding, inexperienced and with generally low expectations

Whatever I'd known before, well, never mind because Jessica and I were at it like a couple of lusty Romans: my cock in her mouth, her lips hungrily licking me up and down and then turning round and jamming her hot fu-fu in my face and I found myself fucking her with my tongue whilst she made the most extraordinary yelping noise and then, somehow (in the car none of this was very easy) we'd turned round again so that I inserted one and then, great heavens, two of my fingers into the mossy nest of her anus whilst she rubbed at her swollen clitoris moaning and writhing and yes, it was true, coming several times and then she was on top, grinding me into her and I could hardly remember the last time I'd ever felt so potent, now taking her from behind, the whole car rocking back and forth, the handbrake sticking awkwardly into my thigh, our bodies slapping together and the most astonishing obscenities uttering forth from our lips, "Do you like it, do you want it, do you like my hard cock, do you like me fucking you, are you wet, you spoilt bitch, do you like it, do you want it?" and she, in response, urging more and harder and begging to be fucked and calling herself a dirty little girl and a wanton slut and before I knew it I was overwhelmed with the most almighty orgasm while she told me to "fill her with come," a request with which it must be said, I duly complied.

I disengaged, out of breath, a cramp in my thigh and my heart going like the clappers. Jessica moaned and tried to straighten her clothing. She gave me a look of languid contentment completely at odds with her habitual demeanour of bitter dissatisfaction.

At that moment, glancing in the rear view mirror, I saw a patrol car parked up a few feet behind us and a Sheriff strolling forward, his wide-brimmed hat pulled low over his face.

"Sweet Jesus," I cried, "It's the police!" frantically zippering myself back up.

Nonchalant, the Sheriff rapped on the window.

"'Scuse me," he said.

I quickly wound it down. "Afternoon officer, how are you? We were, um, we were just discussing the route. I was checking the map."

The Sherriff glanced at me. The map was in the back. He looked at Jessica. "Miss, are you all right? Has this man been bothering you?"

"No, no, I'm fine. Not at all," Jessica garbled.

The Sherriff squinted at us. "I was watching back there and it looked like... well, I just wanted to make sure."

"We're all fine, thanks, don't worry, will that be all?" I said.

"Is this your car, sir?"

"My car? No, I mean yes, I mean no, it's a hire car, it belongs to Hertz."

"May I see your license?"

"Is there a problem officer? There's no problem is there? Officer?"

"License, please."

I fumbled around in my wallet, found my license and passed it over. The Sherriff took it and wandered back to his patrol car. I could see him saying something into his radio.

"Jesus Christ," I snapped at Jessica. "I bloody well knew this was going to happen. This is your fault. What are we going to do now?"

"Oh stop worrying."

"Stop worrying! Stop worrying! I've got my career to think about. I've got tenure! I've got-"

"Just cut it out!"

The Sherriff returned. "I'm sorry sir," he said, leaning over and leering at us both. "I'm going to have to ask you to follow me back to the station."

"The station! What! What are you talking about?"

I gazed at the Sherriff in astonishment. Was there any compassion in his leathery face, something, anything I might be able to appeal to? Alas, I saw nothing. "Officer," I protested, "My name is Professor-"

"I know your name sir, it was on your license."

"No, you don't understand, I have to get to North Dakota..."

"North Dakota? What are you doing here then?"

"The point is – oh look – there is an archaeological discovery of unprecedented importance. An excavation. They need my expertise. I'm an expert, you see..."

"Sir, I'm going to ask you to follow me back to the station. It's only a few miles back that way." The Sherriff nodded, briefly touching his hand to his hat in a half-hearted salute and walked back to his car.

"Jesus! What are we going to do now?"

"Well, we have to do what he says."

"Of course we have to do what he says. Oh bloody hell. I hope you're happy now."

"Don't blame me. It's not my fault!"

"You slutty little slag!"

"Don't call me that, you dirty old man!"

"Oh just listen to us!" I banged the wheel with frustration.

Well, I won't repeat the rest of our predictable and tawdry argument. As the accusations bounced back and forth we followed the Sherriff to the deserted looking town we'd passed through earlier and pulled up outside a modest single storey building, the same one I had noticed before, flying a solitary Stars and Stripes. As we got out, I took a moment to survey the scene. There was nothing, just a few rundown buildings scattered seemingly at random around the road, old shops or what-not, shut-up and abandoned. The sun was remorselessly hot and the air very still. I could smell something too, a dried out, desiccated smell, insect-like close and uncomfortable. I saw that we were being watched from across the road – a couple of figures in a doorway, their narrow silhouettes sun-stretched across the hot macadam. The Sherriff put one callused hand on my arm and ushered me into the station.

"Hey Hank," he called out to another officer – his deputy I assume – sat at a table, feet on the desk.

"Howdy Carl."

"Got another two," said the Sherriff.

"So I see."

"C'mon in folks. This here's a British professor."

"A professor?"

"That's right."

"Well I'll be."

"Take a seat y'all." He gestured at Jessica, who sat down on a plastic chair. I just stood there while these two bumpkin enforcers gawped at me, as if they'd never seen a British professor before. Trying to hold myself aloof from their prurient penetrations, I took a moment to assess my surroundings. The office was a dismal little space with a dirty parquet floor, grubby pot plants wilting in the heat and dead flies stuck to the yellowed glass. There were two desks, both piled high with papers and the wall behind the deputy was covered in faded wanted posters, pictures of rather desperate looking African-Americans and mean-faced red-necks.

"Well now," The Sherriff took off his hat and wiped his forehead. He was quite an old man, I saw, almost as old as me, his neck and forehead creased and worn as if he'd been folded up many times over. He exuded a thick-necked masculine quality, a strong odour of tobacco and musty after-shave. I imagined he liked to drink Bud, watch the game and rail against the Federal government, one of those God-fearing Republican-voting American men I've always found rather repulsive. His deputy was also middle-aged, a lanky, squinty-eyed fellow with a narrow hatchet face and a long hooked nose like some sort of grumpy Witch Hunter.

I realised this state of affairs couldn't continue. The time was at hand. I had to take charge. "Officer," I began, drawing myself up and prepping my voice. A superior English accent can do wonders over here, I've found, triggering some sort of subconscious Pavlovian colonial instinct for deference. "Officer, I am the Randolph C Carter Professor of Ancient American Cultures at Cornell University. My scholarship on primitive North American society is foremost in the field. I'm on the board of numerous academic presses and editor in chief of Neolithicus. I'm a recipient of two Leverhulmes, a Guggenheim fellowship and-"

The Sherriff held up one hand. "I'm arresting you, Professor, for an act of gross public indecency."

I felt as though I had been slapped in the face. "Why – how dare you! Absurd. Preposterous. Good god. How dare you!" Flabbergasted, I felt my face burn and my mouth move up and down in imitation of a floundering fish.

The Sherriff yawned, "Our vehicles are equipped with cameras. I can show you the proof, if you want to see it again."

Words came back. I wasn't going to stand for this. "Outrageous. I demand to call my lawyer." I turned to glare at Jessica. The stupid girl was just sitting there, dumfounded, gobsmacked. Wasn't her father meant to be some sort of hot-shot L.A. lawyer? I reached for my phone. "I won't stand for this." I wasn't sure who I was going to call. The police? Could I claim wrongful arrest? I didn't actually have a lawyer. What to do? Anyway, it was all in vain. No signal. In fact, I remembered Jessica complaining earlier about the lack of reception. The Sherriff and his deputy were looking at me with thinly veiled amusement. I put my phone away.

"Nearest lawyer is all the way in Midtown," said the Sherriff, "and he won't be able to get over here until tomorrow morning."

"It's true," his deputy nodded.

Well, I tell you now, I wasn't going to put up with it any longer. This was quite enough. "Indecent behaviour... How dare you! I don't want some two-bit lawyer. Outrageous. How dare you! I'm outraged! Who the hell do you think you are?"

"It's the law, sir-"

My blood was boiling. "The law? The law? Who the hell are you to tell me about the law?" I can't really bare to describe what happened next. My voice rose in pitch and tone and I think I said "bloody hell" quite a number of times. I remember instructing Jessica to go back to the car and told her and the Sherriff that we were leaving. Apparently this wasn't allowed because the next thing I knew the Sherriff and his deputy had seized me and manhandled me into a small room. They slammed the door in my face and turned the key. Great Scot! One minute I'd been driving peaceably through the American countryside, preoccupied with whether Professor Cameron's discoveries would support or invalidate my famous Delaware Hypothesis concerning tool use among Neolithic Amerindians and now I was in a cell. A police cell for criminals! I wouldn't stand for it. I continued to bang on the door, shouting about my rights and other such things. Indeed, I believe I may have recited a large part of Jefferson's declaration, not to mention a good chunk of Rousseau and possibly even some Voltaire for good measure, not that these cretinous enforcement agents took any notice. Eventually, I calmed down. Whilst it was true that Jessica and had been caught en flagrante I was fairly sure the Sherriff's methods were somewhat cack-handed and once I got a good lawyer on the case I'd be out of here with an apology to boot. No, my real concern was the damage to my reputation if news of this got out. The last thing I wanted was scandal. There had, after all, been one or two other incidents. That silly undergraduate girl a few years back and a rather unfortunate episode in the senior common room following a heated exchanged about Cro-Magnon cookery with that ass from Harvard. Well, best not to dwell on such indiscretions. I have been a slave to my research, but I have not always been, it must be said, a perfect man. No, I prefer to think of my life as a checkerboard, the black marks enlivened by enough spots of brilliance to muster some respect, I feel, some acknowledgement that I, Graham Coxworth-Grove have made a contribution, however small it might be, to our civilisation and that the great wall of understanding, the bridge and battlements of knowledge have been fortified by my work. I hope that, thanks to my endeavours, the barbarians may be kept from the gates just a little longer. Generations of young people, instructed in my methods, shown the gifts of my superior reasoning will go forth and continue my work. When I leave this mortal coil my research will endure, I know this much, a beacon to aid those that dare to ascend after me into the foothills and mountaintops of learning.

I was still shouting and banging when the door of the cell flung open – lo – the Sherriff and his lanky deputy. I was about to demand my release when the Sherriff raised his arm and sprayed something in my face. My eyes burned and my nose filled with an excruciating, infernal substance. I couldn't breathe, I couldn't see! My hands went up to my face and I fell to my knees. There was a sharp jolt in my arm, a burning smell and then the void...

Strung out in the cold darkness... I was a press-ganged look-out clutching at the rigging of a ship adrift in arctic seas... I was an astronomer locked in the dungeons of the Inquisition... I was a psychoanalyst fleeing Austria across icy Alpine footpaths... I didn't even know where I was... who I was... As is my habit during periods of stress, I soothed myself by reciting the genus homo, my mind skipping over that long line of evolution that stretched from tender-footed homo habilis and homo rudolfensis stumbling upright through the primeval forest to homo georgicus, homo nonsensicus, homo ergaster and homo erectus – those human prototypes banging bones together and staring into the flickering campfire. How could I forget rare homo cepranensis with your single remaining skull-cap? Or Homo antecessor, homo heidelbergensis and homo rhodesiensis... think of them, waging war on the Neanderthals in the steppes of Gondwanaland... man at the dawn of the human epoch... the ragged edge of possibility. I always found it so comforting to close my eyes and think about these continuities...

And then, alas, my present discomfort grew too much to endure. Floating back to consciousness, I opened my eyes.

Words, at this moment, fail me.

I dislike admitting it. I am not, after all, an inarticulate man. I am the author of four books, not to mention nearly three dozen articles and countless papers and presentations. My second book, Of Acheulean Tool Use in the Lower Paleolithic Era won two major awards and has since been recognised as the definitive text on the subject. I have supervised twenty three PhDs and examined around a hundred. I have taught thousands of hours of classes, seminars, supervisions. I have marked tens of thousands of undergraduate essays. As a diversion from my research, I have also written two collections of poetry, published at my own expense. For the first, Ruminations on the Fall of Darjeeling, I assumed the persona of a melancholy colonialist lamenting the decline of the British Empire and for the second, Big Boom, I became Canetti Cannelloni, a far right Futurist from Bologna. The central conceit of this volume, which most amused me, was the introduction of a second persona, a certain Dr Palimpscheisser, who was purported to have translated the volume from the original Italian on the basis of a single surviving manuscript kept now in the private museum of a Milanese collector.

Unfortunately, I realised none of this was going to be of any use.

I was tied to a stake in the middle of a cornfield. I had been lashed up quite thoroughly and was stuck fast. It was dark and surprisingly cold. Indeed, the inclement air was more suggestive of a damp cellar or tomb than the open-spaces of the Mid West. On the horizon, a faint blue light was flickering like a distant TV set or neon sign, but I couldn't actually identify the source of the illumination. No moon graced the heavens and the few stars seemed very faint and far. I could see several more stakes stuck at intervals in the field. One or two appeared to have things hanging from them, tatty rags like bits of scarecrows. Much of the corn had been broken down and I could just discern a motley assemblage of objects scattered hither and thither – a deflated tyre, dismantled portions of agricultural machinery and burnt tangles of clothing.

There was something else. I was not alone.

"Well professor, here we are." The Sherriff and his deputy stood in front of me.

"What's going on? Why are you doing this?" My voice was rather weak. My mouth felt bitterly dry, my tongue stuck like a desiccated sausage in my pensive jaw.

"This here be a region cursed by God."

"Cursed by God? My dear fellow, don't be so ridiculous." I knew I had to keep reasoning with them. It was the only way. "Its economics, I mean, without subsidies, it's very hard, isn't it? To compete, you know, as a farmer. I daresay people have gone to the city..."

"The purgin' wiped out enough of 'em," said the deputy.

"I beg your pardon."

"There's a war across these plains."

"War? Between whom?"

"Between those that are saved and those that choose the other way."

31

I gazed at the two men. They must be joking. I wanted to say something, but what to say in such a situation?

The deputy took a step forward. "Now, as you probably guessed, somethin' bad is goin' to happen."

"Right. I mean, no. I don't follow."

"Well now, you're tied to a stake in a field in the dead of night. It don't look no good, does it now?"

This much was true. "So, what are you going to do?"

"We ain't goin' to do nothin'."

"You's is an offering. A sacrifice," said the Sherriff. "As we said, this here be a region cursed by God."

We weren't getting anywhere. I found my voice again. "Chaps, look here, I'm afraid I still don't quite follow. I do rather need the toilet and these ropes are hurting my arms. Can't we be reasonable?"

"This be a haunted region."

"Please, spare me this nonsense."

"Could be the restless souls of dead Indians or pioneers who were killed by Indians when they first came to the region or else it could be settlers what froze to death in the winter or else the ghosts of outlaws and bandits killed in fights with the law or the vengeful spirits of abandoned orphans or maybe it's got something to do with runaway slaves. We don't know."

"We don't really care," added the deputy. "We do what we have to."

"And what's that?"

"We leave you here 'til mornin'."

"What about Jessica? What have you done with her?"

"My wife's lookin' after her."

"But..."

"Her fate depends on yours. Hopefully, come morning, it will all be clear. Have a good night now." The Sherriff doffed his Stetson and the two men turned away, disappearing into the dark corn.

I hung on for a little while, waiting. My bladder was fit to burst. My thoughts, by this stage, had become rather discombobulated. I was sure I could hear something, shuffling and sliding like a great serpent through the corn. It must be the Sherriff and his deputy, come back to cut me down having satisfied whatever malicious spirit had led them to treat me with such cruelty. My word, when I got out of here, there was going to be hell to pay!

From: Cameron, P (patrick.cameron@cornell.edu)

To: Coxworth-Grove, G
(g.coxworthgrove@cornell.edu)

Coxer!

Where the blazers are you? You were supposed to get here two days ago. What's going on? Do you never answer your phone? Did you get the e-mail I sent? We need you here. I've made a rather troubling discovery. I haven't even begun to absorb what it could mean but we might have to re-think our assumptions. Anyway, I'm worried. There have been numerous unforeseen problems. The graduate students I brought along to help have all fallen ill and we don't know what's wrong. Some sort of skin

*irritation coupled with distressing hallucinations. And
that's not all. I knew I should have never hired those
Mexicans. They refuse to work anymore even though I've
offered to double their wages. They seem to think we've
violated a sacred place. There is more, but I'll have to tell
you face to face. You won't believe it until you see what
I've found. Hurry!*

Patrick

ACTION TV NEWS!

NEWSFLASH!

This is live!

We are going to an interview with Jessica Bray,
the Cornell student who, as viewers will be aware,
went missing with her Professor, Graham Coxworth-
Grove in Iowa three days ago. Let's go live to
Midtown, Iowa.

Jessica!

Jessica, tell us what happened?

Oh my God it was horrible. I've had, like, a totally
awful time. Professor Coxworth told me he needed
me to come with him to some archaeological site and
he said like I could totally assist in the excavations
and everything. He said it would help with my
dissertation.

What happened, Jessica?

What did he say?

What did he do to you?

Lies! He lied to me. We never even got to the site.
We just drove for days through state after state. He
wouldn't tell me where we were going or why. And,

like, it's totally gross but he made me do things to him at night, in the motels and sometimes in the car. One time, well, we stopped in the middle of nowhere and he opened his trousers.

He didn't!

No!

That's horrible!

Disgusting!

What did you do?

I opened the door and just like totally ran away. I mean totally. I just ran. He came after me so I ran deeper and deeper into the fields. He kept calling me but I wouldn't go back. Eventually I got away from him, but I was totally lost. I mean Iowa right? Like, totally empty. I spent the night out there. Eventually this nice Sherriff found me and brought me to safety. I just want to thank Sherriff Hank Williams and all the good people of Hope's End, Iowa. Oh my gosh they are just about the nicest people I've ever met anywhere. Thank you all so much for your support and help.

Sherriff!

Sherriff Hank Williams!

Tell us your story Sherriff!

Well folks, when we found Jessica she was in a state of shock. From what we can tell, she was lucky to get away from this pervert. Hope's End is a nice small town full of good clean people who mind their own business and we all want to make sure it stays that way.

What about the pervert Professor?

What you going to do about him?

We've circulated his details to the FBI and all the relevant authorities. The net is closing. He won't get far.

ACTION TV NEWS!

Police have given us this new photo fit of the pervert Professor. Check it out! Anyone with information about his whereabouts should phone the number below. And now, with reports of mass hysteria and human sacrifice in a remote part of North Dakota, we cut to our reporter Jed Blankman. Jed, what's the story out there?

PROSTHETIC MIND
Ele-Beth Little

A man had somehow forgotten how to live, misplaced his passions somewhere beneath an important document in his filing tray. If living is the part that happens prior and post-reflection, then he was like a faulty pendulum that had stopped ticking between these two modes of being. His incessant reasoning would ironically conclude 'a good dose of the irrational is essential in life,' and yet his reasoning couldn't help him obtain it.

For a year he devoted himself to debauchery, assured that this would overwhelm him into a 'moment' similarly to how a large wave knocks you rolling to the shore. However, his meticulous exploration of all the perversions on offer failed, and only left him with an increased immunity to life.

Feeling defeated into inertia, he next spiralled in to the vice of ambitious distractions; he earned himself a promotion, took on more work than he could manage and wasted his free time tangling himself in all sorts of voluntary projects and social affairs. This proved effective at halting his thoughts. And when any spare hours snuck out at him, he combated them with a self-induced (albeit thoroughly insincere) addiction to soaps and celebrity gossip.

The heart of the matter was this: that he intended to forget completely his own beliefs and all the paths of reasoning that led him there. He dreamt of that part of his mind withering in to a neglected stump. Perhaps he'd become sub-human or animal; be alive without being conscious of it. And those were the last thoughts he'd had on the matter, the last thoughts he'd allowed himself to have.

And now, weighted under his overgrown coat that had become wet in the rain, he stood crumbling like damp cigarette embers, beneath the empty bus shelter. His day had been like a mathematical equation. Its legitimacy was irrefutable, though it seemed to run parallel and detached from anything of consequence.

The crows scattered like darts of ink. They cluttered branches, shielding themselves from the rain which tapped with increased ferocity upon the steel roof. His pulse began to replicate the speedy drumming. And next his mind, as if caught in its slingshot, had no choice but to follow suit.

Ravenous thoughts were born and – sifting through the desert of his mindscape – they inevitably ended up circling the memory of a woman he passed each day on his journey to work. Seeing her face gleaming like a moon from her window had subtly developed in to the only glimmer in his day. She seemed to be waiting there only for him, and that notion revitalised him, reacquainted him with his own presence.

He stood for a moment, trying to recollect the first time he'd noticed her watching him, and what he could piece together of her features, or perhaps make a guess of her age.

It was a Friday, and on Friday's in particular he often had an indecipherable, and incredibly tenuous, internal zing of rebellion. It was as if the dreary symmetry of his week begged him to take a hammer to it. The liberation he felt on a Friday could be likened to a spiralling speeding belt to the surface of the ocean to gasp at air.

This zing occasionally brought about a semi-rash decision on his part. And, twinned with the mental stirrings for the stranger at the window, he now felt compelled to walk to her house where he would look upwards, devilishly, accusingly, in search of a possible moment – a meeting, or confrontation.

Even if only their eyes met and maybe an unreadable smile came of it, well, a smile could last him a month at least. He'd learnt to digest things slowly, as his life so far seemed only to offer him scraps.

And, if the window just so happened to be absent, then it wouldn't necessarily be a disappointment. Because even then something could be gleaned from it. Evidently, it would imply that she wasn't always at her window, watching the world. No, she purposely went to the window to watch for him.

At this conclusion, he leapt forward in to the rain, almost in to the speeding shadow of a car that ripped through the world like paper. The hollow beats remained for a moment, making him feel alarmed and untamed in his rashness. The perched black-birds shrieked and dove up into the dark clouds.

He continued again, and this time he was halted

by the vision of the face he recognised. His silent watcher, the woman at the window; she was hurrying through the rain on the other side of the road. He squinted at her flickering form; her heels digging at the concrete to give her speed, her hands clenching her coat tight at the neck. And, she was dressed in a nurse's uniform.

After pausing whilst she turned into an alleyway – which he knew led to the local hospital – he to follow her to her workplace.

His compulsion had grown to unearth the secret of his watcher, his metaphysical lover. This shielded him from his own angst at entering the hospital; a portal – he'd always maintained - to death and all the horrors of human existence.

However, upon entering, the filth he found there exceeded his imaginings. He found there a dripping, destitute hospital bed, deserted in an ocean of excretal mess. The surrounding space seemed wormed with the cavities left behind from the deceased. Everything stunk of negation; dusty silence and shadowed walls. An atrophied wilderness, purposely fucking its own oblivion.

Even the drips seemed hollow. Yet the wet tiles embraced them, like a virile corpse, excited at each watery serenade.

A half-vanishing creature, only aware of her shame, scuffed past him, shit slopping down her leg. The rows of beds brought to life their lost lovers amidst the stale burrows of sheets, where sickly stringy muscles had fornicated with their host.

Some comatose animal, foetal and gasping, raised a dying arm. "I'm melting in to my bed." Her words swarmed to him, as the whites of her eyeballs sank to the floor like discharge. He forced his gaze to the floor, internally screaming the mantra 'Don't read the ghosts. Don't read the ghosts.'

"Stop hiding boy. We're all of us bound to matter and decay. Men can hide from it easiest, but you can't hide for ever!"

He clasped at his forehead; claustrophobic within his own skull and wishing it was malleable to prize open like gates. Her blood leaked through his mind like dye.

The bed sheets swaddled her like the rigid cocoon of a spider's prey. Someone once told him that spiders gain sexual pleasure when they consume victims and he imagined the shadows beneath her bed, with woven tongues, drooling expectantly over her death. She would evaporate, leaving only stains behind.

The tight shriek of trolley wheels ended the spell, as the nurse – his nurse – mechanically handed out grey jugs of still water, sometimes popping straws in the patient's unresponsive mouths. She marched past the other staff as if they were weeds in her path, and they scowled and shared whispers about her before returning to their clinically sanguine eagerness to clean up shit.

Still sunk in his corner, neurotic and now tensely clutching his knees, he was farcically overlooked, as if his outburst was as commonplace as the disinfected floor tiles.

And so he had time to make a few hasty guesses at the nurse's character, and her relationship with the others. He decided that the other nurses judged her to be a solemn bitch, because she refused to integrate with them through their banal humour. He also had time to ask himself what might become of a mind like her, exposed daily to the grotesque and abject, never allowed to forget her own physicality and inevitable expiry. Would these visions be heavy to carry? Would such a woman need a mental retreat, so that she didn't... sink like a flooded vessel?

His put his questions on pause, as he tried to calculate how much time had passed. He expected an uncomfortable greeting to happen soon – surely his nurse-watcher would have found a free moment to deal with his presence. And, since those other bitches that worked here hated her so much, they'd probably jibed and nagged at every chance so she'd be eager to get him to leave.

It struck him that he'd never rehearsed a greeting that was based on two months of shared 'watching' and he felt a pang of nausea at the prospect of being unrehearsed in his speech.

Eventually she approached him with the clinical indifference only a nurse can possess. Her words tumbled from her with little expression, her tongue were a blank receipt. He took note of her greying brown curls – some were an enchanting pearly white – all static as a wild animal's tail. Her brown stocking ankles swiftly perched before him like chicken feet.

She handed him a cup that smelt of bleach and bile, poured in steaming water and then pushed her trolley away, leaving him with a jumbled collection of her presence and the echo of her shoes tapping on the tiles. Lifting up his cup, he found a folded note, damp with steam, stuck to the palm of his hand.

Come and see me tonight. At home.

He fled, breathless through the swinging doors of hospital. The world dipped and creaked like a lost boat as he wheezed.

Out on the open streets, his shadow crept the distance of desolation, but his hope became a prominent beacon, pulsing, as if he'd swallowed a live bird. It seemed he was the only movement in an inert space, where every sound thanked him for its birth.

He walked until he reached the lady's home, where he had grown accustomed to noticing her watching him from her dirty window. There she coiled amidst the stained glass, a step back from the social world.

Perhaps she would consider his presence an intrusion. Perhaps she preferred only to gaze within the embrace of her four walls. If you gaze long enough, then when the actuality presents itself, it can somehow seem less real. Or at least a clumsy replica, lacking in the kind of magic that is brewed in solitude.

Anxious to step out of the purgatory of this anonymous blackness, he strode purposely to her door, hesitated, and then tapped with the bone of his knuckle.

Was she still fixed at her viewing spot, willingly paralysed? He envisaged her dark pupils, rapt, piercing small holes through her window. Perhaps she watched everyone, and he was no exception.

He scraped a last disheartened drawl of a tap, against the splintering wood of the door. And this time, his call was answered. She opened the door to him in her white nightgown, and stepped back to let him enter. The trails of her gown danced in dust, her blackened heals peeking from the lace trim. He followed her steps, which led them to the room where the window was focal; the window that had been familiar to him only from the outside, which he was now entombed behind.

She retook her place there, and he observed that her actions held no warmth to them. Instead she glided solemn and broken. Her body had an untouched purity, glistening like snow and she fell in to the chair like stars. The scent of stale petals made a whirlwind around her. He was captivated and yet he wanted to vomit out every scraping impact she'd made on his insides.

The clock cracked time like a hammer upon ice until he could hardly bare it. Sweat began to surface on his palms leaving handprints on the table where he'd rested them.

He turned to his hostess for console or distraction from his irrational terror, but she set a dead gaze on him, as if she'd been stuffed in that very chair. Her features appeared to be subtly sinking as if they concealed a great void. He stammered "What is this...?"

Her mouth, widening and darkening, began suddenly to miscarry. Blood bubbled and erupted, her eyeballs boiling and shuddering like a horrific orgasm. A witch. With bird's feet. Bird's feet peeking from her white nightdress.

Insistent, through the blazing blackness, the heat, the fluidic boiling matter, his hands gripped tight to his face, he bawled "What is this?! What drug... or curse."

"It's your cure" she snapped, as if scolding an ungrateful child.

He blinked, and the clock struck – its pendulum wiping reality clean and returning him to a blank canvas, where new nightmares simmered below the façade of forms.

"Everything is disgusting. Even being with you is disgusting, and you're the only one who talks to me..."

"I'm the only one you want to talk to"

"...Just make it stop"

She threw back her head to laugh, and as she did so a rain of flies fell dead to the floor, as if her breath was noxious.

"This is what you want to see. Don't tell me it isn't. You spoilt little voyeur, you want a window to perch at, you want a world that lives up to the artificial carnality you've brewed in your solitude."

"Make it stop" he repeated, humbly pleading.

She retaliated then, maternal embers in her voice.

"Come with me to the kitchen and drink some water. It will clear your head"

She led him out of the room, down a dusty wooden-panelled corridor that smelt of the honey of pine cones. She seemed quite titillated to be entertaining a guest, despite his apparent misery. Black feathers clung to his feet like oil, but he was grateful to leave behind the malicious clock-beat, that had started to cause a terrible sea-sickness which fortunately abated as he entered the kitchen.

Propelled in to motion, like an electrocuted doll, she battered round the piles of dirty crockery, scavenging for a clean glass. She broke away from the task briefly to scoop out the rotting food that was blocking the sink and, clenching it until it squelched through her knuckles; she swiped it at the dogs that yapped round her ankles.

"There. Have that, you fools... Can't you just tell these pups are all men. Tsk. Never ashamed by their own need."

She continued to prattle on contentedly as she poured him a glass of water from the tap.

"Now, listen. Immunity is the worst kind of sickness I could ever diagnose. I know this from experience; my job allows me to become immune to the most violent truths of life. It has made me selfish. Now I only fear my own death, my own pain – but am unmoved by others. I could quite easily kill a person. In fact, the moment I became aware of this disability, this apathy, I contemplated doing so, to jolt me out of it. And my work environment would allow me to get away with one... crafty death. As long as it's just the once, you see, it would be considered an accident."

She kicked away a dog that was pawing amorously at her slippers.

"Well, but then I went and had a change of heart. I thought, if only I cared enough for a person, were intimate with them. Then I wouldn't be acting out of obligation or for a wage, I'd really feel it."

He nodded sulkily, and tilted the swamp in his cup from side to side, transfixed; a severed robin's head came bobbing to the surface.

"Don't be dispirited, the hallucinations will subside. Follow me. I have something to show you."

With a naive light in her eyes she led him silently to her bedroom.

"I saved this little treasure all my life. I had it since being a babba."

She reached for a cluster of shell chimes that hung from the window frame, and let them clink in delicate harmonies.

"It still comforts me. Better than any man sharing my bed. I watch this and it sends me straight to sleep. No ghosts."

"... No ghosts" he echoed, drained from his visions.

"You want to feel real, don't you? Listen, I'm like you. I know that when you look out of the window it may as well be a child's sketch and you're wondering when the outlines are going to fill up with substance."

47

She accentuated her next line, as if secure in her role as wise prophetess. One finger rose knowingly.

"When... will there... be meaning?"

She'd caught his attention now, and he perched himself upon the windowsill, enthralled. His thoughts however – now cleansed of torturous visions – was impatient for her to arrive at the conclusion, the cure. And this was the cause of his silence, an attempt to forge a direct path through the winding trail of her talk.

"You know, the world will always be there waiting for you. Well... what's left of it."

She joined him at the window. Rested her head in her palms and gazed out of it, in a way familiar to him as he had peered up at her from the outside.

"You don't talk much do you? I was hoping for more from my friendly stranger"

"What's... the cure?" he asked directly, wanting to take her knowledge and run. Even his routine of soap operas and morning coffees at work now seemed to magnetise him back to their tranquil glow. The flickering tv, calling to him like a siren. His lonely bed, like a post-bickering apology, lay outstretched in wait of his embrace.

"I told you the cure already!" she hissed. "I showed you it. Those moments of horror in my own front room where life happening. It's only since you snapped out of it that you've started rationalizing again, wanting to be back there secretly, back in the moment"

He ventured "But can a moment not be...

48

pleasant!"

"Pleasant? Pleasant?! How sickeningly dull!"

Her eyes became the black pearls of a crow, inspecting him sideways in sly flickering motion. Grand wings unfurled behind her, shadowing the room.

"How could anything 'pleasant' send you spinning in to oblivion? What you need from your nurse is a good hard dose of... HORROR"

Her white gown spilt like sour milk upon the floor, revealing a crawling mass of maggots where her stomach should me. And beneath it, propped upon her pelvic bone, lay a nest-like womb, where bald headed chicks pecked greedily at her stringy flesh.

"And..." she added indignantly, "I am a woman after all, which means essentially I'm infested"

Her two black eyes dropped to the floor like marbles and rolled along the wood to nestle by his feet. Wind wailed through her blooded sockets and ash rained like Armageddon; a small hell conjured in the haze of her room. The door slammed shut...

CORRUPTED FROM MEMORY
Christopher Nosnibor

I couldn't stop myself. I suppose I've always had something of an obsessive side, which from an early age manifested itself in collecting things. As a child, walking along the beach on family holidays, I would pick up stones and shells, and want to keep every last one of them for their different colours, different shades, textures, lustres. As adolescence hit, my appreciation of books bloomed. While the rest of my peers were just bored teenagers, I was feeding my mind. Then I discovered music, became lost in music and there was no turning back. Record collecting, I soon learned, was not merely a hobby, but an obsessive's paradise. Of course, it's all about the music, but it's also a whole lot more besides. Some say collecting is a manifestation of the mild autism prevalent in most men. Maybe it is. Whatever, it's who I am. Or was. Something changed.

It all began with the death of my father. I can see now that this single event was the catalyst. I had a trigger inside. Now I'm not quite how I should be, been finding tricks too hard. I'm thinking something must be broken, because it wasn't like this before. The beginning of the sequence of events, as I recall them, began innocuously enough. On my return home from another taxing day at the office, I had cracked open my last can of a four-pack of Marston's Old Empire and just taken my first long draught down from it when the phone rang. So I answered the phone. A voice came over clear. It was my mother.

"William," she said, and from the tone of her voice I instinctively knew that something was awry. No one called me William, not even my mother. At least, not since I was in my early teens. There had been a lengthy pause, dead air, hanging on the telephone, static over the airwaves, even after I asked her what was wrong. "It's you father."

The fact she never referred to him as such only compounded the sense of foreboding, and I felt as though my pulse had stopped and the air pressure in the room had dropped even before she finally managed to utter the words that carried such weight. She didn't say much, really, other than the fact that he was dead. I recall her being somewhat vague, even evasive, regarding the cause of death, but at that point, I wasn't taking much in.

Hanging up the phone, I had sunk the Empire down, then gone to the kitchen, where the knives are, and poured myself a very large gin. Part of me had craved a decent single malt, but I had been going through a tight patch and pay-day was a long way off. I had knocked it back in a single gulp and poured myself another before making my way back into the living room. I tried to leave it, but I couldn't forget about it. I knew that the more I drank, the more I would think, and that over time the guilt would get me, the thoughts would wreck me, praying on my mind. But these were exceptional circumstances. Questions began circling like vultures around carrion, wheeling and diving, swooping their way to the fore of my consciousness and gnawing away at my frontal lobes before careening out of sight, only to resurface later, back for a second helping of anguish. I was suddenly achingly aware of how little I knew him, as a person. Had known him. So many questions... so few answers. Some of the facts would, of course, emerge over time – irrefutable facts, like the cause and time of death. But within only an hour or so of hearing of his death, I found myself wondering about the whys and wherefores, and, above all, the hows – how would I be able to uncover those details with which the fabric of his being could be stitched together? As I sat, knocking back my third and fourth vodka, time began to warp beyond recovery, and I knew how the remainder of the night would pan out: I would drink, drink, drink and be ill... Beyond that, I saw nothing but confusion and fear and empty space stretching out to infinity and beyond. At the end of the great white pier I saw... nothing. I had nothing with which to start on in my own mind – there were not enough details, no fucking details, no facts, just the loud noted absence, some family snaps...

* * *

The night was young, the moon was mellow and I decided to take a walk. I wasn't in the mood for company, but the prospect of remaining at home, alone, was even more unbearable. Leaving the house

I wandered, without aim, with only the vague notion that I wanted to drink, copiously.

My mobile phone rang.

I picked up, but then the line went dead. I called back.

"Hello?"

"C, it's me."

"Will! Good lord! What news?" Caine sounded strained. An epic pause while he left me hanging on the telephone. Then: "Is... is your dad alright?" he asked tentatively.

"What?" I ask. I'm shocked.

"I don't want to sound like I'm completely off my fucking rocker, but if I didn't know better... I had this dream – more like a nightmare – even though... I don't know, I must've dropped off without realising it. Anyway, I saw him, and..."

"What the fuck? You must be fucking joking!" I was aghast. "He's dead. You know that."

No sooner had I begun to offload than he cut me short. "Will, look, er, a bit busy right now. Can I call you back tomorrow some time?"

Caine may have been a dear friend, but he was also a complete pussy, hopelessly under the thumb of his passive-aggressive girlfriend. Why did he put up with it? Simple: she's got legs, and knows how to use them. And he was in a rut. And when you're in a rut, you've gotta get out of it. But he showed no sign of doing so at present. Oh well, whatever, never mind. I headed home and hit the vodka, hard.

While nursing my hangover, I recalled my resolve from the night before, whereby I had decided to pay my mother a visit, under the guise of mutual consolation. I phoned her up and told her I would be there by lunchtime the following day. Usually I would consult, give more prior notice, but these were exceptional circumstances. I called work and told them I would be taking a few days compassionate leave and would be in touch if I was likely to be off more than a week. My boss is a cunt and was overtly sniffy at my insistence that I would not be in until at least the middle of the following week. It was Tuesday now.

"There's a lot of work in at the moment," he said dryly, verbally situating my arm behind my back and slowly applying the pressure. That's me in the corner, but I won't back down, and I won't be going to work.

"I appreciate that," I replied firmly. "But I don't think I'd really have my mind on the job anyway." As if my mind's ever really on the pointless job of passing pieces of paper around and stuffing envelopes.

"Well I hope you're back in soon," he huffed, adding, "Your pay review's coming up soon, you know," by way of a closer. No concern, no sympathy. Just cuntiness.

I spent the remainder of the day doing very little. As evening fell, I moved on to the vodka. Flicking through the channels I happened upon the opening of an episode of *CSI: Crime Scene Investigation*, which after the obligatory cheese-line kicked in with The Who's Who Are You? It seemed a most apposite question. Who was he? And consequently, who am I? I really wanna know... the programme passed in a blur as I drank until such point that the walls and ceiling moved in time.

I slept very poorly that night: my cerebellum was aflame with lines of inquiry, futile, flailing musings that refused to recede, to let me rest. When I did fall into fitful, troubled sleep, my dreams haunted me with images of my father, clearly dead, in some horror-film cliché of a partially putrefied, maggot-ridden corpse, skin taut, luminescent in its pallor and flaking, popping out from behind every door, on every street corner, looming over me as I slept. His beard was grizzled, as I have seen in life, a sable siver'd.

The following morning, I got my last clean dirty shirt out of the wardrobe and made ready with a quick shave and by throwing a change of clothing into a bag, grabbing an eclectic handful of CDs for in-car entertainment on the way out.

Sometimes I'd rather not be the one behind the wheel. It was the road to Hell. Six lanes of traffic, three lanes moving slow. Pulling off down a B-road to take a less direct but altogether more free-moving route, I felt my tension ease a little. Pedal to the metal, the tinnitus-inducing treble of Big Black's *Songs About Fucking* might not have been the best hangover cure, but it certainly kept me awake for the journey. After the closer, the CD-bonus cover version of Cheap Trick's 'He's a Whore' – originally released as a double A-side with a storming rendition of Kraftwerk's 'The Model' – crunched to a halt, I skimmed over a number of the discs I had grabbed, including Manorexia's *The Radiolorian Ooze* and – rather incongruously, perhaps – Leonard Cohen's *Death of a Ladies' Man*, which is almost without doubt his worst release, irrespective of one's opinion of Spector's production, and instead slipped in another ear-splitting top-end biased soundtrack in the form of the Metal Urbain compilation, *Anarchy in Paris!*.

On my arrival, I was struck by just how old my mother looked. She always had, it was true, but she looked particularly haggard, which was probably to be expected under the circumstances. But look at those clothes. Look at that face, it's so old. More than her tired features and drawn expression, I was struck by just how fat she had become. I tried to calculate how long it had been since I had last seen her, but soon cast this thought from my mind. It was irrelevant, and, moreover, completely removed from the purpose of my visit.

She bustled around, busying herself with tea, biscuits, any number of diversionary activities, all that cal. She asked how my journey was, about work, prattled on about the weather, wheeled out every displacement tactic under the cloud-covered sun. I sat at the kitchen table, sipping the tea, which was overly strong, and, being made with full-fat milk, not particularly appealing. I didn't really want tea and biscuits: I just wanted to drink. But I needed a clear head for this.

* * *

"Can't you just sit down?" I say.

She begins to make some kind of excuse and tries to offer me another biscuit. She's mumbling, "ease my worried mind..." or something, but it's barely intelligible.

"Oh, sit down," I reiterate with a sigh. "Sit down next to me."

After some more protestation and some further procrastination, she acquiesces. She sits at the kitchen table across from me, tight-lipped, her face drawn and ready for the next attack. It's clear to me she doesn't want to talk.

"I want to know," I begin, but she cuts me off.

"I can't believe it," she says.

She started crying. I could not bring myself to look at her. She was crying regularly in little sobs: I thought she was never going to stop. I said nothing: there was nothing to say. We sat like this for quite some time. She began to sigh and sob less often. She sniffled for a while. Then at last she stopped. I was tired and my back was aching. I decided to defer my inquisition and once I had calmed her down enough to know she would not drown in a pool of her own tears and snot, I fucked off down the local boozer.

On my return, my father's brother, Tom, had

arrived. Tom is my third uncle. He was accompanied by a man in a suit who I recognised as being late father's accountant. He in turn was accompanied by a younger man, dressed in smart-casual attire, tall, clean-cut, a rugby-player to be certain. I listened to them speaking and then it clicked: this was Julian, Jim's son, now in university and... a hardline bible-basher, and also the brother of a girl I know, Katrina. She's part of my wider social circle, one of the university crowd, quiet, a little reserved, but given to the occasional flash of dry wit, moderately pretty and attractive in a shy sort of a way and maybe I'm interested, but... Yes, now I can remember, now I can remember... Julian is on his university rugby team in Loughborough. There is a round of handshaking as Jim takes his leave, and Julian with him, before Uncle Tom turns his attention to me. I may be pissed, borderline gashed even, but even in my inebriated state I think something's a little strange in the way he and my mother are behaving toward one another, a little too close, occasional contact, sidelong glances... at the mention of my father's name – and I blame the drink for this, of course – I break down and cry like a woman, no particular woman.

Tom steps forward. "My cousin, William and my son," he says, emollient, placatory, flashing a cherry ice cream smile.

I'm having none of it. What is this shit? The old bastard's there with his arm round my mother's waist while my father's body's barely cold. "Let it be," I caution.

"How is it the clouds still hang on you?" he asks. The insensitive cunt. It's been but days.

"Not so," I reply, unwilling to give too much away in such a strange situation. "I am too much of the ale. Loneliness is the cloak I wear."

"Everyone dies," said my mother evenly.

I ranted at her for a while. In retrospect it was probably a load of incoherent drunken bollocks. The death of my father's bad enough, but this... this is like a slap in the face, this is like an amputation. I can love my fellow man, but I'm damned if I'll love yours, I thought. Perhaps I said it, too. I can't remember.

"Really, it's sweet and commendable of you," Tom patronised. "But there's no need to be such a fucking girl about it. Wrap up, pull yourself together, you're a fucking disgrace. Be a man!"

With that, he and my mother said goodnight and I found myself alone in the kitchen with my thoughts. How long has this been going on? I wonder. I headed upstairs to crash in the spare room I had been designated, which was, once upon a time, my own bedroom. On the landing I hear grunting and moaning emanating from what used to be my parents' room. My guts are achurn at the thought of my mother having sex. The thought of her fucking my father's brother between the incestuous sheets is all too much.

Flicking through the names in my mobile phone, I text people, almost at random. Caine, Katrina, names I don't even recognise or recall adding to my phone book. I'm not myself. I'm more myself than ever. Move back, step outside yourself. Look down on the world, and, more specifically, your own minuscule microcosm. How do you look now? How do you see yourself? Do you see yourself the way others do? What do you think of yourself?

That night I slept fitfully, my rest rent by ugly dreams that caused me to wake with a start, my body dripping with sweat and my head in a spin. I'm burning with anxiety. I knew that this would be the first of many nights like this, and that while the present was bad, it was better than living in what would come. The ghosts of my life blow harder than the wind, and again my somnolence is interrupted by my father's presence. He's signalling something, trying to speak... 'One look could kill...' Suddenly, his face transforms, his eyes are streaming black kohl... he's transmogrified into Alice Cooper. 'Poison running through my veins...' Now he's biting the head off a live chicken, the blood spurts and he's aiming the gore into his mouth, rivulets of plasma and platelets flowing down his chin in an all-too-real display of ghoulish theatricals...

I woke up with the sheets soaking wet and a freight train running through the middle of my head.

* * *

"I am murdered..." the words reverberated around my cranium the entirety of the following day.

Tom was in the kitchen making busy with

60

breakfast when I arrived downstairs. He was bright, he was breezy, he was cool, he was calm, he was always in command. But mostly he was lying like a son of a bitch. I made like I was busy reading the previous day's paper, anything to avoid eye contact and conversation with the man. Not a man, not a man, but a slimy deceitful roach. I stare at the walls, there's nothing to say, not now at least. I glance around the room, it's a mess of souvenirs, here to remind you. My mother entered the room and seems to sense the tension, and takes a diversionary course.

"Here comes the rain again," she commented to no one in particular. And so no one answers. "Humidity is rising – Barometer's getting low…" she mused. "Who can stop the rain from falling? Who can stop this pain that's drowning me?" Her voice tapered to a whisper.

I decided to brave the weather and take a wander round the garden. Things grown in the garden… then they die. Although my father had been active and his death sudden, the garden, quite meticulously maintained in life, suddenly appeared to have become untended, with the trees all bended low.

I don't know why I went into the garage. It had always been a complete shit-tip. Standing there now, amongst the piles of boxes, containing wellington boots, maps, rotting fruit and vegetables, the stacked pieces of timber, dust-covered bottles of vintage wines, the tools, rusting as they hung from nails on the walls, I was swept back through the years. In a whirl, I'm peering down a tunnel, and I look back upon my life. I'm out of my body, perhaps out of my mind, looking down. My father's with me, he's in the vicinity, he's here, I can feel it.

The temperature changes, becomes suddenly lower and I intuitively know there's a pressure drop, I can feel something, something quite bizarre I cannot see. Somehow, I know he's there, and he was reaching out to touch me, he was reaching out...

I made a dash back to the house through the siling rain, which was growing in intensity rather than easing off. By the time I had traversed the fifteen or so yards from my car to the conservatory, I was drenched. On entry, I found my mother bustling around in the kitchen once more, seemingly more interested in appearing busy than actually having anything to do. Grief affects people in strange ways, I reminded myself. But this... this was downright weird.

"Are you alright?" I asked her.

"Yes," she replied, a note of surprise in her voice.

"No, I mean really," I pressed. "Talk to me. Tell me the truth. This smells sour."

She sighed and her shoulders dropped. She looked tired. "What have I done to deserve this?" she uttered in a careless whisper.

Uncle Tom strolled in, smiling as ever. My distrust of him was deepening by the second. What lay behind the mask? I don't know, but there and then I knew I had to find out. Sensing that I was attempting to wring information from my mother, his face turned and he shot me a look, as serious as cancer, as subtle as a heart attack. But it was fleeting, so transitory, my mother missed it and, like a subliminal message cut into a film, it was unclear if I had really seen it or if I was projecting my suspicious opinions onto his calm, tranquil physiognomy. There's the rub: I had no real way of knowing, let alone proving it. One thing was clear: something was rotten here, and the atmosphere was fuelling a deep sense of dis-ease somewhere down in my core, deep, deep down. It was time to go.

* * *

I wound up, sometime later, in the Frog and Parrot on Division Street. The pub has the claim to fame for appearing on the inner sleeve of the Arctic Monkey's debut album, but more importantly, I was assured of a decent pint. Being a Thursday night and out of term-time, it was pretty quiet, so I just walked on in. There were a few faces I recognised at the far side of the room, but I elected to keep myself to myself. It's better this way. Sheffield's a prison. I needed to get out, or at least out of it.

I caught sight of Katrina as she made her way to the bar and almost involuntarily took a grip of her arm. She looked at me a little strangely. I was starting to feel some kind of love buzz. I gave her a lascivious wink. Dutch courage? I gotta stop drinking around. But for now... I needed more yet. All in good time.

* * *

I had to confirm his guilt, somehow or another, and I had the very thing... after the funeral, scheduled for Monday afternoon, the wake would provide me with the perfect opportunity to expose the devious philandering motherfucker to whom I was shamefully related.

The following morning – Friday – while Tom was out, I went over to visit my mother, and while she was faffing around with some newspapers, I made my way into the spare room that Tom had already made his office and lifted his iPod. Shortly after, I made my excuses and raced home, where I plugged his iPod into my own computer, deleting all of his files and replacing them with a few choice cuts of my choosing, kicking off with Talking Heads' 'Psycho Killer.' I then uploaded the whole of Nick Cave's *Murder Ballads*, and 'Murder Song' by The Cooper Temple Clause followed. Cheap Trick's 'He's a Whore' went on, too, for good measure, along with 'Tonight We Murder' by Ministry, 'Another Body Murdered' by Faith No More and Boo-Yaa T.R.I.B.E. and 'Murderer' by Grammatics. After all, subtlety wasn't Uncle Tom's forte. The plan was simple. Return the iPod to its owner, and at the party, once the Pod was docked, simply wait for him to hit play and... bang! If the wanker bletched, I would know for certain.

* * *

The funeral passes peacefully enough, I'm struggling to hold it together as the procession of tearstained faces and other voices blur and I try to stay focussed on the moment while being painfully aware of what lies ahead, to forget the night ahead. The funeral party is where it all happens. You could call it a success...

"Are you mad?" Caine asked me in disbelief as Roberta Flak's hit 'Killing Me Softly' began to run from the speakers.

"What is love?" I retorted. I paused. "It's all a front," I said, sinking a cold gin. I took it quick, took it neat. Did it again.

"Are you drunk?" he pressed.

"Hell, I was drunk at the pulpit," I rejoined.

"You're in a bad way," Caine interjected.

He was right. I was too drunk to fuck. I can't dance. I can't talk. I can barely walk. Anxiety was building. But I ain't fallin' down bro. 'Murder' by New Order, ripped from the Substance compilation, came on. Being an instrumental, it was far too subtle to achieve by objective, but I glimpsed Uncle Tom looking perplexed. This was supposed to be a collection of his brother's – my father's – favourite songs. My father had liked Mod and 70s rock, so what was this?

After 'Killed by Death,' 'Killing an Arab' and 'Killing in the Name,' I could see that Tom was deeply agitated, and was fumbling with his iPod, fingers trembling, his face flushed. Seconds later, a pallor descended over his physiognomy as Alice

Cooper's 'Poison' rang out from the stereo that the MP3 player was docked to. Perspiration sheened his brow.

"What's the matter?" I asked him, "you look as though you've seen a ghost."

* * *

A few hours later I'm gallon drunk and most of the mourners have made their excuses and left aside from a few who are still dancing at the funeral party. I wander out to the garage. My father was a hoarder and the place is rammed with his stuff. I want to be close to his belongings right now. I sniff the air. It's as though he's there beside me. He's in the vicinity. I can sense him, almost hear his breathing.

In the far corner is Tom. His back is toward me, and he seems to be lost in thought, unaware of my presence.

Flashback... I'm nine years old ... I glance down. By my foot there's a hammer, the very same one that lay on the top of the toolbox when I was a boy. There's also a light dusting of multi-purpose compost, and from my floating position I watch my father as he's pricking out seedlings and some of the earth is spilling over the edges of the pots onto the concrete floor.

This is my opportunity. I gather the hammer and make my way silently toward Tom.

I can't do it. I return the hammer to the floor and make my exit. Returning to the house I head upstairs for a piss and find my mother on the landing.

"William," she said. Her tone alone told me I'd had my last chance on the stairway.

"This is bad," I told her, "real bad. We need to talk."

She led me into her room – the room she used to share with my father, and now shared with that incestuous motherfucker whose name I can barely bring myself to utter.

"You've gravely offended your father," she intoned.

"You've gravely offended my father," I retorted.

Just then, I heard a sound, and sensing the curtain that hung across the bay window move, I dove across the room and came face to face with Jim. I reacted in an instant, instinct driving my actions as I grabbed him about the shoulders and dragged him out. I landed a punch in his face, then took his hair in my fist, thrusting his face into the dressing table mirror, not once, not twice, but repeatedly until his visage was ribbons and he was sprawled, lifeless on the floor, his blood pooling rapidly on the carpet beneath where it spurted from his severed jugular.

* * *

I awake the following morning in a cold sweat. Not only had I killed a man, but I recall through the purple haze dragging his lifeless corpse down the stairs by the feet like a sack of grain, and depositing it... where? All I know is that it had been a reflex action. Don't wanna be around when this gets out... and yet, I feel no remorse.

My phone rings. The line's fuzzy, but the voice in the distance, quiet and clear, tells me what I don't want to hear. I'm needed back at work. But more than this, I'm needed on a project and urgently. I must leave for London that very afternoon. I'm too fucked for this, but I'm into autopilot. I shower, pack and am out the door before I have time to think.

It's only on arrival in London that I realise I've been stitched up. The call was a hoax. The project doesn't exist. Worse still, on walking out of the office, where I'm met with bewilderment and blankness, and into the street, my car's been stolen. And I've either had my pocket picked or otherwise dropped my wallet, too. This is fucked. I'm fucked. So fucked I can't believe it. My head is full of chopstick: I don't like it. Call me paranoid, but I suspect Tom's got something to do with this. I curse the cunt as I head for the nearest station and wonder who I should call. I was riled up, fired up now. My thoughts were bloody alright. Fucking bloody.

* * *

I eventually managed to get hold of Caine and to convince him to sort me out with a train ticket home with the strict instruction that no-one should know of my whereabouts or of my return to the Steel City.

On my arrival after a long and turgid journey, most of which was spent being crushed against the window by a big girl who was anything but beautiful, I should have gone straight home. But instead I rang Caine. I needed his counsel. I needed a drink. He was concerned for my wellbeing, and rightly so, and as his other half was round at her sister's, he agreed to meet me.

* * *

The Grapes, Trippet Lane. I've offloaded onto Caine while he's kept a steady flow of pints of Abbeydale Absolution – a pale, light and easy-drinking ale that belies its powerful 5.3% ABV. We've been huddled in a corner, avoiding the people we know and half know who are also present. The selection of punk and new wave tracks on the rebellious jukebox always draws the cool people, and I'm in with the in crowd.

Something isn't right with Katrina. I could feel something coming in the air tonight, something building. I guess this was it. The confusion in her eyes says it all. She's up and dancing – after a fashion. Her moves are strange, and she's swaying a little, but more as though in a trance than drunk. Somehow, in agonising slow-mo, she clambers onto a table and continues her curious dance, a slave to the DJ and out of control. It's painful to watch, her ascent to her elevated position being anything but graceful, her movements anything but smooth, but it's like a car crash and I'm rooted to the spot, transfixed, out of my body again, like in a dream, unable to connect, to make contact, to be anything other than a careless fucking onlooker.

The jukebox falls silent, but Kat's off singing her own tune anyway, this time it's Kelis' number, 'Milk Shake,' and yeah, she's shakin' it alright. She's got a body under that chiffon blouse, and in this light and on this evening it's quite apparent.

It really is truly fucking tragic to see it: she's no longer the reserved, demure girl I know. Right now, the best I can say is that she's a maniac, and when I notice the look in her eye I fear she is locked into the danger zone where the dancer becomes the dance. I can't help myself. I know it's wrong, and she's clearly vulnerable, but I just want to give her my love action. She's beckoning to me, but I can't dance and right now I'm just standing here. Young punk spilling beer on my shoes as he's trying to inch closer for a better view. I want to pull him back, to get her down but I'm as transfixed as the rest of them.

"Nothing to see here, people, keep moving on," a guy is saying as he tries to guide the baying crowd away from the fractured girl while simultaneously attempting to communicate with her and bring her down.

It's time to leave.

* * *

Days pass. I'm so messed up. I'm so fucking alone. I remain in hiding, knowing there's a world outside. The music is outside. There's a voice in the

70

distance, quiet and clear saying thing I never wanted to hear. Yet I must bide my time. Revenge will be mine, of this I am convinced, and every day it's getting closer. The timing, however, would be crucial. I've arranged to meet Caine at the cemetry gates with a view to visiting my father's grave. On arrival, I see there's a funeral on. I consider leaving but feel a compulsion to move closer. What is this? There are faces at the graveside that I recognize. Closer still and I can hear hushed talk at the back of the group of the drowning, a rumour that someone drowned in my pool. Then I overhear Julian asiding to some posing prick in an ostentatious peacock suit.

"Yes, she did drown, after a fashion. Choked on her own vomit after a fucked-up crazy bender. Over William, definitely... well, maybe. I'm sure. And I'll see that he follows her into the grave."

My blood runs cold as my fears are confirmed. It's Kat they're burying – and Julian's set on my being next. Welcome to my nightmare. Something came over me and in a flash I find myself in her grave and howling like a banshee. The mourners stare at me like I'm out of my mind but I'm having none of it.

"I loved her!" I screamed as I was hauled out of the pit, only to find Julian's fist in my face. So that's what I get. I make to retaliate, but find myself being hauled off by some other rugger-playing cuntfuck who's six feet ten. I guess you could call it cowardice, but I'm not prepared to go on like this and so I beat a retreat.

71

I return home, but I can't shake the feeling that there's a ghost in my house. I'm not buying Caine's rationalisation that there's a rat in my kitchen, either. He's clearly no interest in this ghost talk and instead has been pushing me to straighten up, pull myself together.

I lie low again for the next couple of days, but it's no good. I'm haunted by memories, and the death rattle 'n' roll of my father's dying moments echoes around my cranium without end. It's a living hell. I'm staring down the barrel of a gun.

I make my way directly over to my mother's, knowing I'll find both Tom and Julian there. Some kind of gathering had been planned, and when I arrived it was apparent that some heavy drinking and more was already under way.

"Look, we need to put this behind us," I tell Julian, extending my hand.

"I agree," he says, returning a firm shake. "But we still need to settle things once and for all. Like men." Call it instinct, but I can feel a setup here, and my instinct can't be wrong. Perhaps it's Julian's earlier threat that was playing on my mind. "You'll be sorry you crossed me," he'd said. "You'd better understand that you're alone."

"Take it outside, Godboy," I sneer. Like rats, more like.

"You bastard," he spits.

I'm hanging by a single stitch, laughing at the

stony face of gloom. He comes at me, and now we're coming face to face. I'm faster than the speed of sound and I show him no pity. I've smashed a bottle and slam the shards into the fucker's face, but he's had the same idea and I feel the hot trickle as my face is torn in shreds at the same instant. We both fall to the ground, blind, destroyed.

"You've got glass in your mouth... maggot," he snarls.

Out of the corner of my eye, I see my mother sink a large glass of vodka, a full half pint. She tanks her poison, takes it quick, takes it neat, falls to her knees and in an instant her eyes bug and she's lying glassy-eyed on the ground. Something tells me the sun ain't gonna shine any more for her. A ghastly gurgling wheeze and she is still. Momentarily I enjoy the silence.

I look back at Julian as he stands before me: he looks good in ribbons. There's no love lost, but he begins to speak.

"You think you've got it all worked out," he gurgles as gouts of blood spume forth from his lips. "It was a plot... you reap what you sow. I must learn to accept my reward... Tom's to blame for all of this."

Tom has rushed over to see what the commotion is, and with my last remaining strength I plunge the makeshift blade into him, once, twice, three times. He stumbled and fell, blood pulsing from his carotid artery and spraying like b-movie gore. Then he hit the floor, snuffed.

"Justice is served," Julian croaked as he slipped to

his knees. "Forgive me, William..." he stopped. He slumped as h bled out at my feet.

Realising that my own blood loss was heavy, I began to feel myself fading.

"Caine... I am dead." I could not hide the surprise in my voice. I hadn't expected to go down like this.

I can feel that I'm slipping away. Nobody cares when you're gone... The last thing I see is Tom's glazed eye and I realise he has my father's eyes. I close my lids across my eyes, and wish to see no more. As the light pours of out me, I hear my father's voice once more... Oh, to sleep... to dream.

BUTTERFLIES
D M Mitchell

You walk down the flight of steps following the sound of the machinery, to a large oaken door. You have a dim notion, somewhere in the darting shoal of fish which constitutes your consciousness, that you shouldn't be here – should, in fact, be somewhere else. Doing other things. But the momentum of the moment carries it away, or rather propels you to a point where notions have no import.

Opening the door, you find a dimly lit chamber filled with gears and machines which chatter away like hostile pygmies, in a foot or so of stagnant water. Suddenly you realise you're dreaming, but unlike the popular myth regarding dreams, you don't wake with this realisation. From above you somewhere sounds the booming of titanic waves, which you eventually recognise as the sound of Mahler's First Symphony. In the apparent absence of choice, you comply with the dream's logic and cross the threshold, wading through the water in the dim, stroboscopic flicker of strip lighting. You momentarily remark to yourself that it is impossible to smell things in dreams, then push through the rusted dripping chains and arrive at the lip of a sunken arena.

A caterpillar of fear crawls along your neck and down your spine. In the centre of the open space are three draped mortuary slabs, outlines suggestive of human figures beneath each cloth. Something small and white flits through a beam of diffused light and one of the drapes begins to slip off, revealing the prone form of your wife. She wears the wedding dress she hasn't worn for fifteen years. You stretch out a frozen arm and a cry turns to a dry insect rattle in your throat.

Above you, the Mahler climbs to a crescendo as the second drape begins to slide. As you suspected, your daughter lies naked beneath. Before the third pall can move you turn and crash through the chains, leaving them swinging. You wake soaking wet.

(it began the day i arrived home to face the news that the doctors' diagnosis and our own worst fears were confirmed my mother had cancer and within six months would be dead – we pulled her through pneumonia by suctioning the mucus from her lungs – the intravenous tube had been removed)

"Where the hell did you sleep last night Jonathan?"

Amy stares coldly at you across a vast desert of kitchen table. You cough and frown, sip your coffee without answering. Fighting the hangover is taking all your energy.

"In a hedge, a field?"

Despite the harsh words, her voice is flat and calm, almost bored. She's delivered similar harangues so many times, that this one slips off her tongue with practised ease.

"Oh, what the fuck do I care?"

She slams a cupboard door. A token gesture. She doesn't care. She stays because of your income. You've never offered her violence, not even verbally. She stays.

"I rang Trevor and he said you were steaming when you left the club – couldn't even walk straight, he said. And when he begged you not to drive, you told him to fuck off! Do you realise how often I have to apologise for your behaviour? You've lost all your friends. Are you even listening to me now?"

"I'm listening." you read the back of a cereal packet

"Good job you're insured because it's only a matter of time..." her voice becomes a blur in your head, like the beating of some huge insect's wings. Knotting your tie you gaze out of the window at a distant hang-glider making an early start. You try to kiss your wife, but she side-steps with practised ease. As you leave the house and open the car door you hear the television come on. Ricki Lake? Oprah? Or some other vicarious substitute for real emotional contact. This is the way we live our lives, you think, and it's probably better this way. At least it doesn't hurt. Not really hurt.

(the sixth week she looked better each day i watched and wondered at the flesh in her cheeks dulled to what was taking place and what could it mean but grateful all the same to the nurses who seemed genuinely concerned – the sixth week she looked better – each day i watched and wondered at the flesh in her cheeks – oh mother i didn't)

You're back at your father's sick bed. Unlike dreams, memories carry smells. You stand again, over the old man who lays coughing blood and shivering. At the time, you felt frozen, paralysed inside by the fear of death – not your own death – just death in the abstract sense. Nothingness. Most of all – loss. You realise now that you stopped feeling altogether on that very day. The numbness seemed somehow preferable to the tide of grief which threatened to engulf you.

They'd thought at first it had been food poisoning but it was the final stages of a fatal disease nobody had even suspected. You'd watched blankly as your father tossed and sweated all night like a woman in labour, only finding relief in the morning when the doctor had finally arrived and given him a pain-killer. When your mother turned back the sheets a huge, horned green caterpillar had crawled from the bedding. Several weeks later your father died and when the remains were planted in the soil like some grisly seed, a single white butterfly had risen from the still open grave, gleaming in the dying sunlight.

In your childhood you had a recurring dream of the old flour mill near your home. In the dream, you found green bones deep in the basement, faintly glowing. With the strange incongruity of dreams, this discovery had impressed you with the force of a revelation. In the dream, if not in life, vistas of possibility had opened – vast horizons of Nietzschean proportion. Yet always in the back of your head was that dead weight which brought you crashing back down – taking the form of a menacing presence lurking Leviathan-like within the walled-up section of the old building. You felt its stifling breath and heard its colossal shifting.

Panic-stricken, your dreaming self would search for an exit, eventually fastening on a hole in the structure's inner wall, and wriggling through. The dream logic, however, always twisted and trapped you. You discovered, with a cold shock, that instead of escaping, you'd actually gone deeper in, getting closer to the thing from which you were attempting to flee. Down crumbling stairs, between hanging chains and rusted grain-chutes where a swastika was painted crudely on the wall. Finally into the chamber where, above the rusted remains of gears and mechanisms, was suspended the enormous cocoon, throbbing claustrophobically with its own light.

Crying for your mother, you'd awake.

(as i went in a seething anger swept over the room where mother was it was a fetish nothing less yes that was the word for society to worship the flesh while it was still alive imprisoned again the tube was in heedlessly to prolong life she was receiving the destroying spirit her hands were tied again not to measure the semblance of life but to confirm that the machinery her squirming had caused to be brought was functioning it sat there maternally watching – disheartened desolation in the mist of infinity – a searing anger swept over the room – to worship the flesh while it was still alive still imprisoned)

79

You wake slowly, taking time to focus on the room. With a sudden jolt, you notice your daughter, Stephanie, is sitting on the bed beside you. You have the unnerving certainty that she's been sitting there a while, just watching you.

"You shouldn't sneak up on people like that, love!"

"Daddy, what's wrong with you? You were making an awful noise in your sleep."

"Bad dream, love. Too much cheese last night. What have you been up to?"

"Just been shopping with Annabelle. Bought some new outfits."

"Jesus, Steph! You bought one yesterday. You must be spending a fortune on clothes!"

"You used to tell me that I was worth more to you than all the money in the world!"

Her words are light, but her tone is flat and heavy.

"We don't have all the money in the world, Steph... Where's your mother?"

"She's gone out with the dogs." She looks down at her lap, then back again with penetrating directness. "What's wrong with you and Mum? You're not going to split up are you?"

The question takes your breath away for a moment. You'd hoped your daughter hadn't noticed the tension between her parents.

"I don't think so love. It's just a little patch we're going through. It'll all blow over soon, you'll see."

(now mother's position in bed was changed and a

catheter tube was introduced to catch the urine and chemicals that dripped through on schedule to prevent bedsores and a tube fastened in her nose passed to provide comfort another tube hung through her body from a bedside stand for intravenous feeding and emptied efficiently into a pouch at the foot of her bed – disheartened desolation in the mist of infinity – it was a fetish nothing less – receive the destroying spirit)

You walk, yet again, down the cellar steps, listening to the dismal sound of the machines below stirring hateful memories from the dim recesses of your childhood mind. When the door below begins to open, panic grips you, slapping you backwards up the stairs, through a door and into the hallway of your house. A grandfather clock you don't actually have ticks discordantly. You run into a dream-distorted living room knocking into furniture you no longer own. The room is bathed in a pulsating green light, stretched and distorted. The Mahler booms and echoes, dribbling caustically in a nitrous-oxide parody of your favourite recording. You force your hands into your mouth to stop from screaming as the door opens and a withered hand comes creeping insect-like round the jamb. Childishly, you throw yourself behind the sofa and wait, trembling as the rasping breath you've been dreading approaches. A thin quivering voice calls your name.

"Jonathan, you naughty boy. Where are you?"

Urine trickles down your leg as thin bony hands grip your wrist and spin you around to face gaping insect mandibles. You scream yourself awake again.

"What the fuck are you screaming at?"

Reality floods back into you with the pain of blood returning to a constricted limb. You look at your wife's concerned face and wonder from what ocean of unconscious experience she's just risen. Vomit rises suddenly to your throat and you catch it in your hands as you run for the bathroom.

"You're a stupid drunken bastard Jonathan and I'm leaving you. Do you hear me? I'm taking Stephanie with me tomorrow and I'm leaving."

Your head feels like it's full of broken glass as you stagger back to the bedroom.

"I'm not drunk. I only had the one with Clive at lunchtime. It must be flu..."

"You lying bastard. I rang the office this afternoon and you hadn't even come back from lunch. Clive answered the phone. Where the hell have you been all evening? What time did you sneak into bed?"

Shock settles on you as you realise you can't remember.

"What's happened to you, Jonathan? What's wrong with you?"

She turns her back on you, pulling the duvet around her like a cocoon. You stare at her impotently for several minutes, then go downstairs, dress, and take the car keys from the sideboard.

(we pulled her through pneumonia by suctioning the mucus from her lungs they said how thoughtful i reflected and gave each one ten bucks then i entered the room and

was startled to find that the intravenous tube had been removed from her arm – a sheet had slipped off and she was lying there nude – i kissed her degradation that made a mockery of living – the pain threatening to consume us all – what does society want – oh mother i didn't mean i didn't)

The cat's eyes rush and vanish in a blur of green as you push the car like a weapon along the narrow country lane. Every so often you thump the steering wheel and swear. After a while you wipe tears from your eyes. You're pleasantly surprised. You cannot remember the last time you cried. Buildings and then trees fly past and then the old woman steps out in front of you, so suddenly that there's no possibility of avoiding her. Bones crunch audibly as she hits the bonnet and flies over the roof.

You stop the car and numbly step out. Her dark huddled form lies just outside the pool of light cast by the headlamps. A thin white hand stretches out towards you, picked out feebly by the beam. With a shock of recognition you leap back into the car and pull away at breakneck speed.

No blood! You keep thinking to yourself. There should have been some blood, but there was no blood!

(a sheet had slipped off and she was lying there nude i kissed her degradation that made a mockery of living what does society want and the nurses again were kind and in heavens name why the anger has not left me still it will in time mother was suffering the pain threatening to

consume us all why are those who value living so
insensitive then i was privileged at last to watch her die a
tired defenceless body laid out against the machine –
terminal two hours – give death its dignity – oh mother i
didn't mean)

In your dream you run from the house into the snow. Behind you the house is burning with a green flame. You know you're fleeing something impossible to face but can't remember what. Your face and hands are sticky. You run from the house between two rows of cedars. Glancing up at the sky, you're shocked to see a vast black sun. So numb are your feet that you don't feel the old lady when you trip over her. You look down at her pitiful frame lying face down in the snow and reach out your hands to turn her over. For an instant you hesitate – she looks as brittle and dry as an old stick as though she'd crumble under your fingers. Finally you touch her and she turns with blinding speed, her insect jaws opening towards your face.

You lie awake, body wet and shivering. You remember your mother in the lonely sanatorium, a tube in her nose, another removing waste chemicals at regular intervals. Her skin, almost transparent, revealed the network of blue veins beneath and, at the extremities, the soapy flesh seemed almost to glow from within. What metamorphosis did she undergo in that place? If they'd cut her open, what marvellous creature would have emerged from the putrefying cocoon of her body, spreading kaleidoscopic wings in the light of its brave new world? You dress and walk out to the car.

(at first she seemed to be able to withstand the daily agony but gradually the pain got so bad she was taken into the local hospital and drip fed pain killing drugs and watched constantly twenty four hours a day she lay on her back in the bed while each evening i tied her hands to the bed rails – oh mother i didn't mean it – oh mother)

You pull up and search the undergrowth until you find what you're looking for. Something has dragged itself through here recently. You follow the trail, twigs and branches tagging your hair like withered old hands, scratching your face and tagging his clothes. You step in something soft that gives off a foul smell. Something in your stomach and chest feels like it's about to rip. You think you're going to start screaming. You glance around. Nobody in sight, so finally you let it all out. The trapped thing in the brackets of your chest – the small thing with no identity that has been flapping there for as long as you can remember. It has gotten bigger lately, too big to contain any more, so you let it out to fly away to wherever it belongs.

When it finally comes, you are pleasantly surprised. Instead of a scream, there is laughter. Not unpleasant hysterical laughter, but laughter, so golden and joyful that you don't want it to stop. Eventually it leaves you and you start to cry, sitting down and rocking back and forth hugging your knees.

It's almost an hour later that you reach the clearing where a large white shape flaps brokenly at the centre, looking like something trapped beneath the folds of a parachute. All fear is gone, replaced by a calm acceptance. Only for a moment do you consider getting a can of petrol from the car, deciding that the reunion is long overdue. As you approach the flapping thing becomes agitated.

"It's ok. I'll never leave you again."

What will they do when they find your car? You no longer care. Bending down, you lift the corner of the white canopy and the form below reaches up with its snapping jaws to kiss you and you embrace your guilt, fully, finally in the cold light of day...

CAVEMAN
(A WICKED CHILDHOOD TALE)
Lana Gentry

I often refrain from telling my truths for two reasons. The first one being that they are so bizarre I fear people will not believe them. The other reason is that my experiences are so full of unthinkable darkness they are much like a sponge that has found its level of liquid and is now dripping like a caustic acid onto the flesh of those who read them. In the end, it is my way of being. So you have been told now that you may not want to read this and you will make your own choice. I will however, proceed to tell it as was, believed, appreciated or not.

Caveman...

When I was young enough to wear patent leather shoes, I would sometimes go with my mother to her part time job where she answered phones at the local Salvation Army. For those in my area, it was behind what was 'The Arena' and is now by the ballpark called the Diamond. It was overseen, as I recall, by a man named Brigadier Ward and his wife. It was, as many are, a thrift store that was run by recovering drug addicts and alcoholics who were housed in dorms at this facility where my mother worked. She managed the mundane tasks of her duties in a glassed in office that overlooked a hallway and then another glass windowed large rec room where the recovered addicts would congregate to engage in simple entertaining activities such as television, card games and the like. My mother worked weekends there and would walk me to the rec room where I stayed while she worked. To be clear, on each side of the rec room, there was a door. One door was to the hallway beside the window where I could see my mother working through the window when she was not up and about, and the other door led to the dorm.

I was pathetically attached to my mother and would often press my face against the window to soothe myself. The dismal rec room was walled with white cold cinderblock and the floors were paved with waxed yellowish tiles. It was a large room and one had to buzz in and out of that room as to keep the tenants incarcerated while they detoxed. The front of that room was where I was able to look out the glass window across the hall to see my mother working, but if you walked back into the room there were billiards, and finally a curtained off area that contained plastic chairs organized in rows before a television. This room was dark and a bit of a make shift theater where the men would gather to watch television while visually obscured from in the remainder of the room. Shuffling duck tailed and flat topped fellows made their way by morning from the dorm to the rec room in their wrinkled flannels and white tees.

I was shy, as you might not imagine, but quickly became comfortable with many of them after several stays at the facility. There was one man in particular who was always friendly and would sit beside me in the room. He was monstrously large, had brilliant white hair cut nearly to the scalp but also had some other distinguishing features. He wore thick glasses, had a severe speech impediment and was missing fingers to the knuckle. I also remember quite clearly that he was covered in the thickest amount of hair I had ever seen, which spilled like cotton from each opening of his shirt.

I was always very lingual and some of the other men found humor in the fact that I seemed to be better able than them to decipher the speech of this man they called 'Pop.' He was one of the older transient tenants and we would look at books together. We often went to the back part of the theater area which was shrouded by the curtain and we sat in the plastic chairs while watching cartoons. This weekend ritual soon became a game of chase as he ran behind me and we giggled while making our circular runs around the chairs. On one such occasion the ritual changed on the turn of a dime and he moved his monstrous body around me as I ran, knocking me down into the darkness of the corner and leaned over me saying these muddied words… "I dwant dit ooo in a deeee dah ole."

And I knew exactly what he was saying, at which time he ran his fingerless hands across my dress and pinned me to the floor baring his teeth like a pincher. I struggled in horror and kicked my shoes against the waxy floor trying to get away from his grasp as he repeated his mantra. "I dwant dit oo in a deee dah ole."

As he heard other men entering the rec room through the buzz door he released his hands long enough for me to bolt from his grasp as I fell but raised to my feet again to run like mad to the lighted area of the rec room where I headed straight for the buzzer beside the window where my mother was sometimes seen. She was not there, but I pushed the buzzer and slapped my hands till they stung against the glass for anyone to see. No one came so I buzzed again... and again... and again. He followed me there.

When my mother finally came, she giggled a bit at the story as I tried to explain my horror... but she returned me to the room in her assumption that I simply wanted to be near her. I did not return to the curtained area. More disheartening days would follow on weekends as I was held against my will in the rec room. I'd go again and again as my mother worked, and despite my avoidance of the curtained area, he would still move up beside me and repeat those words which no one believed I could possibly understand.

Finally one night at home, I would repeat the story to my father who had been a convict at the Spring Street Prison in Richmond Virginia in the sixties. Then and there he called my mother into the room and the real terror began. My mother recanted the actual name of 'Pop' to my father, which I now do not remember and have made great strides to uncover.

According to my father, who explained the story in great depth in my presence, 'Pop' had spent decades in the pen with him and was known to the other inmates simply as 'Caveman', and they all kept their distance. Daddy said he was covered in the thickest of jet black black hair in his youth from head to toe. He had been found in the hills of Virginia tucked away in a dark cave where he had the genitals of a woman in his pocket and was cannibalizing other various parts. His release found him in the halfway house at the local Salvation Army behind the Diamond where we met. My aunt who also worked in the sorting room for the Thrift Store of that same Salvation Army later corroborated the story through her tale of a similar incident she'd had in the hallway when passing him.

She had heard it too... That same dark mantra... thinly veiled by his impediment so clear to my lingual ears, "I dwant di oo in a deee dah ole..." or the clearer interpretation, "I want to get you in a deep dark hole."

A deep dark hole. A cave perhaps.

DEMONS
Claire Godden Rowland

I felt the end of my bed sink; he was here again. The cold shudder of fear seized me, vice like, relentless. He was here. I was too afraid to look and too frightened to close my eyes so I stared, instead, into the blackness of the room around me. I fixed on the familiar shapes, my chest of draws, lit by the pallid moonlight. I felt the bed shift a little as if a body had sat down upon it. I froze, was he coming closer? I could see the little red light on my bed side phone. If I could make my hand reach out from the warmth of the bedding to the unprotected cold I could touch it. I could call my stepdad, Allen, and before long he would arrive. I would hear his key in the lock and he would comfort me and sit up most of the night drinking hot chocolate having searched my flat for a ghostly presence and found none. I wanted to reach for that phone but my hands were unmoving and claw like as they clutched the perceived safety of the bedclothes to me.

Then I felt more movement. He shifted his position. I felt a tug on the bed clothes. He was pulling them from me. I felt them move down over my bare shoulder and the air was icy on my flesh, making my skin prickle. I yelped with fear and grasped bed clothes back to my shivering body. My brain was assaulted by strange pictures, strange flashes, and images from a source unknown. I imagined a form sliding in behind me and holding my body against theirs. It was a man and his erection pressed against my spine. I could feel hands over me and gentle, teasing whispering in my ear. I curled up tighter and coaxing hands reached to my thighs and pulled them back down so my body fitted against his; the eager breathing in my ear, the feral sound of hunger.

I tugged the duvet, desperately trying to re-cover my body, to protect myself with it somehow. How was this possible, what were these visions I was being battered with?

I felt an icy hand on my ankle. This was no vision, this was real. I was being pulled toward the demon at the end of my bed. I squealed and kicked out, only my foot went through whatever it was which pulled me. I heard laughter and a mixture of panic and strange anger propelled me from the bed. As I catapulted onto the floor and landed on my knees I grabbed my phone. I scrabbled to my feet and before I could stop myself I turned to face my attacker.

I screamed! The figure rose slowly and precisely from the bed. It was tall, much taller than me, nearly double my height, and it wore a cloak of black with a heavy hood which covered its face completely. For a heartbeat I was frozen to the spot, my legs like stone, and my heart pounding hard against my breast. I was wearing only shorts and a vest but I was sweating with terror. The demon lifted a hand to me, a long bony hand which appeared human, like a human male's, with dark hair across the knuckles. It seemed so real that for a moment I paused, but as I watched the demon I realised I could see my curtains, my window, I could see through him. The hand reached for me and then I realised the creature was making a noise. It was shushing me, a low broken hiss to silence me as it approached. I spun around, slammed into my bedroom door and fumbled helplessly with the handle. The thing was behind me, so close I could hear its breathing, deep, laboured breathing. I could feel it, all of it, its presence too close, far too close. Then my mind disappeared to another place once more. Tearing between my legs, repeated ripping, sharp, acute pain. There was a hand covering my mouth to stop me crying out for help, and a shushing, a low hiss of shushing hot on my ear.

I screamed with fury and dread, and with a violent wrench, my bedroom door burst open, hitting my face and arm clumsily as I burst through it.

I erupted into the open space of my apartment and flew across it, past the table, toward the kitchen area. I began to dial frantically on the phone, fumbling the numbers in my haste with shaking fingers. At the kitchen I spun around toward my bedroom door, I couldn't see the demon and I couldn't run any further. I could hear the agonising rings down the phone, each one taking an eternity, torturing me with its rhythm. I strained my eyes toward the blackness of my bedroom door and what I knew lurked within. The phone continued to ring and I began to plead with it out loud, desperate for rescue, for my mother or Allan wake up.

As the phone continued in my ear and I began to openly sob at the thought of them having gone out somewhere, another sound joined the cacophony inside my head. It was a thudding, a padded thudding, rhythmic and continuous and the sound clawed at my brain. The drumming grew louder, closer, and I wailed in fear as I listened helplessly. Then it struck me; it sounded like feet on carpet.

At the same moment the thudding stopped, the creature appeared at my bedroom door and I heard Allen's voice sleepy and distracted down the phone. The sight of the creature was too much to bear and I began to scream hysterically down the phone.

'Help me; help me … hurry … please God…'

The creature moved toward me, its hands outstretched, almost as if I may be persuaded to take them. It was still shushing me as it approached.

Allen was screaming my name down the phone, over and over, the panic cold in his voice. Then the phone went dead and the momentary silence was filled by a dial tone. I threw the phone at the creature and it sailed straight through it smashing against the wall by my bedroom door.

Then I was somewhere else. My flat was gone, evaporated, the scene changed to a new venue. I was in my parent's house, I was upstairs and it was dark. I could tell it was late at night, I'm not sure how, perhaps it was the stillness. Then the thudding began, softly at first then coming closer, heavy portentous footsteps. I rushed along the corridor and tried my parent's door. It was locked. I couldn't believe it was locked. There wasn't even a lock on their door. I began to pound on the door but it was lost in the thunder of the footsteps along the corridor, getting closer, louder, closer, and louder. He was coming. He was coming for me and I knew what he wanted. I began to bleed from between my legs. I sobbed a heavy, desperate sob and placed a hand to myself. It was so painful, so sore, as the blood sticky and hot trickled through my fingers. The footsteps grew louder, closer, and the blood was no longer a trickle it was a torrent, gushing through my fingers and smearing over my thighs. The pain was intense and I collapsed to the floor screaming, kicking backward, pushing against the locked door at my back as I watched my blood pool mercilessly around me, gleaming black in the moonlight. Then the creature was above me, its face hidden but I knew it was smiling down at me, with a twisted fondness. It was on me and the blood poured faster, I was drenched in it, my shorts sodden. The door opened and I burst through it and was back in my apartment.

I was no longer bleeding; my legs dry and I stumbled to my feet and reached for a vase which sat in my front window. I leapt to my feet and turned to face the creature which stood before me.

I was panting hard and crying hysterically, all reason given way to panic and fear ricocheting around my skull. The visions continued to assault me. Rape: But the strangest kind, administered with gentleness, almost nurturing. Tears poured down my cheeks and I wiped at them frantically, the glass vase raised above my head like a cricket bat, ready to strike at my ghostly assailant.

Finally the creature stopped approaching. It stood on the other side of the coffee table, the orange light from the street lights outside giving him an eerie glow.

'Stay the fuck back,' I ordered through gritted teeth, struggling to keep my voice steady, adrenaline shooting through me.

Was he laughing? It sounded like laughter, or was it sorrow, was he crying?

Standing my ground felt so good, it was empowering, it was euphoric and the creature seemed to shrink slightly.

He held out his hands, those human hands, in a gesture of peace, visibly growing smaller, becoming my size now.

Curiosity crept into my brain, and there was another feeling, another notion I could not yet grasp but it hovered close, just out of my conscious reach. 'What are you?'

The fear, although still pumping through my veins, was being surpassed by the other thing, the sensation which lingered just outside my reach.

'Are you sure you want to see?'

The voice, although whispered was so familiar. Still that whisper clawed at me, just out of range and I narrowed my eyes at the spectre before me, concealed beneath the heavy hood.

'Tell me,' I found myself screaming. 'Tell me.'

'Are you ready?'

'Fucking tell me!'

'Are you sure, you want to see?'

'Fucking tell me,' I repeated furiously, my voice rising to a screech.

I heard the key in the lock. The creature grasped its hood. The door began to open. The creature lowered the hood. Allen burst into the room, his face stricken with fear. I saw the demon's face. Recognition like a tidal wave assaulted my brain, thundering in with all natures' force, barriers of repression crumbling beneath its power. I remembered everything, like a hideous dream bombarding my brain with its unforgiving garish colours. The footsteps along the hallway at night, clutching my covers to my body as I listened to them grow louder, the child's need to please, to cooperate. The bed moving as another body sat upon it, pulling down the covers, exposing my naked body and climbing in behind me, and the pain, followed by the brutal and diminishing shame. The misery of everyday at school knowing you were different but being uncertain how, knowing it was wrong but not knowing how it could be. The pain of it all so exquisite it had been blocked out all these years.

I stared at the exposed face in utter disbelief, my own memory rediscovered from its dark hiding place. I stared at the face, my tormentor, my abuser and my step father. As the demon vanished I turned to Allan and I swung the vase and brought it down on his skull, the shattering of glass and cracking of bone resonated around the apartment. I saw the look of comprehension on his face. As he lay on the floor, staring up at me in surprise I leant forward and, raising my fingers to my lips, I shushed him just before he died.

HAUNTING
Andrew Maben

Last night.
Last night,
As I slept.
Last night,
As I slept
She came to me.
After so many
Years.
Her memory,
Her soft voice,
Her gentle
Curls, those
Blue eyes…
Her face
Has haunted
All the long
And oh so
Lonely years.
A love that,
Unreturned,
Had left me,
Until now,
Incapable
Of love.
Her cold words
Have followed me.
Her cold words,
Her devastating

Superlative,
Convince me,
Until now,
Convict me
To unending
Solitude.
Until now.

And now?

At last I have
Dared
To love
Another.
And now those
Words
Echoing across
Those long
And oh so
Lonely years.
I hear
Again
Those cruel
Words
Echoed in
Another's
Soft voice,
Another
Whose
Blue eyes,
Whose face...

But last night.
Last night,
As I slept.
Last night,
As I slept
She came to me.
She came to me
As I saw her
That morning.
The words
I spoke
That day,
Those long
And oh so
Lonely years
Ago,
Were not
The words
I should
Have said:
"You look
So old."

But last night.
Last night,
As I slept.
Last night,
As I slept
She came to me.
She came to me,
And in my dream

The words
I spoke
Were
The words
I should
Have said:
"You look
So young."

But when,
Last night.
Last night,
As I slept.
When
Last night,
As I slept
She came to me,
And all
Those long
And oh so
Lonely years
Ago,
The words
Trapped in
My heart
Were the same:
"You look,
You are,
So beautiful."

RESISTING PERSISTENCE
Kimberly Dallesandro

The phone rang.

I had just found a photo labeled "Jessie S. 1970" in the cellophane packet in a box from the closet. I ignored the call, staring at the young man of 20 or 21 with an aggressive stance, thick premature gray hair almost chin length, wearing a camouflage jacket and pointing to dog tags that glittered around his neck. There were obvious injuries on his face and neck, though they appeared to be healing, and his right hand was wrapped in gauge and held a cigarette. I kept the photo out so I could look at it when I listened to the man's voice on the tape.

The phone began ringing again.

I was hesitant to answer because of the early hour, afraid of what news the call might bring. I sat down at the desk and reached for the phone. I heard a dial tone and placed the phone back in its cradle. "Should have taken the call" I thought, the rest of the empty day looming ahead of me.

The phone rang again.

"This is Kathy."

I was staring at the cellophane packet filled with photos while opening a pill bottle. One rolled into my palm as I picked up my diet soda and took a drink washing down the first of many I would take throughout the day.

"Good morning Kathy, I'm calling about Jesse Smith. I got this number from a friend of a friend. I was wondering if you have seen Jesse or have a current phone number for him."

I physically bent from the waist, both hands crossed over my stomach when I heard the name, my heart began to beat faster, and I noticed my hand shook as I brought the phone back to my ear.

"You have a wrong number."

I hung up.

I don't know if the caller heard my voice get smaller and crack- if he realized the effort it took to hang the phone up- the sweat on my palms, my dry mouth, or the sensation of dizziness that had come over me. I checked caller ID and noticed that the last 3 calls had come from the same number. I walked to the front window and looked out through the closed blinds at the street. Neighbors were walking their dogs, cars were parked, traffic was stopping at the 4-way. Everything as it always was. Except for me, I thought. I walked back to the desk and sat down. There are moments in life that duplicate what some have described as the process of dying. My mind moved through a series of people, places and events, pushing faster towards the light that was the face of Jesse Smith.

I went to the closet and removed a tape labeled #22 from the box. I pushed it into the recorder, took a deep breath clicked it on and listened.

"I like small spaces, I require very little just me 2 weapons, one loaded under my pillow, the other a 12" knife, blade down leaning in the shower, in case they climb through the window, ease under the door

when I'm in there and try to catch me off guard-
never will catch me off guard (laughs). My piles of
laundry folded precisely-there and there- surround
me- clothes hanging just right easy 1" between each
garment so I can see between them in case one of
them is hiding- always 1" between them. The dust
doesn't matter to me, the filth of this place, my
ashtray always overflowing, I should empty it but I
don't give a fuck about that. Stacks of advertising
shit- buy this buy that, I date and keep every piece of
mail in those boxes, takes me forever to figure out
my bills, what I owe what they want-- I read every
single line every piece of mail date it and keep it as
evidence, just in case they come say I did it wrong, I
have the proof. Here, look. This calendar records
everything; information moved from the front of
each envelope to the day on this calendar, I spend
hours every day fucking with this pile of mail. Then I
lay down here on this pallet with my loaded gun
under my pillow; leave the TV on all day all night to
wipe out the sounds of guns (tat tat tat) I hear in my
head. I find it calming the companionship I have
with this TV. Over there I have stacks of money
zipped into that cushion. The US Government gives
it to you then they try to steal it back so I cash every
damn check as soon as it comes and hide it in that
cushion. They're always waiting to find some way to
insist I owe them, have to beat them at that game. I
pay for this room, these cigarettes, little bit of food
and stuff- you know stuff (laughs). I guess I'm
content in here. Honestly, when I stay alone too long

the voices get louder and I pull the gun out all night and wait. They're everywhere, Baby Doll, can't bear to be alone, don't trust anybody, either way I'm fucked."

I shut the recorder off and removed the tape and put it back into the box and shuffled through the photographs stopping at one with the same aggressiveness, but the eyes were empty. On the back was written "Jessie Smith 1971".

The phone rang.

(Excerpt from *Mad Dog Tag*)

CONFESSIONS OF A
TEENAGE GHOST-HUNTER
Charles Christian

It was one of those autumn evenings that catch you out. When the clocks have just gone back on to daylight-saving time and you forget how quickly a late afternoon can switch from bright sun to dusk... and then total darkness. One of those evenings when, almost the moment the sun falls below the horizon, the temperature plummets and a fog starts to roll in across the open meadows and farmland.

Georgia and I have been out walking the dog along the farm tracks and bridleways behind our house and are just cutting back through a spooky little copse call Websills Wood when the light starts to go. Then it happens.

Perhaps it is only my imagination or the sudden chill in the air but all the hairs on the nape of my neck begin to tingle and I just know we have to hurry back home – to safety – and that, whatever else I do, I must never peer behind me. I can tell by the way Georgia has increased her pace that she is also aware something is amiss. Even our dog Woolfgang (I know, why do we give dogs these names) is straining for home with more determination than usual. Pulling at the end of his leash – and barely visible in the increasingly dense fog – Woolfie's ears are slicked down onto a head that never once glances back in the direction of the wood.

Later, as we sit by the fire at home, Georgia asks

me what I'd felt when we were in the wood. "Go on," she says, "the honest truth, not some macho bullshit."

"OK," I say, "the truth. I had this sensation – stupid though it now sounds – that I was being stalked by some foul fiend that would snatch my soul away to Hell if I ever looked back and caught sight of it."

Georgia laughs. "A bit late to worry about that," she adds.

"What about you?" I ask. "I noticed you go tense – well as tense as you ever can go tense – as if something had unsettled you,"

"Just feminine intuition," she replies. "We women can always tell when our menfolk are worried."

There's no answer to that but I still push the point. "So what did you think I might be worried about? Come on, you be honest as well."

"Well, it crossed my mind that a dark, foggy night like this would be ideal cover for any mad axe-wielding, psycho serial killers who might be on the prowl."

Now it's my turn to laugh. "Serial killers! In the depths of the Norfolk countryside? You can wander along those tracks for miles, for days on end, and never meet a living soul. In the fog on a November evening, your serial killer's more likely to break his own neck falling down a rabbit hole. If there are any serial killers on the loose, you'll find them lurking in backstreets of Norwich. There are plenty of places to hide – and no shortage of people to kill. At least my fears have some foundation, you know those woods are supposed to be haunted by a headless monk."

Georgia throws a play-punch in my direction – it doesn't make contact. "Haunted by a headless monk! You know the woman who told you that is away with the fairies. And where did this monk come from, since we're miles from the nearest monastic ruins. But tell me," she continues, doing that eye fluttering thing women do when they are signalling they are interested in what you have to say yet simultaneously humouring you "have you always had this thing about ghosties, ghoulies and things that go bump in the night? When did my little Alexis" (that's me by the way) she pats me on the knee as she says this, "first start to be fascinated by the supernatural?"

"That would have been when I was a little kid, back home in Scarborough," I say. "The house was an old building – a Georgian frontage on a medieval core – with an interior that ignored the normal rules of architecture and seemed more influenced by the principles of non-Euclidean geometry. There were concealed doorways leading down into catacomb-like cellars. There was a blocked off passageway leading nowhere. My grandmother said it headed off towards the old castle on the headland and was once part of a network of secret tunnels used by smugglers.

"And then there were the attics. The roof timbers were from old ships and according to one of my more eccentric aunts, who claimed to have

110

clairvoyant powers, she could hear the ghostly footsteps of long-dead sailors in their seaboots."

"Oooo, spooky," says Georgia, "I can hear dead people." We both laugh.

"This aunt," I add, "lived in a little house jammed packed with her collection of china teapots."

"Sounds like she had one too many teapots with a cracked lid," says Georgia. "But let's get back to your ghosts, was that it? Did you ever hear these clumping seaboots?"

"No, I didn't. But, there was this weird thing that used to go on with my bed. On certain nights I'd be woken by the sensation of someone – or something – shaking the foot of my bed. Of course there was never anything there for me to see but it happened far too often for it to be my imagination or a bad dream. It used to wake me when I was young – and it was still waking me when I was a teenager. My father suggested it was gusts of wind hitting the side of the house and shaking my room. Plausible, I'll give you. But it also happened on still nights, when there was no wind.

"It did cross my mind that perhaps it was my parents playing some kind of trick on me." Georgia gives me an incredulous look. "So, on a couple of occasions I dusted the footboard of my bed with soot to see if whatever was shaking my bed was also leaving fingerprints."

"Soot? Fingerprints? What is this CSI: The Childhood Years?"

"Yes, soot," I reply, refusing to be drawn by

Georgia's teasing. "We still had coal fires and a sweep would come to clean the chimneys a couple of times a year. I scrounged the soot from him. Said it was for a school science project. Didn't do any good though. I never found any fingerprints."

"That's the trouble with ghosts," says Georgia. "Their totally inconsiderate tendency to not possess fingerprints. Or fingers. Or any other corporeal presence. So, are any there more confessions of a teenage ghost-hunter forthcoming tonight?"

"How much do you want to hear? When I moved to Leeds, to go to the university, I used to share a house with a medical student who also had an interest in the supernatural. We used to head out on nights to stake out supposedly haunted graveyards looking for ghosts. We had cameras. We had tape recorders. And plenty of flasks of coffee. But we never saw diddly-squat.

"Although we both nearly caught pneumonia sitting out in the grounds of Calverley Old Hall trying to catch a glimpse of Sir Walter's ghost. That's Sir Walter Calverley, he was crushed to death, on the orders of the Court of Star Chamber in 1604, because he refused to confess to a crime he was suspected of committing. And then there was Ethel Preston."

"Ethel who?" asks Georgia.

"Ethel Preston has a spectacular memorial in the Lawnswood Cemetery. It's from the Edwardian era, well anyway early Twentieth Century. It takes the form a full size house front-door, complete with a few steps leading up to it and is topped by portico.

But, the statue's the thing. At the top of the steps – and standing in front of the partially opened door – is a life-size in white marble statue of Mrs P in her prime. And I can tell you, the first time I saw this statue – in the fading light of a winter's twilight – I thought it was a ghost."

"So who was she," Georgia asks, "and why such an elaborate memorial?"

"There are two explanations," I reply. "The sanitized version is her ever-loving husband had it erected in her memory, to commemorate her loyalty and the fact she would always wait up for him on an evening, so she could greet him at the door when he returned from one of his business trips. The alternative version is Old Man Preston ran off with a chorus girl, so Mrs Preston – using her not-so-ever-loving-afterall husband's money – had the tomb built as a taunt from beyond the grave to say that despite the fact he had abandoned her, even in death she was waiting for him to return."

"I like her style," says Georgia, "a woman after my own heart."

"Georgie dearest," I reply, "you don't have a heart." Georgia gives me what my mother used to call an-old-fashioned look.

"But," I add, "the story doesn't end there, for over the past few years somebody has started placing bunches of fresh flowers in the arms of Ethel Preston's statue. Which is kind of odd as all her family are long dead and mouldering in their own graves by now.

"There was also the time," I continue, when I was cutting across the campus by way of an old graveyard – the St George's Field Burying Ground – which is now surrounded by university buildings. It was about midnight when something swooped down out of the inky-black night sky and knocked me to the floor. I could feel that whatever had attacked me had drawn blood. And, when I got back to my flat to clean myself up, I could see, reflected in the bathroom mirror, three parallel gashes in my scalp. Like something with sharp talons had slashed at my skull."

"You are making this up now?" says Georgia. "That, or it was an owl."

"That's what they said when I took myself down to A&E. Mind you the stitches and the tetanus jab they gave me hurt more than the original wound. And then it was on to London."

"You'd have been in your early twenties by then," asks Georgia, 'when you were attending law school?"

"Correct. By this time I was a member of the Society for Psychical Research and I also belonged to this outfit – called the Ghost Club – that used to meet in one of the Pall Mall clubs to discuss apparitions and hauntings. It was full of ghost story novelists and Madame Arcati – the Margaret Rutherford version – look-alikes.

"Anyway somewhere along the way I found myself on an expedition to look for a nest of vampires in Highgate Cemetery. This was the spooky, overgrown Western Cemetery with its crumbling family mausoleums and gothic vaults, rather than the smarter and tidier Eastern Cemetery that houses Karl Marx's grave."

"But vampires don't exist," says Georgia interrupting me mid-flow.

"I know that – and you know that," I reply "but that doesn't stop people believing in them, acting as if they are real and going the whole Van Helsing nine yards with the pointy wooden stakes and everything."

"So did you find this vampire infestation?"

"We did, there was an underground vault that had been broken into and inside we could see one of the coffins had been prised open and its contents sowed with salt before being set ablaze. All that remained were some gobbets of melted lead, from the coffin lining, embedded with flakes of charred bone. Oh yes, and there were about a dozen bulbs of garlic strewn around the tomb."

"Well that's one vampire, which never existed in the first place, that won't be returning to plague the living," says Georgia.

"Of course," I go on, "I was still a feckless youth back then, which is probably why I pulled a lump of the coffin-lead from the grave and took hit home as a souvenir. I used it as a paperweight."

Georgia winces, then pokes her fingers down her throat to simulate retching. "Where is it now?"

"I dumped it years ago. My first serious live-in girlfriend said it was gross, freaked her out and wanted me to get rid of it. As she was providing me with pretty much on-demand sex, as well as catering and laundry services, I certainly wasn't going to protest."

"Always the New Man, eh? And then what?" says Georgia.

"And then nothing," I reply. "The day job took over. And there was the first wife. And there was a mortgage to pay. You know, all those little distractions that suck the life out of us mortals.

"So that was your last encounter with the supernatural?"

I laugh. "You know that's not true." I haul myself out of the chair and head for the kitchen. "Do you want a glass of wine?" I ask out of habit, before remembering. "Of course not," I say, "you're not drinking at the moment are you?"

The kitchen is unusually cool, as if a chill has crept in with the night.

"No wine," says Georgia, "but I'd sell my soul for some chocolate. Ideally a 70 percent cocoa-solids bar of dark chocolate."

I nearly jump out of my skin. I hadn't realised she'd followed me into the kitchen and is now standing immediately behind me.

"Oops," she giggles, "I shouldn't have done that. I've scared the dog."

I look down. Woolfie is in his basket looking terrified, his eyes rolling white in fear.

I smile. "What do you want to do now? Mythbusters are running a feature on horror movie special effects. Should be right up your street."

Georgia laughs. One of her deep, down, dirty laughs. And then she vanishes. A split second later I hear her call from upstairs, from our bedroom. "You bring the soot," she says. "And I'll show you how to really make a bed shake."

A DREAM OF STONE
Craig Woods

"It's me! It's me ..."

Sarah's urgent but calming voice dragged me from the hyperreal panic of my dream and back into the composed reality of our bed.

"It's me, babe. Relax."

Heart still thundering from the fear of whatever peril had pursued my dream self, I paused for a few confused seconds as Sarah cradled and caressed my temples in her warm hands.

"What...?" I stammered, struggling to evaluate the sudden invasion of reality around me, flooding my ill-prepared senses with the fact of its existence.

"What indeed," Sarah replied, her voice soothingly husky from sleep. "That was quite the drama you put us through there. Looks like I have a few bruises to look forward to."

Dazedly, I brought up a hand to Sarah's face, returning her caress. "Shit, did I hit you?"

"Not 'hit' exactly. But you were pretty rough."

"Fuck. I'm sorry."

Her mouth curled into an affectionate grimace, revealing the crooked front teeth I so adored for their distinctiveness and which she characteristically detested. "Don't sweat it. I was just trying to restrain you. You had me pretty worried. Thrashing around and shouting at someone to tidy up their mess." She laughed at this. "Kind of funny that you should be so house-proud in your sleep."

Sarah and I had lived together for four and a half years and in that time had never felt the need to tidy the apartment or indulge in spring cleaning. As the home of musicians and artists, the apartment's every spare inch of floor space was typically occupied by art supplies, finished works, partly finished works, musical instruments... 'Tidying up' in such a climate would indeed constitute something of a subversive act.

"Can you remember what you dreamt?"

"Not really," I yawned, scouring my hazy post-dream psyche for any images or sounds which could shed light on the impetus for my violent outburst in the harmony of our bed. "I just remember panicking because of something someone else had done. Like I was scared of it being discovered ..."

"Mmmm ..." Apparently already dismissing the dream as an irrelevance, Sarah yawned and rubbed her eyes. "I'm going to go out to the Old Town today. Or what's left of it. Get some photos taken of those wonderful old buildings before they disappear for good."

The Old Town was the name given to the many blocks of tenements on the east side of the City, their sad grey silhouettes laying claim to much of the view beyond our windows. Ironically these glum structures were not particularly old at all, most of them having been built after the Second World War. In comparison to the stately manors of the city's more prosperous outskirts and the positively ancient sandstone block in which we ourselves lived, the buildings of the so-called Old Town seemed in fact quite youthful.

These brick and concrete tenements had been built as council accommodation; owned by the government and generally occupied by the elderly and those on low incomes or benefits. Over the course of the previous decade however, and with a decrease in the need for arduous physical labour, the government in collaboration with the most significant members of the country's corporate sector had rapidly rolled out a plan to incorporate the working classes and various other demographics deemed to be of minor productive value into its many High Rise Workstations. These colossal monoliths of concrete and steel had sprang up in swift succession and now dominated much of the urban landscape. At eighty storeys high apiece the Workstations were visible from every corner of the city and for miles beyond. Their rigid outlines loomed above the tenements like imperious sentinels, their glacial sheen and flawless symmetry an example of civil engineering perfected to the point of madness.

Each tower accommodated somewhere in the region of 25,000 Workers, all full time inhabitants who at no time left their respective complex. Each Worker was assigned a live-in Workspace of equally modest proportion, comprising a computer and telephone desk, a mini-kitchenette, a shower stall, minimal toilet facilities, enough floor space to roll out a sleeping bag, and the all-important television screen. Within the confines of these glorified alcoves, these most lowly paid of Workers used their telephones and computers to undertake the generally menial tasks of society now that manual labour was largely a thing of the past. Since the Workers' needs were provided for by the Workstation itself (mainly in the form of televisual diversions and the infinite cornucopia of predominantly fictionalised real-life material available on the internet), the concept of Worker's solidarity and Unions were likewise safely confined to the past. In short, life had become work and vice versa. Now that such tasks as home shopping were achieved without the customer ever having to leave their home, the occupants of the Workstations were by no means unique in their forsaking of the outside world. Supermarkets, along with all other corporate entities, now served the public via the Workstation staff who logged and electronically processed each customer demand which was then delivered by teams of specialist drivers. These ghosts of the ancient roadways would embark on weekly deliveries to each neighbourhood, depositing an entire block's worth of goods in the street for the occupants to collect. Since few people rarely crossed the threshold of their block or tenement other than to collect the week's rations, the fear of goods being stolen before they could be brought inside was a relatively minor one. The drivers would then tear off along the empty streets, eager to be done with their deliveries in the oppressive open air and to return to the interior familiarity of the local Emergency Rations Centre (E.R.C.). The conclusion of each transaction came at the end of the month when each customer would receive a statement of their account. These unwelcome reminders of debt left the way for the legions of loans and credit companies to prey on the fearful homebound consumer with seemingly benevolent offers of financial assistance which ultimately led to an increased popular debt to the Sate and its corporate cronies.

Living in the sandstone tenements, Sarah and I were among the minority of citizens who dwelled on that ethereal grey area between the New City and the Old Town; a thin fringe of stone streets where the ghosts of the industrial age merged in an uneasy marriage with a cold vision of the future. From here we enjoyed the ease with which we could slip from one world to the other, imagining easily that we were tied to neither.

The brick tenements of the Old Town, soon to be wiped out as the government's demolition plans crept ever closer to fulfilment, held a particular fascination for Sarah. To the nervous horror of the few neighbours who bothered to watch from their grimy windows, Sarah would stroll regularly into this vista of urban ghosts, patrolling its tenebrous recesses with camera in hand, exhilarated at the possibility of the anti-government squatters who were rumoured to dwell within the crumbling walls. After each visit she would return with a wealth of photographic material; sublime monochrome landscapes of glass and stone, iron and wire mesh. It seemed she captured within these images of gloomy apartment blocks, rusted rail tracks and crooked pylons a far more truthful vision of existence than that which permeated the encroaching backdrop of technological efficiency and material comfort. In a world increasingly dominated by uniformity, Sarah found in these decaying streets an effigy of her own uniqueness; the myriad facets of her psyche reflected in the geometry of each moss-furred stretch of tarmac, in the angles of every grimy wall, busted drainpipe and broken window.

As Sarah showered, I occupied myself in the kitchen with the task of reheating some of her excellent homemade vegan pancakes and brewing a pot of tea. True to her established routine, Sarah sang in the shower this morning; the melody of a piece we had composed the previous night. As usual, I found myself going about the business of breakfast in perfect time to her voice, using the percussive rhythm of the running water as my beat.

Sarah and I had first met as members of a musical ensemble, fairly prominent in the City's underground art scene of several years ago. All such movements had long since fallen casualty to the prevailing trends across the country and were driven so far underground as to be irrevocably atomised. Nonetheless we continued to indulge in our passions undaunted. Sarah believed earnestly that as long as even two people could remain true to their obsessions in this fashion then a more macrocosmic resurgence could still follow. For my own part, I continued to create music and art simply because I had to. And because Sarah's unwavering faith in the artist's ability to effect true social change was irresistibly seductive.

"Smells good," she exclaimed as she entered the kitchen, dressed casually with her hair tied in a loose ponytail, its dirty-blonde shade turned almost black with dampness.

"They should. You made them, remember?"

"Uh huh." She stretched her thin arms around me, planting a firm kiss on my lips. "But preparation is just about everything."

I welcomed the embrace almost childishly. To my slight unease, the spectre of my dream still hovered on the fringes of my consciousness, its undefined malevolence nagging at the back of my mind like the repressed suspicion of an illness or the memory of an unpaid debt.

"You okay?" I could never hide anything from Sarah. Her fathomless, melancholy grey eyes seemed to contain all the wisdom of the universe.

"Fine. Just tired. Don't think I slept too good."

"Well, you didn't wake too good either. Maybe come along with me to the Old Town today? Relax your mind a little among the psychic zero of the crumbling streets?"

"Is that really how you think of it? Psychic zero?"

"Mm, in a sense," she shrugged. "But sometimes zero is the biggest number there is." She leaned in for another kiss, her warm tongue penetrating my mouth by a tantalisingly slight fraction. "So, what do you think?"

"No, I'm going to try record some parts of what we composed last night. I just want to get started on it while I have the enthusiasm."

"Or you just want to prove to yourself you can keep up the enthusiasm without me around, eh?"

"A little of that too, yeah," I replied truthfully. "Call it my tragically male need for independence."

Sarah's sly grimace made another appearance, teeth emerging in all their imperfect and reluctant beauty from their shy scarlet confines. "Well, I think I can deal with that."

Clearing space to sit at our dusty kitchen table, Sarah moved the obstructions of my battered Telecaster guitar, her grimy cello, and a plethora of her paintings and sketches into an untidy pile.

"Shit. Either we're gonna have to quit this art nonsense or I'm certainly gonna have to throw out some of my old work."

Aware that this statement was made partially in jest, I nonetheless experienced a stab of sadness in reaction to Sarah's uncharacteristically negative proclamation. "Oh I don't know ..." I muttered in an attempt to diffuse the melancholy. "You can always use the walls as your canvas."

After a nonplussed pause, Sarah's face brightened. "Actually, that's not a bad idea. It's not like we ever have inspections from the council anymore."

It was true. Such public appearances by any

administrative representative of the government were a thing of the past.

We were no more than two minutes into our breakfast when the doorbell rang.

"Ah, here she is," Sarah exclaimed shrewdly. "Her Ladyship, no doubt looking to complain about last night's noise."

"Fuck. I really can't face her right now. You want to speak to her?"

Sarah shrugged. "It doesn't matter which of us answers the door, she'll walk right past and into this very room regardless."

Recognising the truth of this observation, I got up from my chair with a resigned sigh. "Brace yourself."

Inhaling deeply, I unlatched the door. I had opened it by barely a crack when it swung inward from the force of a blustering tempest which exploded into the apartment in the form of a diminutive middle aged woman. Pushing straight past me, the woman strode into the kitchen.

"Good morning Mrs Gilman," I announced to the already empty doorframe, "won't you come in?"

Mrs Gilman was our nearest neighbour, occupying the apartment on the opposite side of the wall from our bedroom. More precisely, Mrs Gilman was in effect our only neighbour since she was the only other living soul in the block whom we ever laid eyes on. Over the past few years, in accordance with the dwindling need for anyone to exit their home for any reason, our other neighbours had gradually vanished from view, forsaking the archaic customs of neighbourly familiarity for the self-contained havens of their apartments and stockpiles of consumer goods. Moreover, Sarah and I had speculated that several of our former neighbours, many of whom had been self-employed semi-professionals, had surrendered to the impossibility of maintaining such an outmoded lifestyle and that each had moved out to assume a position in one of the Workstation towers.

I followed Mrs Gilman into the kitchen where she was already haranguing Sarah who merely sat in tolerant silence; a marble Venus weathering the worst of the elements, safe in the knowledge that the sun will eventually return to undo this torrent's violent handiwork.

"For the love of God, young lady! I just can't believe it!" Mrs Gilman was already in full flow. "It's the absolute height of ignorance! And so irresponsible!"

"Mrs Gilman, we are sorry ..."

"I mean, I'm a vulnerable woman. I live alone. I need simplicity and routine in my life! I can't afford this kind of disruption!"

Tentatively, I intervened. "Look Mrs Gilman, have a seat. A cup of tea. Relax. We can sort ..."

"Relax?!" The exasperated woman cast an incredulous glare in my direction. "Don't you patronise me, young man! I'm about as close to breaking point as a woman can be forced to go."

At this absurd outburst, Sarah emitted a strangled smirk. Attempting to conceal this expression of amusement, she erupted in a series of muted pantomime coughs, upsetting the morsel of pancake lodged in her throat which precipitated a succession of new coughs very real and visibly painful.

Apparently hypnotised by Sarah's predicament but disinclined to assist, Mrs Gilman watched absently as Sarah spluttered through several large gulps of tea while I caressed her back.

"I'm fine," Sarah croaked feebly as eventually the spasms subsided.

Mrs Gilman took this as her cue to continue her outburst unabated.

"I mean, it's ridiculous. It shows a complete lack of respect. I can't be expected to live this way, with my daily life thrown into such disorder. I won't stand for it."

"Mrs Gilman, please," I finally managed to interject, "there's really no need to get so upset."

"It was disrespectful, you're right," Sarah added. "But we promise you, it won't happen again."

A look of confusion crossed the woman's reddened face. "You promise? How in the Lord's name can you promise anything? What's it to do with you?"

Now it was our turn to be confused.

"Uh well, I think we can at least claim to be responsible enough for our own actions," I struggled to keep the tone of condescension from my voice. "We're sorry about last night's noise levels and ..."

"And it won't happen again," Sarah interpolated mercifully. "We promise."

Mrs Gilman rolled her eyes in derision. "Oh for cry eye! That's not what I'm talking about. Not at all, dear." She lowered her voice in a tangential aside: "Although you're right, your racket last night was intolerable. Hardly the kind of behaviour becoming of responsible neighbours, hmm?" Sarah made to respond but Mrs Gilman went on; "No, indeed not. But no matter, I'm afraid we have a more pressing concern to address. My week's supply of oatmeal has not arrived! It was not included in this morning's delivery!"

"Oh," I muttered, struggling to present a façade of concern, "that is bad news. Well, we have plenty of cereals stocked away, you can ..."

"You're welcome to help yourself to whatever you like." Sarah, asserting her position as the more diplomatic between us, tactfully finished my sentence once more.

However, the offer fell on hostile ground. "That's no good to me, dear. No good at all. I can't eat all that heavily processed garbage. Plays havoc with my bowels don't you know?"

Sarah laid her fork to the side of her plate, appetite evidently decimated by the mere reminder of the fact of Mrs Gilman's bowel movements. "I see. Then how may we help?"

"Well clearly someone is going to have to walk out to the Emergency Rations Centre to pick some up, aren't they? I mean, I can't be expected to go out there. Not with the things that go on ... not with those ... people around! It's not safe."

The 'People' to which Mrs Gilman was referring were the Old Town squatters; an unseen and as good as mythical demographic of supposed socio-political mutineers who were portrayed by the government as dangerous, immoral and literally inhuman. Having rejected the materialist and hierarchical conventions of mainstream society, these fabled bands of ragged miscreants purportedly made their communal homes in the dilapidated hinterlands of boarded up tenements, derelict warehouses and the blackened shells of factory buildings dotted around the former industrial hubs of each city across the country. While there was no doubt that the government capitalised on the fear invoked by such a lawless force, using it as a means to push an increased number of citizens towards a life of economically productive work within the material safety of the Workstation towers, no plan to engage this supposed insurrection was forthcoming. Instead the government were clearly confident that the urban landscape's gradual consumption by the towers would ensure that all viable squatting space would be safely bulldozed into oblivion, annihilating the silent revolution in the process.

"Well, not to worry," I strove to be conciliatory, "I'll go down there straight after breakfast and get you sorted out, okay?"

All the bluster suddenly drained from the woman's face and she exhaled a voluminous breath which seemed to reduce her overall mass, as though her balloon of worry and stress were suddenly deflated. "Oh thank you so much, young man. You are an angel, simply an angel."

"Actually, I'm going out anyway," Sarah offered, "I'll go to the E.R.C. while I'm out. It's no problem."

With that, Mrs Gilman's face froze once more, the tension and rigidity returning. "Oh no, dear. No. You can't do that. It's not right that a young woman should go out there. I mean, anything could happen ..."

"I think I can manage, Mrs Gilman. I go out there two or three times a week you know."

Our disapproving neighbour looked as though she had been slapped hard. "Oh but dear, you shouldn't! It's simply not safe. You watch the news, you know what goes on ..."

Sarah waved a dismissive hand. "Well, the 'news' is full of speculation and not very many facts, I ..."

Mrs Gilman suddenly erupted in distress. "How can you say such a thing?! These are very dangerous times my dear! I of all people should know that ..."

"Well, look ..." Sarah stammered, "I didn't mean ..."

"How can you sit there and talk to me about speculation? After what I've been through!"

I stepped forward, attempting to diffuse the sudden friction in the room. "Mrs Gilman, please. Sarah didn't mean anything ..."

"How can you young people be so ignorant? After the kind of thing that's gone on around here! After what happened to my poor sweet Martha!" Mrs Gilman sobbed, choking with an abrupt onslaught of grief.

"Please, Mrs Gilman. I'm sorry," Sarah's voice resonated with genuine regret, "I didn't mean to upset you."

Wrapping a nervous arm around the weeping woman's quivering shoulders, I attempted, in my own awkward manner, to console her. "It's okay. Just relax. No point in getting yourself upset ..."

"Oh Martha," the woman continued to sob, dabbing at her reddened eyes with a soiled hanky, "My poor sweet angel ..."

About twelve years previously, Mrs Gilman had suffered a double tragedy from which she had understandably never recovered. Her husband had worked for the government as a land surveyor. It was his duty to investigate the deserted buildings and wastelands of the Old Town and file reports on which sites were most suitable for the construction of new Workstation towers. It was a well-paid job and one of the few remaining exterior occupations valued by the government.

One cold misty October morning, Mr Gilman kissed goodbye as normal to his wife and their young daughter Martha and walked off out to the Old Town. At this time, Mrs Gilman had only recently been diagnosed with M.E. and was largely housebound with pain and fatigue. Not that this presented any major issue; already the number of people spending most of their time indoors greatly exceeded that pursuing exterior interests. Mrs Gilman's predicament was therefore by no means unusual and she routinely dedicated as much time and energy as she could afford to keeping house for her husband and home-schooling their daughter.

That evening, following a typical day of math lessons and subdued playtime punctuated by sporadic napping, Mrs Gilman was disturbed by the first break in a solid routine which had run like clockwork for the preceding months. In fact, for the first time in their tem year marriage, her husband was late in coming home from work. She became anxious at the absence of the familiar rattling sound of his key in the lock at precisely 5:46pm. This anxiety had escalated considerably when, almost half an hour later, Mr Gilman had still not appeared.

Worse still, the incessant calls she made every two minutes to her husband's cell phone were to no avail, the electronic ringing sound repeating into eerie infinity. Fraught with worry and bound helplessly indoors, Mrs Gilman decided on her only accessible course of action. Knowing that her husband's site was but a few blocks away, she pressed her own cell phone into the hand of her young daughter, supplied the girl with specific instructions on where to find her father and to have him call as soon as he had been located. Although unnerved, Mrs Gilman had believed that her husband had simply mislaid his phone and been waylaid with some complication at the site. With that, she sent her daughter off into the urban mist which hours before had claimed her husband.

Mrs Gilman saw neither her husband nor

daughter alive again.

In a society where a tangible police presence was already becoming a relic of a bygone age and government representatives were reluctant to venture into the public eye in any event, there was nothing unusual in the two whole days which passed before the senior officers and accident investigators from the Urban Development Council materialised to investigate the site of their employee's disappearance. Anxious to retreat back to their headquarters as quickly as possible, they conducted their investigation rapidly and efficiently.

The row of tenements had already been razed to the ground by government bulldozers. Although the drivers had no recollection of seeing Mr Gilman onsite at the time of demolition, his body was soon discovered, crushed and pulverised among the rubble. Piecing together the evidence the investigators ascertained that Mr Gilman had re-entered the tenements prior to their destruction in order to warn a group of squatters he evidently believed to be residing there. Ironically the main stairwell of the sagging building had collapsed as he ascended, dropping him to the concrete floor in a shower of stone. Crippled and in agony, the surveyor had lain helpless as the bulldozers arrived to level the structure. A victim of his own humanitarian impulse, Mr Gilman died attempting to save a ragged band of vagabonds who had either managed to flee the scene or had already vacated prior to this fateful day, if they had indeed even existed.

Martha was never found. Her mother's cell phone was discovered lying in the centre of a nearby deserted street of empty apartments and warehouses. Evidently the girl had not attempted to make any calls. There were no obvious signs of a struggle and absolutely no trace of Martha whatsoever. Mrs Gilman's daughter had quite literally vanished into thin air.

Since then, Mrs Gilman had apparently become more paranoid, prone to stress and generally uptight. (Although, since Sarah and I had only known the woman for a few short years, this was merely guesswork on our part. It seemed at least possible that she had been slightly less unbearable prior to this tragedy, and we saw fit to grant her the benefit of doubt). More importantly, she held the squatters responsible for the ruin of her life and gladly supported the government line that they, and indeed all dissenters, constituted a sickness to be eradicated from the nervous system of our society. Not only had her husband's unreciprocated concern for the squatters cost him his life, but Mrs Gilman was convinced that the same ragged band had abducted her daughter; snatched this pure and beautiful angel from the warmth and decency of society as a plaything to corrupt and sully before sending her to some unimaginably ghastly fate.

"It's alright Mrs Gilman," I said in the most reassuring tone I could muster, "I'll go to the E.R.C. for you. Don't worry." I cast a wink in Sarah's direction which she accepted with a lazy knowing smile. "Sarah will stay here, safe and sound. There'll be no tragedies today."

"Oh, thank you." The woman made a last dab at her eyes with the hanky and straightened herself. "You are very kind. And clever too. Both of you. Very clever young people."

Sarah emitted a self-effacing smirk. "Thanks, Mrs Gilman. Nice of you to say."

"I do admire you both you know. I do hope you get out of this building soon and make something of yourselves. Talented young people like you should be using your abilities to the betterment of society."

"Yes," I said resignedly, "we know. All in good time, eh?" Unseen by Mrs Gilman, Sarah rolled her eyes. We knew this lecture by heart.

"This art carry-on doesn't really pay the bills anymore, does it? You have to be responsible."

Actually, Mrs Gilman had a point here. In recent months it had become increasingly difficult for Sarah and I to make a living without the additional aid provided by state benefits.

"And you can't rely on handouts forever," Mrs Gilman continued, seemingly predicting my thought. "It's not right that hardworking people should support you when you both have so much to offer …"

"Thank you, Mrs Gilman," Sarah said with finality. "Always a pleasure."

I began to escort our neighbour back to the door. "Now if there's anything else, don't you hesitate …"

"Yes, of course. Thank you." She paused at the

doorframe, then looked me straight in the eye with a pointed expression. "Seriously. You both have to think. I mean, you can't live this way forever. And you must have heard the rumours."

"Rumours?" I murmured absently, willing her to step away from the doorframe and out into the stairwell.

"Looks like these old sandstone buildings here may be considered Old Town as well. They're debating it this week. Got to make room for the towers you know."

"Yes, of course." Her presence was beginning to make me nauseous.

"So, maybe soon we have to relocate too, eh?" Her dry, lined lips opened out into an absurd toothy grin. A silence followed.

"Goodbye Mrs Gilman."

"You will remember my oatmeal."

"Of course."

The sound of the latch clicking into place as the door finally closed behind the woman was a blessing.

Sarah got up from her chair with a furtive grin and began to clear the table. "Better tidy this lot up; wouldn't want to waste any of my valuable talent in idle repose."

*

"I don't know how long I'll be. But I'll call you." Sarah eased into her coat and scarf, then leaned forward to embrace me. "And I'll be sure to

137

remember Dame Drama's fucking oatmeal."

"No worries." I nuzzled into Sarah's neck, enjoying the scent and sensation of her warm skin. "I'll hopefully have something half decent to let you hear by the time you get back." I leant in and kissed a patch of pale skin.

Sarah moaned lightly in pleasure and returned the kiss upon my right ear. "Gotta go."

She withdrew and cradled my temples with both hands, addressing my gaze directly. Looking upon the familiar planes of Sarah's face, I was struck as I often was by the way in which I could read so much of myself in every detail. It seemed my past and future were encoded within the contours of her nose and cheekbones, the myriad pathways of my psyche mapped in the elegant ridges of her brow and eye sockets. There in the open geometry of Sarah's features, the very essence of my identity could be traced in a biologic map which transcended the conventional boundaries of time and space. I noticed a stray bead of moisture in her tied back hair, quivering just above her left ear, suspended like a jewel of time crystallised in the wake of her betrayal of time's primitive law.

She leaned in once more to plant a parting kiss upon my lips. "See ya later."

With that, she shouldered her camera bag and left.

For much of the day I occupied myself with the task of recording some guitar and percussion parts based around the previous evening's experiments. Our recording equipment was characteristically rudimentary, both Sarah and myself more than willing to tolerate the shortcomings of largely analogue technology in light of the pleasingly dirty organic results. We were want to think of ourselves as two artistic gardeners cultivating what we could from the raw components available to us, eager to see what results might bloom despite the treacherous soil and often harsh psychic weather.

In its bare form the piece boasted a relatively minimalist harmony of which I could only barely scratch the surface with my limited arranging skills alone. As I strummed and plucked and altered settings, I did so in the knowledge that, upon Sarah's return, the piece would blossom into an entirely different entity, spiralling off into a cornucopia of rhythmic syncopations and profound dissonance. Sarah's skills on the cello and piano were not technically adept from the strict perspective of a musical purist, but she possessed an uncanny ability, comparable to the greatest of jazz experimentalists, to strip a melody and rhythm to its bare elements, tearing them to shreds in a gorgeous cacophony, redefining noise and chaos as the most acute harmony. In the process it seemed she rearranged the basic components of our shared reality, altering our perceptions to reveal something far closer to an existential truth behind the façade of our everyday existence in the surrounding urban sprawl.

As I played, my eyes were drawn repeatedly to the distinct silhouette of Sarah's cello which sat propped against the bedroom windowsill, the elegant outline of the instrument's neck set against the vista of faded tenements beyond. The cello seemed to assume the position of a surrogate Sarah, its curved figure staring at the doomed buildings in some trancelike reverie, surveying this dilapidation through the prism of the grubby windowpane which, standing in for Sarah's camera lens, framed the scene in a pleasing composition.

Looking out at those condemned structures, I was struck by the way in which their very existence seemed to defy not only the law of the state but indeed the laws of time and space. Standing inert, boasting their rebel dress of vines and weeds, the tenements rejected the dominant vision of material and technological progress espoused by the encroaching Workstation towers, and appeared to suggest an alternate universe wherein the passage of time was meaningless. Their functional urban architecture was now working hand in hand with the underbelly of nature to create a post-organic landscape where there was no longer any life or death, no past or future, but an eternal present. If the rumours were true and the rebel squatters truly did exist then I began to fancy the notion that the true nature of their rebellion lay in their ability to transcend to something resembling a mineral state; the last truly subversive act imaginable in a conformist world geared earnestly towards the onward thrust of linear time and a lust for sensation.

I envied the landscape for its temporal tenacity as I noticed the light in the apartment begin to fade notably. Turning my eyes to the treacherous clock, I was surprised to learn that it was by now early evening. Since I largely set my daily habits around Sarah and our joint activities, I had little regard for the telling of time. However, there was no question that Sarah was later than usual in coming home this evening.

For the next hour or so I stood by the window, looking out at the post-industrial panorama into which Sarah had wandered that morning. An alien feeling began to well up inside my stomach, a sensation of profound emptiness, deeply unsettling in its unfamiliarity. In the five years that Sarah and I had been a couple, this stretch of hours was by far the longest period we had yet spent apart. Perhaps due to the long established laissez-faire nature of our union, I found myself entirely unequipped to deal with this unexpected and prolonged separation. I spent the entire hour rigid and motionless bar the almost unconscious caressing of the cello's slender neck, watching for some sign of Sarah to emerge from the evening mist, waiting for her to regress from that timeless vista and back into our temporal prison.

Shaking myself finally from my lethargy, I picked up the phone and dialled her cell number. The insect buzz of the ringing tone began already to set my mind at ease and I was pre-emptively thankful for the sound of Sarah's melodious voice as she answered to tell me she was sorry for taking so long, she'd gotten rather carried away with photographing, she'd be home in moments. But to my confusion the ringtone finally ended not with Sarah's voice but that of an androgynous-sounding computer in an automated message:

The person you are calling seems to be unavailable to take your call. Please try again later.

Bewildered, I merely stared at the handset for a few moments. In all our years together, Sarah had never once failed to answer one of my calls. Gradually I mustered the will to redial. And again I was met with the disheartening echo of Sarah's phone ringing out to oblivion, culminating in the same robotic voice with the same negative message. As the light in the apartment retreated further from the advancing night, all of the furniture, bookshelves, musical instruments and art supplies – all the signature symbols of my life with Sarah – receded from view and I suddenly felt as though I had somehow fallen through some fissure in the time-space continuum to land in a vacuous mocking reflection of the life I had come to know.

Panicked, I stood up to look out at the hungry darkness beyond the window. By now, Sarah's beloved dilapidated landscape was scarcely visible and I was filled with the knowledge that, were it to disappear completely, it would surely take her with it. Half-blind in the gloom, I stumbled through the apartment and pulled open the door out to the stairwell. Instantly, I was blinded by the glare of the evening lights which were timed to come on automatically with the onset of nightfall. Unprepared for the dramatic shift in light, I stumbled backwards against the door which lay ajar to my back. As my eyes grew accustomed to the electric brilliance, I looked down at the stairs before me.

Inexplicably, I was paralysed. The concrete steps, the same ones I had lived with for over four years and traversed countless times, now seemed strangely hostile and alien. While my straining eyes still recognised the unshakeable familiarity of the stairwell, my psyche interpreted an entirely different scenario. As I followed with my eye the sloping descent of the steps, in all their mathematical exactness, I was struck by the notion that they no longer led to the ground floor and thus the outside world but in fact culminated in a cold and complex geometric puzzle which my abstraction-obsessed mind could not possibly fathom. Focussing on the fine detail of the steps, I noticed each and every fleck of crumbling stone, bombarding my psyche with the fact of their existence. As though the night had conspired to swallow Sarah and prevent me from following, it had sabotaged my only route by establishing a barrier comprised of the very time-defying essence of which both she and it were constructed; a gate I could not pass without the sublime key Sarah possessed in her melancholy grey eyes and timeless cheekbones.

Nauseous and terrified, I retreated back inside the apartment, slamming my back against the closed door, attempting a flimsy barrier from the invading force of the geometric nightmare beyond. Frozen in fear, bewilderment, shock and devastating heartache, I stood in that position for what seemed hours, my mind an agonised quagmire. Realising that the only other human life in the vicinity comprised Mrs Gilman with all her dead hidebound customs and banal rhetoric, I fell into a tenebrous abyss of unimaginable loss and loneliness.

In this dark place, it seemed the concepts of logic upon which I had previously relied had been swept away like the insubstantial stage sets of some movie melodrama. Although I later attempted to call Sarah's phone several more times, I did so lethargically and with the unquestioning expectation that the sexless robot of the automated message would surely provide the only respondent voice. Moreover, despite her completely unannounced disappearance and supposed solitude among the dark tenements, I was inexplicably unafraid for Sarah's safety. Indeed, for reasons I could not quite yet understand, I found myself envying her sudden and seemingly effortless immersion in that spectral world of decaying concrete and rusted metal.

That night I stood for several hours by the window and stared into the fathomless blackness beyond, a cold vacuum in place of Sarah's timeless dimension which had now left the brutal linearity of this world behind. When eventually I felt my way to bed it was to a largely sleepless night spent staring into the hollow void hovering before my eyes and aching from the loss characterised by Sarah's half of the mattress as it announced its cruel emptiness.

I was awakened the next day by the intrusive ring of the doorbell. For a few moments I lay immobile upon the mattress, staring at the ceiling. The ringing did not cease but became incessant, increasing in length with each attempt. Eventually I recognised the familiar shrillness of Mrs Gilman's voice as it echoed from beyond the door.

"Helloooo! Are you home? Did you get my oatmeal? Helloooo!"

For the first time I could remember, I was not affected by the woman's voice in the usual unpleasant way. In fact it had no detectable effect on me whatsoever. Already the established emotional conventions through which I had previously understood my life had been seriously destabilised. I would very likely have gone on ignoring Mrs Gilman's cries were it not for a stray speck of peeling plaster which I noticed hanging precipitously from a random patch of ceiling. This single fleck imposed itself on my consciousness, its jagged edge piercing my psyche and repelling me with the fact of itself within the oppressive confines of time and space.

Suddenly queasy, I rose swiftly from the bed and stumbled from the room towards the front door. The effort of pulling it open seemed to require all my reserves of physical energy and I succumbed to a wave of dizziness as the puffy and imposing face of Mrs Gilman came into view.

"Ah, you are home. I ..." She paused mid-sentence and eyed me up and down. "Oh dear. Someone appears to have had a rough night, hmm?"

In my mental shock, I had lost all sense of my physical appearance and only now, under my neighbour's scrutinising gaze, did I become aware of being clad in yesterday's wardrobe which was now crumpled and stuck to my body in sweaty patches. "Oh," I somehow mustered the strength to mutter, "Yes."

Barely disguising her disgust, Mrs Gilman went on; "Hmm, well, all harmless fun in the privacy of your own home I suppose. Now, may I pick up my oatmeal?"

Bringing a hand to my suddenly aching temples, I inhaled deeply and, with some effort, summoned the energy to dispense with Mrs Gilman's unwanted presence, the proximity of her fleshy solidness impressing upon my psyche with the force of a juggernaut. "Mrs Gilman, I'm terribly sorry but I'm afraid I don't have your oatmeal."

"Oh no." The woman's face twisted into its default expression of chronic constipation. "But they must surely have had some at the E.R.C. I just don't believe that they didn't. That's ridiculous."

"Mrs Gilman, I'm sorry," I raised a hand to silence her, "but I'm afraid I didn't get a chance to go. It's been something of a hectic twenty-four hours. You see, Sarah is gone."

"Gone?" A completely incredulous look crossed the woman's face, as though I had just told her that I was Jesus Christ and she was to become the first of my new disciples. "Gone where? Young man, what are you babbling about?"

"She's gone to work. In the towers." Hearing these words fall from my mouth, I was struck by a sensation of almost complete disembodiment. This unplanned, spontaneous and completely ridiculous lie spilled forth with an astonishing ease which suggested a new prevailing logic at work, one of which my subconscious was entirely cognizant but had yet to inform my conscious mind of the details.

Unsurprisingly a wide approving smile erupted upon Mrs Gilman's bloated face. "She's gone to work? Oh, that's fantastic. Really very well done. I'm so glad to hear it."

"Yes, it's great," I forced myself to concur "We've been planning it for a while. It just seemed the right time. I shall be joining her soon enough. But unfortunately I'm not feeling too well. Some kind of bug or something ..."

"Oh!" The woman recoiled slightly, her hygiene-obsessed mind clearly perturbed by the thought of any infectious illness festering on her doorstep. "Nothing serious I hope?" she asked with poorly feigned concern.

"No, no. But it's routine procedure. Each new inhabitant of the Towers must pass a simple health exam. So I have to wait until this clears up before I can join Sarah."

"Ah, I see." She was evidently less than assured.

"Anyway, I'm afraid I can't very well risk going out alone in my condition. So I'm not going to be able to get that oatmeal for you, sorry. You'll have to make other arrangements."

At this, Mrs Gilman became visibly deflated, irked not so much by the inconvenience to her but rather by the absence of anyone to blame. "Oh. Well, I suppose I can wait a couple of days. It usually takes a couple of days for the people at the E.R.C. to make a home visit, doesn't it? Not the end of the world I suppose." Despite the sentiment, her tone suggested that all out Armageddon was precisely what this minor nuisance in fact amounted to.

As my gaze drifted slightly from the woman's face to the stairwell which loomed behind her, my nausea increased sharply. I remembered the vivid terror which had seized me when faced with the stairs' transformation the night before and I had no desire to face it again.

"So anyway, Mrs Gilman, if you'll excuse me ..."

"Oh, of course. You get yourself some rest young man. And in no time you'll be fighting fit and working away alongside that young lady of yours," her wide flabby mouth wobbled in an obscene smirk. "I always said you talented people would make good. Just a matter of time. No point in limiting yourself to that silly art nonsense when it makes no money for you or the economy, eh? There's no limit to the possibilities, I always said ..."

"Thank you, Mrs Gilman."

"I mean, after all, there are so many vacancies out there. No point in sitting around on handouts when you could be ..."

I slammed the door shut before she could complete the sentence.

Retreating from this intrusion, I walked back into the bedroom. The contents of the room assaulted me heartlessly with their harsh physicality, doubled with the inseparable essence of Sarah and of our life together. Every object – each item of furniture, musical instrument, piece of artwork – perforated the lining of my psyche with ice cold knives. Each item boasted a billion memories which each inflicted a billion wounds. Every tangible curve and contour recalled Sarah's body and mocked my incarceration within this temporal prison of which I was now the sole occupant.

Aching eyes, reddened from lack of sleep and flooding with bitter tears, drifted across this museum of the soul towards the window. Beyond, the Old Town stood as before; a monument to an alternate existence free from these tyrannies, an ethereal domain which had readily accepted Sarah as its own but to which I was granted no port of entry. Having transcended the shackles of this world, Sarah had shed the superfluous bonds of our love in favour of total and absolute freedom, leaving me to rot in the merciless flow of time among the detritus of her former life with me.

During the next week or so, my daily routine consisted of wandering in hopeless circles around the asphyxiating boundaries of the apartment, inspecting the various items scattered throughout as though seeing each one for the first time. These symbols of a spectral past had metamorphosed from benign entities into agents of supreme malevolence devoted to the complete evisceration of my soul. As the days progressed, the items seemed to multiply, spreading across the floors and furniture in an attempt to drown me in their malignance.

The food which continued to arrive in weekly deliveries despite my increasingly overdrawn account was deposited by my door, presumably by Mrs Gilman who mustered enough of a concern to ensure I ate, but stopped short of making conversation and thus risking the contraction of my fictional illness. I no longer cooked, instead dazedly gobbling the individual raw ingredients of Sarah's speciality pancakes which bubbled and swirled disagreeably in my stomach.

Dazed, I would often switch on the television set, dusty from lack of use, and allow the banal and insipid tones of largely fictional "news" reports and government propaganda wash around the rooms in an attempt to numb the pain induced by the contents of the apartment, so venomous in their distinctiveness. Occasionally I would pick up the phone and dial Sarah's number, no longer in the hope of hearing her melodic voice, which I now knew was lost to me for good, but simply to provide an alternative soundtrack to my existence now that all the music I owned had become aggressive and antagonistic in its recollection of the past.

From time to time I would pause before the bedroom window and gaze upon the forbidden realm of the Old Town. Although my heart ached at Sarah's absence, the view of this stubborn landscape seemed to quell the onslaught of lovelorn agony. The audacity of the grey tenements and crumbling warehouses as they flaunted their time-defying power before the looming silhouettes of the encroaching Workstation towers seemed to recall Sarah's spirit in a way which was devoid of pain. Every edge and angle of each structure appeared as a component in some psycho-geographic map of a world without time. Just as I had previously read the infinite possibilities of my life in the contours of Sarah's face, so too could I identify if not decipher a latent code for a post-emotional liberation within the grubby walls and shattered windows of those defiant buildings.

Finally, as the Old Town eventually escaped into the darkness of night, I would back away from the window without drawing the curtains, stumbling hopelessly to bed where I would grip the sheets, still rich with Sarah's scent, fiercely to my tearstained face and sob myself into uneasy sleep.

It was by about the tenth day that the bed began to bleed.

The previous evening I had drifted off to sleep, sobbing; my grief unperturbed by the audible commotion from Mrs Gilman's bathroom. Clearly suffering the effects of a few days deprived of her precious oatmeal, Mrs Gilman had made several trips to the bathroom in the space of an hour or less. While the repugnant noise of each of the woman's troubled bowel movements would have been cause for disgust in the past, they were now catalysts of sheer terror.

Over the course of the previous few days, my own bodily functions had begun to appal me in ways I could not wholly intellectualise. These crude episodes of physical excess seemed to express all that was oppressive about linear time and solid space; trapping the psyche in a cage of fleshy compulsion beyond its control. As I finally succumbed to slumber, the vile impression of Mrs Gilman's lavatory ordeal saw fit to pursue me.

I woke early in the morning, gasping in terror from a dream wherein I had become a proxy for my neighbour's lavatorial needs. In the dream, Mrs Gilman stood over me imposingly in my own bathroom as I sat helpless upon the toilet seat. "I need to go NOW!" she would scream maniacally into my upturned face, after which my body would erupt in painful defecations, each one threatening to tear my anus to shreds. The toilet's flushing mechanism appeared to be absent and with each excretion a mountain of swill rose ever closer to the surface until finally it exploded sickeningly around us.

I screamed as I woke and panicked at the warm dampness I could feel all around me, convinced that I had somehow dragged the mountain of faeces out of my dream and into the bed. As my vision cleared however, I saw that the viscous matter which soaked the sheets and coated my skin and clothes was not the filthy brown of excrement but a deep liquid crimson.

Leaping from the bed, I rubbed my eyes furiously

but the vision of horror remained. A deep puddle of fresh blood, apparently originating from the side of the bed once occupied by Sarah, saturated the sheets. I quickly tore off my clothes in alarm and inspected my body desperately. But there was no wound and, other than the nausea and heartache which had permeated the days since Sarah's departure, I felt no particular symptom of sickness.

Although disturbed by this development, I was surprised to find that it did not alter my routine. At least not at first. Somehow I was able to accept this bizarre and macabre phenomenon as an integral and unavoidable facet of my ongoing malady, which seemed to progress according to its own peculiar logic entirely irrespective of my reactions.

Having stripped the mattress and replaced the sheets (my first real domestic act in Sarah's absence), I slept the next night as before.

The following morning I was soaked yet again. This time the blood covered almost the entire bed in addition to much of my body. Second time around my fear and revulsion were intensified significantly. Once more I changed the bedclothes, attempting to assert a modicum of authority over the bizarre sequence of events unfolding in this treacherous grotto I had once called home. But I did so in trepidation and it was with a profound sense of dread that I drifted off to sleep the following night.

When I woke up drenched in tepid red blood the third consecutive morning, I succumbed to a sudden epiphany amidst the fear and revulsion. With each changing of the bedclothes I had regressed towards a pre-solitude mentality of domesticity, and with each repetition of this act the blood had materialised in increasingly copious amounts. I was beginning to realise that the apartment was mirroring my psyche in Sarah's absence; it too was injured by the constant reminders of a life and love lost and was now declaring its desire to move beyond its established spatial and temporal boundaries. In that instant I reeled from the recognition that in order to attain a state closer to that which permeated the portentous buildings of the Old Town, I had to free myself and the apartment from the shackles of the past.

I spent the rest of the day demolishing the furniture. Using an old rusty claw hammer and saw I found in the cobweb-infested storage cupboard, I broke up the bed, tables and chairs, depositing their skeletal remains down the garbage chute, safe in the knowledge that there was enough waste space to accommodate it now that the majority of apartments lay vacant. The shattered remains of guitars, cello and piano promptly followed.

Steeling myself, I ransacked the wardrobes and sideboards, spilling the contents into the chute. Thereafter, eyes filled with tears and choking with grief, I swept every book from every shelf, scooped up every CD and vinyl record, retrieved every single item of Sarah's beautiful artwork and sent them all hurtling towards the darkness of the building's musty basement. Now that garbage collection occurred on a sporadic basis, I had no way of knowing how long this weighty gallery of memory would fester below me, but it seemed that it could do me no more harm as long as it remained safely beyond the walls of the apartment.

With each jettisoned item, the apartment seemed to sigh with relief as though a huge burden had finally been removed. Finally I came to the final item; a self-portrait of Sarah rendered in charcoal. Gazing upon this inert likeness, I recognised once more the fateful trajectories imprinted within the contours of her beautiful and proud features. Holding back a cascade of tears, I made a silent vow to honour those portents before sending the sketch down into oblivion.

With the exception of minimal electrical appliances (which were spared the cull merely due to the practical problems posed by their disposal rather than out of any need or desire to keep them), the apartment was now entirely empty. Exhausted, I stretched and rubbed my aching back, surrendering myself to the apartment's unadulterated essence. Already the rooms had expanded under their liberation from the despotism of memory. The walls seemed to stretch ever further up towards a ceiling which now spread out in dimensions seemingly so vast I could not look up for too long without succumbing to a mildly vertiginous queasiness. As I looked out through the bedroom window, the faded buildings of the Old Town shimmered in the afternoon light, as though signalling their silent approval.

It was as I returned the rusty tools to the storage cupboard that I found her.

Wedged in between the stone wall and an old rusted pet cage, a small figure of about one foot in height stood upright, unblinking eyes reflecting the light from the bedroom window. Leaning down, I reached in and wrenched the figure from its dusty prison and lifted it out into the light.

I held in my hands an antique ornamental doll made of porcelain. The inanimate girl was dressed in what resembled a blue Victorian era party dress, now filthy and tattered with age and neglect. The girl bore a sharp alert expression, a vaguely coy smile haunting the edges of her cold lips. A thin ribbon of blue cloth only barely held in place her once blonde hair which was now almost colourless and thick with the stale smell of mould.

Judging by the design and condition of the doll, I surmised that she had once belonged to a previous occupant, long since forgotten in the heartless shifting sands of linear time. Staring into her pale marble eyes, cool and reflective as gemstones, I was struck by the sheer audacity of such a lifelike (if miniaturised) imitation of the human form. I contemplated the generations of women and girls who had invested immeasurable time and effort into collecting and caring for these inert figures, projecting on to them their own particular psychologies and latent sexualities. It seemed these inanimate ceramic mannequins, with their dichotomous combination of juvenile charm and ageless wisdom, presented to their owners a surreal psychic canvas upon which they could identify and trace the myriad possibilities of their own existence.

Stuck here in this empty apartment with only the time-defying panorama of the Old Town to seize one's attention, the doll appeared a perfect symbol of all that was occurring here. With her human likeness and mineral veneer, she embodied a vision of existence in spite of time.

Eagerly, I propped her upon the windowsill where she could stare out at the defiant tenements as they engaged the approaching Workstation towers in silent battle. Here she would provide the necessary bridge between the lingering fragments of my past and that timeless zone beyond the glass.

*

Following this development, the passage of time rapidly shed its significance. From here on my days were spent crouched upon the floor of what had once been the bedroom, joining the doll in her inert and persistent gaze out at the timeless tenements. The only signifier of time having passed was the undeniable advance of the Workstation towers as they multiplied across the horizon, advancing through the Old Town in battle formation. Occasionally the roar of bulldozer engines and the tumultuous crash of collapsing mortar floated towards me through the still air. From these simple sensory cues I was able to gage that weeks and

157

subsequently months were expiring before my immobile gaze.

The minimal movements I allowed myself were restricted to the retrieval of the food parcels which Mrs Gilman continued to leave by the door. Noticing that I was accepting the food into the apartment, she very likely believed I remained too beleaguered by illness to venture outside and therefore refrained from bothering me for fear of contracting the plague.

As the days progressed I consumed less and less. It pleased me to notice the flesh recede from my body, freeing my skeleton from the cage of its superfluous weight and edging me tantalisingly closer to something resembling a mineral state.

The doll remained silhouetted in place against the window and, from my perspective upon the floor, she seemed to dominate the skyline, looming like a ceramic leviathan against the insignificant columns of the Towers. The angles and contours of her artistically crafted figure seemed to contain the code with which I would finally gain entry to a time-free realm.

After an almost indeterminable period of this minimalist daily routine, a rock was finally thrown into the tranquil pool of my consciousness.

One morning I awoke to the sound of a tremendous crash, so loud I half expected to see the entire façade of the sandstone building collapsing before my eyes, opening the apartment to the grey sky. I gathered myself feebly from my foetal position upon the mildewed carpet and staggered towards the window where the doll, rigid and alert, surveyed the scene of carnage beyond.

Two blocks away the bulldozers had begun to demolish the brick tenements. From behind a row of weather-beaten slate roofs I could clearly make out the thick plumes of black smoke expelled from the machines' mighty engines as they roared in triumph, an animalistic battle cry which set the entire neighbourhood trembling. As I watched, the familiar jut and angle of a grey roof suddenly sunk below that of its neighbour as the unseen structure was razed to the stony ground with an apocalyptic thunder.

Entranced by the devastation developing before me, I noticed my pale reflection in the foggy glass, an insubstantial emaciated figure mimicking the rigidity of the doll who stood to my side, her timeless grace announcing its insubordination to the monstrous demolition machines. Finally I became aware of the sound of the doorbell being pressed repeatedly in urgent and thoroughly unwelcome bursts of shrillness which perforated the calm of the apartment ruthlessly. The ceiling and walls heaved and groaned their displeasure at this affront which dragged the apartment temporarily out of itself and back into the malignant vortex of time and space.

With a great deal of effort I traversed the enormity of the room, every muscle and joint screaming at the indignity of being forced into the terminally agonising practice of movement. After an age I finally reached the door to the apartment and pulled it slowly and weakly open, interrupting the strident call of the bell in mid-ring.

At the sight of me, Mrs Gilman's face distorted instantly into a mask of horror and revulsion.

"My god!" She raised a swift hand to her mouth. "Dear young man, what on Earth has been happening to you?"

After such a prolonged period of surrendering myself to the apartment's dimensionless vision of itself, I had mercifully lost contact with the conscious fact of my physical self. Forced now under my neighbour's horrified gaze to reflect upon this insubstantial shell of flesh and bone, I was assaulted gravely by the memory of the redundant aesthetic codes I had long since transcended but to which Mrs Gilman continued hopelessly to adhere. Through the prism of this memory, I realised that my appearance must have been quite shocking indeed. Standing before her, naked except for filthy underpants, this unwashed, unshaven, emaciated shell of a human being must have surely seemed a vision of death itself.

"Excuse me, Mrs Gilman," I finally managed to stammer, "forgive my appearance. But as you can see, I am still not in great health. Perhaps this can wait ..."

"No, young man, I'm afraid none of us can wait any longer." For the first time in the years I had known her, it seemed a genuine concern for my well-being could be detected emanating from this censorious widow. "You need to organise. And someone needs to help you, you're clearly in no fit state to handle this by yourself."

"Organise ...?" I rubbed my forehead in a haze of confusion. "I'm sorry, I ..."

"For your move. You can't possibly be expected to handle something so stressful in your condition. You'll need help with packing and the like."

Queasy, I persevered in searching the mental vault of my suppressed memories for some clue as to what Mrs Gilman was referring, but came up short.

"I'm afraid I don't ..."

The woman's mouth and eyes widened in a grotesque caricature of alarm. "Oh my God! You don't know?! Haven't you been receiving the emails from the Council?"

As with all of the apartment's electrical appliances bar the refrigerator, my computer had lain dormant since my cull of the contents and subsequent immersion in the liberated apartment's expansion. "Emails ... I ... let's see ..." I feigned a recollection of emails I had not read, leaving my sentence open for Mrs Gilman to provide the necessary information.

"This building is now officially part of Old town! They're demolishing it next week!" she shrieked in rapid staccato bursts. "We have to be out of here within the next five days! The Council has assigned us placements at one of the new Towers! Haven't you heard?! If you don't turn up for your placement you'll be classified a squatter! You'll lose all your rights! Haven't you prepared?!!"

Reeling from this onslaught of information, I

paused for a moment to gather my thoughts. Finally, clearing my throat, I managed to force both a pantomime smile and an assuring tone. "Of course, Mrs Gilman. Of course I'm prepared. It's all organised. I've been assigned a placement next to Sarah actually."

Mrs Gilman's face relaxed a little, although a shadow of doubt continued to darken the edges. "Oh. Well that's good." She coughed and shifted uncomfortably, clearly unsettled by the concern her outburst had betrayed. "That'll work out nicely then, eh?"

"Indeed." I moved to close the door.

"Oh, but ..." the woman leant in, imposing herself upon the apartment. "You'll still need help to organise, though. I mean, a sick person can't be expected to ..."

"Actually, it's under control." I moved my aching body slightly to the side, allowing my neighbour the merest glimpse of the gutted kitchen and its unequivocal emptiness. "As you can see, almost everything is safely packed away already."

"Ah. Fine." For once, my meddlesome neighbour appeared lost for words. "Well, it seems you have more stamina than I gave you credit for. Jolly good. Glad to know you're okay." She squinted. "You are okay?"

Straining, I forced yet another movie star grin. "Never better. I'm sure I'll be fighting fit for work next week."

At that, Mrs Gilman visibly melted, regarding me

with the adoring gaze of a proud parent at their child's graduation ceremony. "Oh, that's wonderful to hear you say. I'm so glad you've seen sense and decided to make the most of your potential. It's really the best thing."

"Thank you. Now if you'll ..."

"I mean, everyone can make themself useful. The council have even been kind enough to grant me a prescription for new drugs which will ease my pain as long as I work a certain amount of hours. It really seems like a bright new day ..."

"Goodbye, Mrs Gilman."

Standing once more by the window, the timeless and queenly figure of the doll by my side, I looked out upon the shifting landscape. After weeks and perhaps months of surrendering myself to the apartment's unbound dimensions, I finally realised exactly what these empty rooms and expanding walls were preparing me for. Unconsciously, I had placed the doll by the window as a signal to that timeless zone of crumbling tenements and empty warehouses; an outward proclamation of my desire to be assimilated by its dimensionless sprawl. What I had mistaken for a complex entry code embedded in the geometry of the buildings was in fact a response signal, a clandestine communication from an ageless realm announcing its approach towards my apartment.

As I watched another portion of brick and concrete structure tumble to the ground, I was reminded of Mrs Gilman's husband who had long since surrendered himself to the dream of stone which blossomed in the rubble and dust. It seemed clear to me now that this faceless man's disappearance was no tragedy but in fact a triumph. Having been seduced by the Old Town's spatial and temporal defiance, I surmised that he had in fact remained within the condemned building by his own will, following its collapse into a boundary-free mineral world. In this audacious realm it seemed one would surely discover an image of oneself entirely free from the hazards of time and space. It was here that Sarah had settled; liberated in a post-emotional state among all the last true rebels who had forsaken the physical and temporal world.

Watching the monstrous government machines go about their work in the shadows of the dictatorial pillars of those emerging towers, I took comfort in the ultimate ineffectuality of this celebration of industrial strength and technological progress. Like the Hydra of Greek myth, the Old Town sacrificed the heads of its crumbling buildings in order to move to the next transcendental phase, where its glorious neutrality would be impervious to the petty machinery of the material world.

Viewing each collapse intently, I could almost count every single particle of plaster dust, each individual fleck of dislodged brick. My whole being throbbed and hummed with the anticipation of the bulldozers' advance on this sandstone enclave. Cursing the lingering grip of linear time, I longed for the days to pass quickly, accelerating the onslaught of those brutal machines which would send me mercifully in an avalanche of stone and glass towards an existence beyond life and death.

The next few days passed intolerably slowly. The apartment's walls grew damp as it wept in longing for the bulldozers to strike. From the window I watched their sluggish progress desperately; each and every brick structure now seeming to demand an eternity for its demolition. To my side, the doll remained committed to her unwavering gaze; the promise of an eternal present reflected in her static marble eyes. Assured that the guardianship of this inert nymph guaranteed the eventual desired conclusion of my ordeal, I curled upon the floor each night in childlike contentedness.

However, my confidence was to prove misguided. In those final days before the merciful onset of demolition, the sanctuary of the expanding apartment was to be violated by the most malign treachery.

Three or four days subsequent to Mrs Gilman's portentous visit, I awoke to an alien sound. The stillness of the room was invaded by a soft but high-pitched whine which set my hair on end. Bolting upright, I looked around for the source of the sound. Honing in, I followed the whining to the windowsill where the doll stood.

To my alarm, the doll was no longer gazing out at the approaching demolition but had evidently abandoned her guardianship and now looked directly down at me. An almost accusatory shadow obscured her inanimate face in the early morning light.

Disturbed, I mustered the strength to stand and approached the windowsill to examine the ceramic figure. She stood coy and proud as before with no sign of having been manhandled. I had no memory of altering her position. Indeed I relied upon her insistent outwards gaze as my beacon to the Old Town and the timeless domain it promised on the other side of the demolitions. I could only assume that this idol had been corrupted by the insidious oppressive forces of time and space which had somehow found a way to infiltrate the apartment.

As though in direct response to this thought, a breeze brushed the hairs of my bare arm lightly, stirring nauseating patterns amongst the greasy follicles. The whining escalated in pitch and volume. It seemed the breeze passed through some weakened seam upon the doll's costume, generating a soft undulating melody. Although only identifiable at an almost subliminal level, the melody struck at my psyche with a cold dagger of familiarity. With its distinct alterations in pitch, there was no doubt that the breeze was utilising the doll as a sinister instrument, replaying that final fateful song I had composed with Sarah.

Sick with the heartache of a lost past and aggrieved by this appalling symptom of time's hateful caprice, I was forced to summon all of my strength and restraint in order to refrain from smashing the doll against one of the apartment's walls which now too were moaning and trembling at this violation of their intimacy. It seemed the egregious forces of time and space had conspired to dupe me into destroying the very beacon which ensured my eventual escape from their destructive clutches.

Regaining my composure I turned the doll calmly back around to her rightful lookout position. Running my fingertip along the edges of the window, I identified the weak portion of rubber lining which permitted the breeze and all its temporal malevolence to enter the apartment. With my bare weakened hands I wrenched a strip of musty carpet from the floor and jammed it into the affected area, blocking the wind's route and sealing the apartment once more from its timely influence.

Troubled by this unexpected development, I was anxious for much of the day, waiting for the material world to launch its next attack at any given moment. Gradually however, the sight of the continuing demolition beyond the window reassured me that I would achieve victory over these moribund forces in the coming days as the apartment fell to join the Old Town in the benevolent rubble.

A further disturbing development occurred the following morning. I was awakened by a thick globule of moisture as it fell forcefully upon my cheek. Sitting up, I cast my eyes to the ceiling and saw that it wept in distress. I cast my eyes instinctively to the windowsill. The doll was gone. She had abandoned her post.

With excruciating effort, I raised myself urgently to my feet. There was no sign of the doll anywhere in the vast blank expanse of the room. Wincing with every step, I traversed the breadth of this enormous space towards the door.

I found her in the kitchen, lying on her back upon the patch of floor previously occupied by the table where Sarah and I had eaten our meals. The doll stared lifelessly at the weeping ceiling, the contours of her finely carved face straining under the pressure of time and space as they launched their brutal assault.

Shaking with grief and nausea, I scooped up the limp form and held her tightly and protectively to my chest as I retreated from the kitchen. The winds of time battered my frail body and abused the doll's delicate features as I made my wearisome way to the storage cupboard. Gritting my yellowed teeth, I wrenched open the rickety wooden door and pulled out the ancient rusted pet cage which still lay rotting among the cobwebs. The cage emanated a foul vermin stench and was generally less than pleasing, but I was taking no chances. I thrust the doll inside and sealed her within the partially corroded bars.

Returning to the vast space which had once been the bedroom, I placed the cage upon the windowsill. Fixed here in her rightful place, the doll would finally conclude her intended mission. Imprisoned within the malodorous cage, the static grey jewels of her eyes surveyed the demolition as it prepared to make its final push. The bulldozers busied themselves now on the other side of the street, providing the Old Town with the final yards it required to claim this sandstone edifice and embrace me in its dusty oblivion.

On the final day I awoke to a cacophony which engulfed the building as the apartment defended itself staunchly against the last ditch assaults by the material universe.

From outside the thunderous roar of bulldozer engines reverberated, echoing through the building's many empty rooms and cavernous stairwells. A man's voice boomed out through a bullhorn, uttering words I could not comprehend through the haze of time and space from which I was now radically dislocated.

Nearby, another more familiar sound cut through the air of the apartment, soiling its stillness:

"Are you in there? Are you? Come on! You need to get out of here! Now! Let me help you!"

The recognisably repellent tones of Mrs Gilman's voice resounded from beyond the door, accompanied by a male voice I could not place:

"You say you know this man?"

"Yes, yes! He's been my neighbour for a few years! Him and his young ladyfriend. She's gone off to work now though ..."

"I see." The male voice adopted a sterner tone with which it addressed the apartment. "If there's someone in there, you need to remove yourself right now! This building is to be demolished. If you're not out on the street within ten minutes then you'll be going down with it. Do you understand?"

Ignoring the inconsequential voices, I looked excitedly up towards the window to view the oncoming oblivion. My elation was short-lived, erased by a cold thrust of terror as my eyes fell upon the windowsill.

The cage lay in disarray, the top wrenched brutally open. Heart racing, I propelled myself towards the window to inspect the violated cell. The floor of the cage was littered with jagged shards of shattered porcelain. Here and there I could just make out the curves of a facial feature, the angle of a limb joint. It appeared as though the doll had exploded from within, obliterated by some sinister force which had risen from the core of its artificial body.

I felt as though the wind had been knocked from me, my chest tight and constricted as I gasped in panic for breath. The voices out on the street and in the stairwell continued, barking orders for me to remove myself from the haven of the liberated apartment. Underscoring this auditory onslaught was another sound which only now in my distress did I identify as emanating from elsewhere within the apartment itself.

Listening closely, struggling to filter out the roar of engines and bullhorns, the incessant cries of Mrs Gilman and the unidentified man, I detected a faint melody violating the air. Following the sound, I staggered away from the window and out of the room.

As I passed the front door, the voices beyond

became more audible and increasingly urgent.

"Please, you have to come out of there. I know you're sick. People can help you."

"Seems like he might be sick in the fuckin' head. What does this idiot think he's playing at? We ought to just leave him here. That is if there's actually anyone here."

"He's here, I know it. I just know he didn't leave."

"Well lady, if he is here, he's not doing much to deserve a rescue."

To my right was the bathroom from which it seemed the intrusive harmony was emanating I approached cautiously and pressed my ear to the door. From beyond the voice of a young girl hummed the same sickeningly familiar melody which had possessed the doll two days earlier. Already the cold daggers of heartache perforated my consciousness, my eyes welling with tears at this cruel celebration of an emotional past with all its temporal constraints. Weakened and agonised, I pushed open the bathroom door. Nothing could have prepared me for the spectacle beyond.

The walls of the bathroom were covered in childlike scrawls and drawings executed in charcoal. I stood aghast at this flagrant violation of the apartment's purity, my head throbbing with the unreal quality of this manifestation. In my daze I reacted slowly to the sound to my right; a high-pitched girlish giggle which seemed to spring from below the grimy sink. Before I could collect enough of my senses to investigate the sound, a small figure emerged from the corner of my vision; a blue and white streak which moved with the swiftness of a cat from a crouching position below the sink to lash out at my crotch with a tiny fist. Stunned by the pain and shock of the blow, I collapsed to my knees with a loud grunt. As I lay crouched in my indignity, my tiny assailant giggled mischievously and ran out of the room, tiny bare feet pounding a hasty rhythm upon the floor.

The commotion finally confirmed to the unwanted voices in the stairwell the truth of my presence:

"What the hell was that?"

"It's him! What did I tell you? Oh, we have to get him out of there!"

"Alright lady, stand back!"

With that, the door began to shake with the force of a series of heavy blows. Sensing that my time was running desperately short, I forced myself to my feet and staggered out of the bathroom.

The girl had resumed the melody and I followed the sound into the kitchen where I was met with the worst of all possible scenes. Each and every wall was now covered in the childish charcoal drawings and the apartment moaned and heaved in distress at this assault on its integrity. In the centre of the room was a large pile of shattered wood and what at first seemed like random detritus. Upon closer inspection I could make out the legs of the old kitchen table, the body of my telecaster guitar, the elegant neck of Sarah's cello. This onslaught of time and memory was like a rusty blade in my heart and I howled in anguish, a primal animal bellow which for a moment overpowered the industrial rumble of engines outside.

"Oh dear God," I heard Mrs Gilman yell from behind the front door as it shook on its hinges with the continuing blows, "It's alright, we're coming! Oh, I hope he's okay ..."

"Fucking idiot ..." the unknown man muttered.

Amidst the museum of wreckage stood a young girl, no more than seven years of age. Her untidy dirty-blonde hair hung over the shoulders of a grimy blue and white Victorian era party dress; a bizarre anachronism set against the ultramodern backdrop of emerging Workstation towers just visible beyond the filthy kitchen window to her back. Her grey eyes regarded me with an unreadable eagerness as she hooked the tip of a grubby finger coyly in her partially open mouth.

"You!" I screamed savagely, spittle spraying from my aching gums. "You better tidy this up right now! There's not much time left! Don't you understand?" Realising the absurdity of addressing this strange child in such a parental fashion, I paused for reflection. Changing tack, I shouted again: "You have to leave right now!" The ironic similarity of this statement to those directed at me by Mrs Gilman and her unknown accomplice was not lost on me.

The girl merely giggled and, in another lightning quick movement, stooped to pick up a random piece of debris at her feet. Without warning, she launched the object straight at me. My reflexes being somewhat out of step, I was as good as helpless to prevent the projectile from striking my forehead which erupted instantly in a pain more real than anything I could remember.

As I brought a hand instinctively to my head, I was appalled by the moist warmth of blood which met it there. Bringing the wet hand to my face, I saw my defeat reflected in the crimson blob. This endlessly fluctuating fluid, which had remained thankfully hidden from view for so long, now seemed to cruelly announce time's killing blow in its organic depth. Adjusting my vision to the projectile that struck me, I saw that it was Sarah's cello bow; red droplets glistening upon its taut edge which grinned with all the murderous pride of a triumphant guillotine.

With a bestial scream and a savage swiftness which surprised me, I scooped up the bow and launched it back at the girl. Despite the velocity of my throw, it was nothing compared to the swift agility of the child as she dodged the missile and leapt effortlessly upon a dusty kitchen unit, still giggling defiantly. The intruder's lithe grace caused the apartment to howl in agony as it yielded to the brutal forces of time and space as they reasserted themselves around her.

Beyond the kitchen, the front door of the apartment gave way with a tremendous crash.

"Right! Where the hell is he?"

"Through there, the bedroom! It's alright, we've

come to get you out of here!"

Comprehending now that the only way to restore the apartment's freedom and thus guarantee my own was to destroy this tiny invader, I launched myself at the girl. Mustering all my strength, I grabbed at her bare ankle, pulling her from the kitchen unit. She did not yell but lashed out brutally, kicking at me with her free foot.

Alerted by the noise, Mrs Gilman entered the kitchen followed by a tall man in an anonymous black uniform which I recognised as that of a governmental officer, most likely the block's assigned surveyor. The stranger scanned and evaluated the scene quickly and bellowed in a voice like a bear: "Hey! Let go of the girl and step away from her right now!"

Ignoring the man, I kept my attention focussed on the task at hand, grabbing the girl by the shoulders and slamming her tiny body against the wall. The impact robbed the child of her breath which exploded with appalling heat across my bare chest.

"Oh my God! Oh my God!" Mrs Gilman wailed uncontrollably. "Martha! My sweet little Martha!"

The officer seemed momentarily confused. "Martha?"

"He's going to kill my Martha! My sweet daughter! Oh Martha, you've come back! Please, please don't hurt my baby!"

The man in black advanced towards me, primed to attack. With that, I clamped my hands around the girl's fragile throat.

"Stay back! I'll fucking kill her!"

Thinking twice, the officer paused and stretched his arms out to his sides. "Okay. Okay. Take it easy. We can sort this out."

"Oh Martha!" Mrs Gilman continued to sob and moan. "Please don't take her from me again. Please!"

"It's alright Mrs Gilman," the man in black said in a calm and reassuring tone, "we can deal with this. Nothing's going to happen here."

"You better get out of here," I yelled at him. "Now!"

"Let's just keep calm," he spoke in the banal tones of a billion faceless TV personalities. "If we all get out of this safe and sound, there'll still be a good, productive job waiting for you at one of the Towers. Now doesn't that sound like something worth living for, eh?"

Abruptly, our standoff was interrupted by the sound of liquid dripping in a steady flow upon the kitchen floor. A stream of dark yellow urine tumbled down the girl's legs as they hung limply in the air, forming a pungent puddle upon the linoleum. As I watched this thick layer of liquid spread out upon the filthy floor, I was struck by the notion that it contained within its sour depths all the oppressive materiality of linear time and the organic treachery of space. The tortured walls of the apartment shook and shuddered in a terrible death rattle.

Fully enraged now, I squeezed my hands tightly around the girl's neck, intent to choke the life from her tiny body and thus restore the apartment to its

176

state of liberation.

"Oh my God! Martha! No! NNOOOOOOOO!!!"

In my peripheral vision I could see Mrs Gilman collapse to her knees in grief.

The man in black hovered ineffectually, unsure of how to react. "Don't do it, Mister. Stop!"

Intent upon my mineral destiny amongst the timeless rubble of the Old Town, I steeled myself and wished for this unpleasant and violent task to be over as quickly and mercifully as possible. I regretted that the old temporal universe had demanded this gratuitous sacrifice, which I would gladly have avoided. But with the clock of time running down, I could afford no -

"Wait!!"

I opened my eyes. This eerily familiar voice which had erupted from the girl's straining throat seemed to blast a gaping wound in my consciousness. Staring into the juvenile face, I suddenly became aware of its fine detail for the first time. There in the strangely recognisable contours of nose and cheekbone, the uncanny melancholy of the grey eyes, the distinctive geometry of the crooked teeth, I saw a reflection of myself in all my myriad forms and guises; a funhouse mirror of the infinite possibilities of my existence ...

As I relaxed my grip around her throbbing neck, the child spoke again in a voice older than time itself:

"It's me! It's me ..."

FEATHERS
Simon Marshall-Jones

All I found of her that morning was a single white feather; just that. A pure, crystal white, damply glistening feather, limned heavily against the black bed linen. A marker of a beautifully-lived life and a memorial to a grief as yet unfelt. In utter silence I looked at it, afraid to touch or even to breathe too heavily, lest I lose even this one small reminder. Time compressed, and eternity was held in every fibre of its whiteness.

Resisting its inevitable magnetism, I rose from the bed, careful not to disturb its repose. I padded out of the room gently, persuaded that my customary heavy morning footfalls would blacken and rot the pristine clarity of that object. Fluttering thoughts, dove-like, broke my reverie's surface and took flight. Even the monkish frigidity of the stone kitchen floor stabbing icily into the soles of my bare feet barely distracted them from their frenzied trajectories.

Mere mundanity ceased to be and fled away. I found myself already back in my room, propped up in bed and under the covers, staring at the feather. Only a steadily insistent stinging heat, felt in the fingers clutching a steaming mug of coffee, brought me back to a world of preternaturally bright winter sunshine streaming into the room. The white walls, broken only by the occasional pressurised burst of painted abstraction, relayed the light endlessly and lent the room a pillowed dreaminess. Its intensity compelled my eyes to seek refuge in the only place they could – the feather embedded within its matrix of black mutely lying next to me.

My thoughts, in that instant, came home to roost. Memories, echoing the dreamy light, flew in on brilliantined wings and perched comfortably in familiar recesses.

* * * * *

Romances are only deemed to be romantic if their very beginnings are so. If that is true, then I would say that ours transcended even that trite utterance. I was living at the time in an almost newly-minted city of steel and glassine angularity, a new town stuck in a cultural no-man's land between two other, larger, older (and thus more venerable) cities. History had yet to bestow its patina on my adopted home, its only buildings of note turned over to the tarnished glory of consumerism and commerce. The massed congregation of worshippers at these particular temples crammed themselves into endless satellite estates of brick and tarmac, of mock Georgian and characterless boxes, outside of which some were festooned with the signs of their gods' favours. Touted optimistically when originally planned as a promised land of multiculturalism, cosmopolitanism, equal opportunity and good living, it had instead over time caught the fashionable diseases of ghettoisation, marginalisation and wary distrust. Communities had willingly imprisoned themselves within invisible yet wholly tangible barriers, erected upon lines of ethnicity, race, culture, and wealth. In other words, the city hadn't yet learned to live with itself.

I had fetched up in this place quite by accident. After an aimless peripatetic existence lasting most of my adult life, I had reached that point where the attraction of wandering had paled into a pastel anonymity, where towns, people and places osmotically bled into each other and lost their significance. After a brief return to my place of birth came a horrendous vacuum of purpose, followed by a lengthy period of fruitless searching.

Boredom and its unwanted bedfellow ennui seeped in, blanketing me with an uncomfortable feeling of claustrophobia. Once familiar and welcoming hometown streets now took on an air of melancholy and drabness, a kind of tangible depression that was beginning to infuse itself into my very marrow. People, with their tiny inconsequential small-town preoccupations and irritations, appalled and disgusted me. It became such that the town itself took on a sense of ignorant, barbaric bestiality, spewing bile and acid; every time I walked its failed streets, or encountered its mean-spirited people, I absorbed more quantities of its stifling airlessness, until it felt like a physical, choking miasma, driving out every atom of life-giving oxygen. This metaphorical smog filling my lungs often brought with it a bright electric fear, inspiring fight or flight, but mostly a ghastly desire to turn tail and run. Sometimes my autonomic nervous system would readily latch on to its animal vitality, sending me headlong into a blind panicked motion. Arriving home after a bout of frenzied leg-pounding, I would collapse in a state of nervous exhaustion on the bed, where within an hour or two the soothing arms of Lady Sleep would thankfully envelop me.

That last time though was the decider – I really couldn't live here any longer; otherwise I would suffocate under its superficially-benign malignancy. The details don't matter particularly – suffice it to say that I ran, unseeing, down streets and unfrequented back alleys, through littered and graffiti-defaced lanes, back to my sanctuary. Once there, I shut away the world, cocooning myself in a shell of books, posters and wallpaper. The moment had arrived – it was time to move on.

* * * * *

Later that morning (how much later remains forever unknown to me) I had risen from bed in an attempt to normalise my day. The sunshine was still eye-wateringly fierce for a far-northern winter's day, but the reason was made plainly obvious once I had thrown back the curtains – sometime during the night a coating of snow had settled and was amplifying the sun's rays. Mountains and hills pierced the expanse of white, seeking perhaps to penetrate the unblemished blue canopy overhead in an act of defiance of the erasing whiteness below. The occasional bird skirled overhead, looking for any indiscriminate movement beneath betraying itself as a potential meal. Winter had been here for some time, marked by the animals assuming their winter colourings, making them easy targets against the heathers and rocks. Nature had now seen fit to restore a semblance of balance, swinging it back in their favour once more.

I stood in the garden outside the whitewashed cottage smoking a menthol cigarette, dressed thickly against the cold in my customary black, staring out at the magnificence paling away into far horizons and a previous life. In a place like this, where time seems more naturally anchored to the land, thoughts become unfettered and are given grace to be indulged. That's where I was now, lost in that previous existence way beyond that distant horizon....

* * * * *

There are times when my committed atheist stance is tested, and what happened after my crisis was one such time. Not many days afterward I got an email, out of the blue, from someone I hadn't seen in a long time, suggesting a reunion at his place. I pretty much pounced on the opportunity, seeing it as a way of relieving the pressure of stress as well as spending some time away from my personal Hell. Arrangements were put in place swiftly for a few weeks later, weeks which couldn't go by quickly enough.

Finally, there I was pumping the hand of my friend on the train station concourse, the gremlins of anxiety having melted away almost as soon as I stepped out of my front door back home. Now, a bus-ride later, I was safely ensconced in his kitchen, nursing a restorative cold beer. As we both sat there talking, sinking a few more beers as we did so, it was almost a blessed relief to unburden myself of the detritus hanging around me. I wasn't particularly looking for solutions then, just talking was good enough to tame some of the legion of demons I'd accumulated.

In the morning, new hope seemed to seep through the curtains as well as the sun, animating the planktonic dustmotes. A good sleep had contributed to a markedly peaceful state of mind. I wasn't even bothered about checking the time – couldn't have cared whether it was early or late, I just revelled in the utter timelessness of the moment underscored by a deep silence. The universe was holding its breath between the microseconds, and the infinitesimal became the infinite at that point.

Pulling myself back from the edge of forever I idly ambled out of bed and downstairs. Continued silence betrayed the house's emptiness. Generosity had left out a bowl and some cereal on the kitchen table, as well as some tacked-on handwritten scribbles on fridge and cupboard indicating milk, coffee and sugar. The silence, leavened only by the occasional creak and pop, eventually requested that it be filled somehow. Just by the toaster and kettle sat a radio; soon the room was filled by the gentle arpeggio of strings gliding and butterflying gracefully. Contentment seemingly had its own soundtrack.

The groove my mind was on was diverted by the sound of the front door opening and closing, and the keys being thrown on a table in the hall. The kitchen door opened, followed by a broad face breaking into a grin. Settling himself opposite me after making a cup of coffee, the grin seemed to get wider, threatening to split the top of my friend's head off. In answer to an inquisitively raised eyebrow he told me that he may have found me a job locally in a mate's music shop. He'd gone down there this morning after the previous evening's conversation, reckoning that a permanent break away from the source of my problems would restore some semblance of equilibrium. He also reckoned that my time should be put to good use at the same time: with a conspiratorial wink, he suggested I stop daydreaming and shuffle on down to the shop as soon as I could.

* * * * *

Once again, despite the freezing cold fingering its way through the fibres of my clothes, I had failed to take note of the passage of time. The sun was by now climbing down the arc of heaven, making sundials of lengthening shadows. I finally shuddered and turned back to the cottage. The heat of the kitchen came almost as a shock, but I was glad of its embrace nonetheless.

I shrugged off the overcoat and casually flung it over the arm of a convenient chair in the living room, returned to the kitchen, and prepared myself a mug of hot chocolate as a further antidote to the chill still hanging about my bones. Setting the mug on a small table next to the biggest armchair, I mused on the idea that a roaring fire in the grate would in all probability be a useful one.

By the time the flames were dancing in the open fireplace it meant that my hot chocolate needed a visit to the microwave. The sun had travelled further down the sky by this time, heading for the western curve of the mountains, and the corners of the living room were starting to fill with a creeping, deepening dusky gloom. As twilight approached, colouring the sky with airbrushed hues of navy, purple and orange, and the sparse clouds with blushes of pink, the darkening gloom in my little cube competed with the warm orange suffusion of firelight until they took refuge in the furthest reaches. The shadows performed an animated puppet play of strange misshapen ogres and phantasmagoria on the wall behind me, the figures feinting and darting in a perpetual dance but never quite meeting. In front, the bright sinuous rhythmic hip-swaying, belly-dancing flames conspired to seduce me, drawing out what I had thought buried by the passage of time...

* * * * *

In very short order I had settled into the rhythms of the city, the job bringing not just useful employment but also a small network of new friends and places to meet them in. The traumas of the months spent back home were washed away in a wave of alcohol and parties, and their attendant pleasures; once again the smile that I had stowed away for better times re-emerged, readily and spontaneously.

Thus I lived this way for the better part of seven months or so, weaving myself subconsciously and subtly into the fabric of the scene. Not a weekend went by without a frantic social whirl, either occasioning visits to local watering-holes or cramming myself along with my friends into some sweaty venue to check out the latest bands. Fridays and Saturdays thus were nothing more than vague memories at the best of times, blurs of indistinct sounds, voices and colours, inevitably followed by sickness and nausea on Sundays.

As summer approached, however, the season called me to its outdoor temples of forest and field. Groups of us, but more often than not just me, would drive or cycle to some beauty-spot in the surrounding countryside, spending a couple of days imbibing the balmy pleasures of warm nights under canvas and sunny days in idyllic settings. Here my spirit would truly be set free, experiencing even deeper happiness than I'd ever thought possible. In just the space of a few days I would feel as though I had taken root permanently, and that any enforced transplant back to 'civilisation' would be a trauma too far. Silently, subconsciously, a vow had taken shape within me; there would be a time when a return would be impossible.

* * * * *

By now, the cottage was wholly in darkness, except for the enlivening fire in the grate broadcasting its womb-like glow of warmth. I shivered slightly despite the comfort it bestowed, perhaps because the warm glowing ambience conferred an unearthly feeling of other dimensions, places where everything exudes a supernatural brightness and time has no grip. With something of a start, the image of the feather, surprisingly unremembered until that moment, leapt onto the screen of the mind; it was still lying there in the bedroom where I had left it untouched, a mute presence that yet spoke more than any number of books could. At that moment, a dam of sadness burst, flooding me with the realisation of what it all signified. Quite simply, she was gone. Deeper, and sadder still, it meant that that absence was permanent. Her spirit had flown from this realm of pain and anguish, perhaps to a more congenial plane, somewhere beyond my mortal ken and reach. Then the grief flowed over me, unabated and unabashed, its liquidity seeking out every crack and

187

crevice, until I could contain it no longer. The tears breached my defences and flowed, wracking my entire frame and laving my cheeks with their stinging absolution, bringing with it a strange comfort and calm in its wake.

* * * * *

I decided on one last solo expedition, before the season's colours turned completely and presaged colder, but no less vibrant, times. It was late September/early October, and the evenings were noticeably drawing in, serving notice that soon would be the time when Nature would shut down and conserve itself for the following year's burst of activity. This was a time that, ever since childhood, I had felt closest to the natural rhythms of life – and the older I got, and the more the modern world seemed to encroach on those rhythms, the more keenly I felt it. As the years had gone by, Nature's sorrow at its greatest triumph's estrangement had grown sharper and deeper. In my own little way I wanted to reassure it that there were yet some who still cared, who still wanted to reconnect to the old ways and open the lines of communication. Indeed, that not all of us had been beguiled by the illusory and transient baubles of mankind.

Taking nothing more than the barest of essentials, paring down even my normal amount of camping provisions and equipment, I had set off late afternoon after finishing work early in anticipation of the weekend. Pointing my bike's handlebars where the mood suggested, I soon breached the city limits and found myself bordered with unfettered green, hedges and fields shimmering in the westering sun. A light breeze took the edge off the sun's heat, although I took things at a leisurely pace, letting the emerald lanes glide by serenely and drinking in the comforting promise of a night under a clear, crystalline sky. Unconsciously, a smile broke out while a delightful frisson of expectation shivered its way from one end of my spine to the other.

Dusk had already started to draw a curtain over the day when I decided that I should find somewhere to bed down for the night. Soon the sun would set completely below the horizon, pulling all the colours of the world with it. There was more than enough light to see that I had arrived at a wooded hill, which rose directly from the other side of a fence immediately bordering the road. To the right of it was a lushly grassed field, inhabited by a few cows already settled down for the evening. One or two raised their heads inquisitively as I hefted the bike over the fence, with me following soon after, but they quickly became bored and went back to their bovine ruminations.

I walked a little way into the field, skirting the margin between forest and field, looking for any suitable spot where I could settle comfortably. I didn't want to go too far in under the trees, but neither did I want to be too near the forest's edge just in case it started raining during the night. About a third of the way along I found a gap in the trees edging the field, and a nice little sheltered clearing, flattish, roughly 6 – 8 feet square and more or less devoid of stones and exposed roots. I walked in under the canopy, propped the bike against one of the trees in the back of the space and shrugged off my backpack. I cleared a small strip of detritus by a sturdy-looking oak, just enough for me to lie down on. I hadn't bothered bringing a tent with me, so I unrolled a sleeping mat and then put my sleeping bag on top of that. With my back propped against the tree-trunk, I took out a little bag of food I'd brought with me and waited while the sun finally disappeared behind the horizon while I ate.

* * * * *

I sat there in the gloom, wrapped in a blanket of silence, the grief having subsided just as the flames in the grate had now faded to mere flickers. The shadow-puppets on the wall behind me had exhausted their frantic dances and lay quiescent, only occasionally showing jerky, nervous movements. Like them, exhaustion had by now settled heavily on me; all that remained of the emotional upheavals were my hot and puffy eyes, and the dry riverbeds on my cheeks where the copious tears had dried and left a salty deposit. I felt flat. The pressurised vessel holding my grief in had ruptured, leaving nothing behind but a space just waiting to be filled.

But even in that brief second, I felt a surge of light and serenity fill the emptiness and with it the feeling that it no longer seemed right to mourn; a sudden realisation that the feather was meant to be a sign of something extraordinary, not a memorial, giving meaning to a hitherto unfathomable event. A symbol, perhaps, that regret and loss were unwanted guests; that nothing is ever truly lost, that it metamorphoses into some new, perhaps greater and more substantive, form.

The softly illuminated living room suddenly felt far too small and restrictive, and I was seized with a desire to go outside into the frigid night air, to let the breeze scratch and sting my face under the sheltering canopy of stars. Going into the hallway, though, before I could make it to the front door, I was struck by a soft, gently oscillating glow spilling out of the open bedroom door; moonlight on snow streaming in through the window wouldn't account for that, I thought. With trepidation and curiosity mixed in equal parts, I poked my head through the doorway, half expecting something to jump out at me. Instead, there was only soft light spilling into the room from the window, fuzzying shapes and textures; but weaving itself through the moonwash, though, was that rhythmic glow, with the feather plainly being the source.

I approached the bed, slowly, reverently almost, afraid perhaps that I was committing some unknown blasphemy in the process, or that my proximity would befoul the feather. I half anticipated that the limpid turquoise light that both caressed and haloed the object would decay into sickness if I got too close, and it would start to disintegrate. I knelt on the bed to get nearer to it, as it was lying on the side next to the wall. As I moved my hand to it, cilia of light curled out to touch it. Involuntarily I jerked my hand back, a move mirrored by the little fingers of light. Hesitating only an instant, I brought my hands closer again, and instantly the cilia wrapped themselves around them until they were completely enveloped. Gently, I scooped it up, and walked into the snowbound night.

* * * * *

Somehow, I had managed to doze off while sitting against the tree in the clearing, and I woke with a start. The long, albeit lazy, cycle ride had tired me out more than I had suspected. The sun had by this time started its journey through the underworld but the air was warm and through the gap in the trees I could make out indistinct shapes bathed in moonlight. My eyes still hadn't fully adjusted themselves to the darkness, but as they did it gradually became apparent that playing over the moonglow was an oddly pulsating light, ranging from greens to reds, yellows and oranges. My only thought was that there was some kind of fireworks display going on somewhere, but I was disturbed somewhat by the lack of cracks, pops and whistles accompanying the entertainment.

My curiosity got the better of me, and I just had to look for myself. When I came out from under the trees, I was rewarded by a sight that I would never, ever, forget. The ground in front of me was alive with sinuous colour and movement, ribbons of colour writhing and darting over the pale white light of the moon caressing the rough grass. Instinctively I looked up, and I found the sky shimmering and cavorting in concert with the kaleidoscope on the ground. This was a sight I had yearned to see for years, the magnificence of the aurora borealis, but never had I expected it to appear this far south. Bright, shyly twinkling stars would occasionally peek out from behind the filmy veils like some nervous debutante making her first appearance in public. The moon, completely full, hovered about like an old chaperone, keeping a watchful eye on her charges as they preened and shimmied in their gauzy finery.

I stood transfixed; my eyes must have glittered as the sheets billowed in the cosmic wind and I felt an uninhibited grin split my face. The air danced with electricity: I could feel it ruffling and spiking my hair. But this wasn't just an incidental electricity, there was something more vital to it, an energy animating the very air around me. I could almost feel the atoms pinging about frantically, ricocheting off my face and scalp. I seemed to be drawing strength and energy out of every breath I inhaled.

The timelessness of the moment lingered, and the whole of the universe seemed poised on a pivotal moment. It felt like something momentous was about to happen, but that it was hung between a multitude of possibilities and I was caught between them. Just then, the electrified atmosphere, already at an elevated pitch, somehow managed to ramp itself higher still. The air positively sparked, sending a delicious thrill through my whole body.

The slight chill that started to settle into the night began to seep into my muscles and bones; I guessed I hadn't moved in quite a while. I stirred, bending down to touch my toes, slowly releasing all the aches and cramps that had accumulated. Straightening up, I started at the sight of somebody else standing quite near, looking right at me and smiling benignly. It was a young woman, around my own age I guessed, yet simultaneously there was something of the ageless about her. Seemingly a blue light wrapped around her like an aura, but whether it was something real or a trick of the light I couldn't be sure. Whatever it was, I found it an oddly reassuring sight.

Even in the mystery of that summer night, with all its wonders, and without quite knowing how, we fell easily into conversation. It turned out that she was something of a free spirit, backpacking down some of the forgotten byways, searching out those hidden treasures of the countryside before they finally disappeared. She'd been at the very crown of the wooded hill when the display had started, and at that point had come down the hill. I laughed and joked that that may be because the view was better down here than up there. Her simple reply stunned me.

"No, it's because I knew then you were here..."

That was the start of it all, right there.

My life had taken off on an unexpected tangent, simply because of an improbable meeting in the most unlikely of places. More to the point she turned out to be the most extraordinary of creatures. In a world where magic and mystery no longer seemed to have a place, she was the most magical and mysterious of beings, and it would be no exaggeration to say that I began to suspect that indeed she was not of this world.

There was an ease with which she negotiated the everyday world, gliding through it with a kind of serenity that a made mockery of even the most taxing of troubles, and all the while she radiated a light that brightened all the lives she touched. Certainly my life seemed to have been sanctified by her close presence, and blanketed every moment of my waking life with a warmth and love beyond even the most ardent declarations of the poet. Every cell in my body jumped for joy, and in all the fruitful years we were together the smile she had brought to my lips never left me. I often used to ask her where she had come from; all I would get in return was a liquid laugh and a smile.

So it was that many years and many miles later, and after many partings from friends and family, that we found ourselves a home where we could both put roots down. The cottage was the perfect place, a simple white house with the simplest of amenities, a simple white structure set against a vale of dark heathers and fortressed by solid mountains on all sides but one, yet more than ample for our needs. There was just the one road connecting us to civilisation far to the south, albeit tenuously. Our only companions in this wilderness were the scurrying, scratching, and screeching wildlife, living out their whole lives in the ageless cycles of existence.

The seasons and the years passed, utter contentment charming our lives together. Never was there a day tainted by strife or disagreement. Even on grey days, she was a reminder of cloudless blue skies and pristinely starlit nights. One day though, those blue skies started showing clouds, and everyday thereafter the banks accumulated until they threatened to obscure everything. The smile came less and less easily to her, pain etching lines in her brow and around her mouth. I would ask her what was wrong, but she would gently bat my worries away by summoning a smile and for a brief moment the sun would poke through once more. Even so, I began to feel the distance building between us and I would be left wondering.

* * * * *

The cold air hit me square in the face as I walked into the night, my vision blurring as it did so. I hadn't even bothered putting on an overcoat to keep the cold out, a distant voice telling me I wouldn't need it. Slowly the cold infiltrated the layers and started biting into my skin. I remained oblivious to it, however; my concentration focused solely on the feather still cradled in my hands. It still pulsed with that supernatural light, but its rhythm had become more intense and my heart quickened in parallel with it. Despite the cold, my hands were warm, as if the feather itself were the source of a gentle, living heat.

I stumbled on, not really caring that much which direction I was going in. The unblemished carpet of virginal snow now betrayed the evidence of my blundering violation of its crystal purity. That snow dragged weightily at my legs, so that with every step it sapped just a little bit more of my strength, until finally I sank heavily onto my knees, gasping for a breath that wouldn't feel like sharp needles of ice were stabbing the interior of my lungs. Through the haze of my exhaled breath I saw a mountain looming over me, signalling that I had somehow walked farther than I thought. Eventually I collapsed onto my back, feeling the chill wetness seeping through my clothing.

My teeth started chattering almost instantly and at that moment I noticed that the sky was alive with colour – for only the second time in my life I was witnessing the awe-inspiring aurora borealis. Those sublime sheets waved magisterially across the sky, animated as if blown by some uncanny wind known only to itself. The night-sky blazed with a startling clarity that was unusual even for these northern climes, and reminded me of nothing so much as looking down upon some lamp-lit city from space. Bisecting this celestial city was the sacred river of the Egyptians, the Milky Way, itself ablaze with a hundred million points of light. Even as the numbness crept up my legs and started spreading to the rest of my body, I imagined the aurora bridging the two worlds, the celestial and the earthbound, and I had a sudden urge to find the place where it touched down.

I struggled to prop myself up while still trying to keep the feather safe. I managed to manoeuvre myself semi-upright by using one arm, but even that had been something of a struggle. Looking down at my free hand to find solace in the one remaining token of her, I was suddenly thrown into a panic. The feather had gone, evaporated into the cold air. I frantically searched for it, frenzied flurries of white powdering the air, not knowing whether the feather's whiteness was concealing it against the background snow. I carried on like this for some time, dangerously exhausting what reserves of strength I had left.

I collapsed back onto the freezing pillow of ice, and the tears erupted uncontrollably, the silence broken by huge wracking seismic sobs. This final loss was unbearable, my one last connection had been taken away from me, and I felt that my destiny was to die a cold death at the foot of the lonely mountains, mourned only by the stars. My whole body was now numb, and I could easily imagine putting down frozen roots right into this very spot. I knew then that I would never move from here.

Contradictorily, that knowledge calmed me down, and the sobs subsided. I sat motionless in the snow for a while, resigned to my fate but even then entertaining a faint hope that in passing beyond I would find her once again. I managed to raise my head, and through the tears still blurring my sight there appeared to be a blue shimmer approaching me. By this time, though, my eyes felt increasingly heavy, and I was just longing for some sleep. Peace, and dreamless oblivion, was all I wanted just then.....

...until I heard a voice faintly calling me, a distant, fluting voice, full of warmth, love and laughter. A delightfully trilling voice full of wonderfully warm and beautiful memories. Memories of times spent together, living together and loving together. A night just like this one, spent under the infinite canvas of the universe, enlivened by the dancing veils of vivid colour. Thoughts of all the countless lives we had touched, or been touched by, during our blessed journey down through the years, and all the smiles and all the songs too. The warmth of those memories seeped into every part of my body, wrapping me in a fuzzy blanket of cotton wool.

Through the fuzz and the warmth, I heard her voice now, stronger and clearer. With an effort I opened my eyes and saw her standing over me, clear as when I had known her. She smiled her ever-serene smile and extended an open hand towards me.

"It's time to come home"

* * * * *

It was a warm, sunny day in early spring, and the picturesque pub down by the canal was filling up like it normally did on days like these. The beer garden, fronting directly onto the water, was full of lunchtime drinkers; young, upwardly mobile people, the girls in bright strappy dresses or smart casual office wear, and the boys in shirt sleeves with loosened ties. The mood was genial and relaxed, a reflection of the clement weather; the chink of glasses and laughter cut through the general chatter, and most of the conversation veered towards talk of the coming weekend.

Sitting over on one of the corner tables in the garden was an exception. A man, young just like the others certainly, but marked out by his dress and his being the only one occupying his table. He was wearing black jeans and a black t-shirt with a band logo on it. Placed next to the pint glass by his right arm was a cycle helmet, and next to the table, propped up against the boundary wall, was a mountain-bike. In between gulps of cider from his glass, he was writing on the lined pages of an A5 book. Occasionally he would look up and stare into the distance, hoping perhaps to glimpse an answer to a puzzle floating on the whispering breeze.

"Anyone sitting here?" a girl's voice suddenly interrupted his flowing pen.

The man sharply refocused on the present and looked up to see a young woman, her smooth alabaster skin an island of white amidst the black of her sunglasses, hair and clothing. She must be near to overheating on a day like this, he thought.

"Umm, no." He replied, recovering quickly from his initial surprise.

"Mind if I join you?" The girl asked, a smile flashing brilliantly.

"No, no, please do!" he replied, rushing to gather up some loose papers strewn on the table.

Still smiling, the girl gracefully slid down on to the bench seat opposite. She looked at him from behind the impenetrable sunglasses.

"Are you a writer?" She asked, settling her elbows onto the table.

"This?" The man let out a small chuckle. "No, I'm afraid not, just a scribbler really. I'm just writing down some thoughts. The name's Mike, by the way."

He extended a hand, an equally broad smile reflecting the girl's facing him. She grasped the proffered hand lightly. Mike felt the cool softness, surprisingly cool on a day like today, he thought.

"That's a nice name... a reassuring one." She said. "I'm Neria."

"Neria? That's an unusual name... nice though. Never come across it before."

"My mother was somewhat... eccentric and loved the exotic, shall we say." She said by way of explanation.

Mike looked back at himself from the reflection in her sunglasses. The girl kept smiling at him, her expression hiding behind her reflective glasses. The moment stretched into an uncomfortable silence. Mike simply nodded at her, not knowing what else to do.

"I'm off to get myself a drink... would you like a refill?" Neria asked, pointing to the almost empty glass by his elbow.

"Nahhh, thanks..." he replied. "Need to keep my wits about me. I need to keep a clear head on me today." He motioned towards the bike with his pen.

Neria acknowledged this with a barely perceptible nod, turned away, and disappeared into the cool, shadowy darkness of the pub. Mike followed her receding figure with his eyes. He rested his chin on one hand and eventually turned his gaze to the slow moving-river and let his mind drift along with the water.

The last few years have seen some strange times, he thought. Warren's inexplicable disappearance was the start of it all, and since then it's been a rollercoaster.

"So, what are you writing then? Is it some kind of story?" Mike jumped , startled, out of his reverie. He hadn't even heard Neria come back, or sit down. She was looking at him in that same unsettling way.

"A story...?" he uttered eventually. "Well, not quite a story, exactly... more like a quest for an ending."

"Oh?" She enquired, tilting her head quizzically.

"Do you believe in ghosts?" somewhat hesitantly, a slight nervousness tingeing the question with hoarseness.

"Well, I don't know..." she replied. "I've never seen one myself, but I suppose that means nothing. Are you writing a ghost story, then?"

"No... well, yes, maybe... depends on how you view things." Mike replied, fumbling for something that made sense.

"Hmmm...?" There was a vague hint of arched eyebrows behind the sunglasses.

"It's an old story for me now, verging on an obsession some would say..." he started. "But it's occupied all my spare time for the last four years. Back then, a friend of mine vanished, so completely and so effectively that he appeared to have never existed. And he's still missing."

"What happened?"

"This friend, Warren, had come to live here to put some space between him and his hometown. I'd known him from college days, and after he'd come visiting he said he liked it here, so I suggested that he move up to this area, if for no other reason than to have a break. He did, and he came to be as much a part of the fabric of this city's life as if he'd always been here.

"Anyway, he slotted right into the scene, he'd made loads of new friends, but, even so, come summer, he would cycle out into the countryside, either with a group of us or more often than not on his own. Then, four years ago, late summer/autumn time, he suddenly decided to spend a weekend away from the city, because the weather was fabulous I remember, so it wouldn't have been a surprise. That was the last anyone ever saw of him, although all his camping equipment was found, undisturbed, in a little wooded clearing next to a field about five miles to the west of here some months later."

"I assume the authorities investigated it thoroughly?"

"Yes they did – but all they came up with was a mystery." Mike replied. "No signs of foul play, or a struggle, or anything that would betray a clue as to what happened. Apart from discovering that his sleeping bag had been sat on and finding clothing fibres on a tree-trunk, it was all just as it was when he disappeared."

"And that's why the end is yet to be found..." Neria said simply.

"Yeah..." Mike replied, sighing tiredly. "And, at this rate, the full story will never be known. I have managed to follow a few trails and gather some clues as to what happened in the years since the initial investigation, but I feel the complete picture will never fully emerge. He could be wandering around out there somewhere not knowing where he is or, as is more likely, lying in an unmarked grave in some godforsaken spot. It grieves me just to think about that."

"So what did you find out?" the girl asked, her china white face an unreadable mask.

"Well, too little, until very recently, that is. As often happens, the trail had gone pretty much cold practically the moment his equipment had been found. Then, about six months ago, just by chance, another old college friend had taken up a job at a newspaper north of the border and that's when things started moving again. Idly looking through their archives on a particularly slow day, he happened to come across a story about some weirdo living in an isolated cottage in the wilds up there. My journalist friend was convinced that this bloke was the missing Warren, so he emailed the whole thing down to me and indeed the photograph did show a man bearing a marked resemblance to Warren. I wasn't entirely convinced, because the man looked too old to be him."

"But was it your friend?" the girl asked.

"Yeah, it was indeed him – I've known Warren for more than a few years and I would recognise him anywhere, no matter how much he'd changed physically. However the story was pretty odd, saying that he was apparently living with someone that he kept looking at and referring to as his 'angel'; BUT, the reporter didn't see anyone else there. At times, Warren would have 'conversations' with this 'angel', the flow of words and pauses suggesting that he was indeed talking with someone. The piece, in typically condescending tabloid fashion, made out was that here was an eccentric, if harmless, nutter, living a solitary existence out in the wilderness who'd completely lost his marbles.

"I couldn't just leave it there, though – I felt I owed it to him to investigate it. I had some remaining leave to take, so I made a little pilgrimage to find this cottage if I could. Turned out locating it wasn't that difficult and it took me longer to walk from where I parked my camper to the front door than it did to hunt it down on the 'net.

"It was in a hell of a sorry state – roof caved in, the garden a riot of weeds and embattled flowers, the front door off its hinges and letting in the elements, with nature and rainwater the new tenants. It hadn't been occupied for some time, judging by the decay and mess I found. By some bizarre miracle though, the bedroom looked as if it had only been recently vacated; just a few stray leaves, a light covering of dust and a proliferation of spider's webs were the only indication of anything untoward. Presumably the wind had blown the door shut somehow. Anyway, the bedclothes appeared just newly thrown aside and even the coffee cup on the bedside table looked recently drained. But even so, the room was unwilling to give up its secrets readily.

"The room felt eerily frozen in time, and I shivered in spite of the warmth of the summer sun streaming through the window. I sat down on the bed and I remember that the air was unnaturally still, with not even the curtains moving. I was half wishing Warren would come through that door to dispel the ghostly atmosphere.

"I sat there for a long while, just looking around the room. Time appeared to flow differently; when I looked out the window again the sun was already heading towards the horizon. A sudden thought struck me, and I started looking for anything that might provide a clue as to what happened here, like a notebook or diary. After pulling out drawers, looking in and on wardrobes and boxes, I finally found it, under the bed: a battered unlined notebook filled with spidery handwriting. Here, I hoped, was where answers lay.

"In the failing light I decided the cottage was getting too depressing, so I left it to the birds and the beasts, and walked back to the camper and headed straight back home. After I got back, I set about deciphering Warren's atrocious scrawl, which made me feel like some archaeologist trying to understand some script from a lost civilisation."

"What did you find out?" Neria's voice unexpectedly pierced through, pulling him back from the past.

"More mysteries I suppose" Mike replied, weariness infusing his voice. "Mysterious events involving meetings under an 'otherworldly' aurora, angelic beings, aimless wanderings from town to town, ghostly feathers being left on pillows and soul-wrenching feelings of deep loss and mourning – it's certainly not your average love story. If I didn't know any better I would have assumed it was the outline for a fantasy story. And who was this girl? And how the hell did he manage to wind up in a cottage right up there in the north anyway? What did he do for food and money? More questions than answers. However, reading it does leave you with the overwhelming impression that everything is real and deeply felt. It certainly appears that he believes everything he talks about actually happened."

"Who's to say it didn't happen in the way he says it does?" Her simple question hung in the air, leaving silence behind it.

"Are you being serious?" Mike asked.

"Yes, I am." Neria stated, in a quiet, controlled voice.

The small laugh trembling just under his lips, waiting to spill out, died abruptly. Her face was an inscrutable mask, betraying nothing. Mike, though, felt uncomfortably like her eyes were boring into him, piercing his soul.

"There's no way it could possibly be true." Mike spluttered. "I mean, there are bits in the story that just don't make any sense. Just as an example, he says he met this mysterious woman while watching an amazing aurora – something that no-one else remembers seeing at all. And he says he saw this display within five miles of here and I am very sure that it would have been a topic of conversation for months if it had happened. No-one said a damn thing."

"Well, perhaps you're right... I was only suggesting that maybe to him it was real." The corners of her thin lips curled upwards into a bright, uninhibited smile. It unnerved Mike, leaving him unsure whether she had been teasing him after all.

"Well, maybe it did." Mike conceded

unconvincingly, shrugging his shoulders. "We have nothing but his word for what happened anyway, and this notebook is the only connection anybody has that proves Warren once existed. In the meantime I suppose I'll keep on searching and hoping for some kind of closure to the story, if for no reason other than to lay his ghost to rest..."

The pair lapsed into a silence, filled with the quiet sound of lapping water and the occasional chirrup of insects. It was only then that Mike realised that the voices of the afternoon drinkers had faded long ago without him noticing, and that the pub garden had emptied and the deepening shadows of dusk had crept into its domain. Light was already spilling softly from the curtained windows of the pub, and little lamps on the further canal-side had started to come on. The sun was well below the houses now, and a sharp chill had cooled the air. Mike shivered involuntarily, whether from the cold or from the realisation that he hadn't been aware of the afternoon going so quickly he couldn't tell, and reached for his hoodie. He eased himself into it and down over his torso, feeling the goosebumps subside almost immediately.

"Anyway, I've dallied here long enough and I'd best be getting home before it gets any darker," he continued, gathering all his papers and the notebook, stuffing them into a document bag. He then drained the last of his cider in one gulp.

"Would you mind just looking after my stuff while I go and relieve myself please?" Mike asked the still smiling Neria.

"Sure, no problem," she replied. "And it was nice to have met you, Mike. I'm glad that Warren has such a good friend who still looks out for him and shows such concern. I'm sure he'll be happy to know that."

Mike nodded his thanks and shook her hand. Mike headed for the now shut pub door, weaving in between the tables and with the empty glass still in his hand. The girl removed her sunglasses and watched him, the smile upon her lips broadening and her blue eyes twinkling.

Five minutes later, Mike re-emerged and hurried over to the table, where Neria, was sitting facing the canal. She looked at him, still with that beatific smile, as he slung the document bag over his shoulder, donned his bike helmet and gloves and grabbed the bike. He wheeled it out slightly and turned to say goodbye to the strange girl. In that instant, she had gone.

In her place, lying on the table and glistening in the faint starlight, was a single white feather.

PROCEDURE 769: CDC# B66883
Díre McCain

A supernatural tale based on real people and events...

> **ANALYST:** The subject was born in Fort Bragg, North Carolina three months premature, after his alcoholic father – a decorated World War II Veteran – had kicked the subject's alcoholic mother in the abdomen so forcefully she began to hemorrhage. An act that would set the precedent for the subject's harrowing childhood, during which he would suffer regular beatings at the hands of both parents.

April 20, 1992 6:26 PM PDT

OPERATOR: "I have a collect call from Robert Alton Harris, an inmate at San Quentin State Prison. Do you accept the charges?"

ROBERT ALTON HARRIS: Eleven hours and thirty-one minutes. Shoulda been five hours and thirty-one minutes, but all them people still tryin' to save me only delayed my fate. Need someone to claim my remains, that's all, ain't askin' for the world. Been waitin' to die since before I was born.

Now the Grim Reaper's knockin' at my door, and nobody'll step up to the plate. Cousin Sam's my last hope, but when he opened his mouth, I knew it was a lost cause. He was fucked up, and I was fucked, destined for Boot Hill, with the likes of Bluebeard Watson and William Kogut, to spend eternity stuck in Hell.

VICTIM: It was the morning after Fourth of July. My best friend and I were going fishing. We stopped at Jack in the Box first to get some food. We were eating in the car when two men walked up.

```
At age two, the subject's father
flogged    the    subject    with    a
bamboo    stick,    breaking    the
subject's jaw. It was the first
of    several    serious    injuries
sustained    during    the    subject's
childhood.
```

All these years, everybody thinkin' I wasn't sorry for killin' them two boys, thinkin' I was chickenshit, not wantin' to meet the maker. Hell, I ain't denyin' what I done was wrong, and I come to terms with dyin', but the stories I heard 'bout the hereafter up on that Hill's enough to make the toughest son of a bitch cringe.

One of them had a gun. He told us to let him in the car, so we did. He held the gun at us and said to start driving. He said he wasn't going to hurt us. The other man followed in their car. I didn't know where we were going or why, but I was really scared.

> Even meals in the subject's home were a continual source of trauma and abuse. While at the dinner table, if the subject reached for something without his father's permission, the subject's father would drive a fork through the subject's hand. The subject would then be forbidden to eat another bite until he had "learned his lesson" – often resulting in several days of starvation.

Goddamn story of my life. Ain't had real food since 1978. Now I got one foot in the grave, and here comes the pizza, the fried chicken, the works. Cigarettes been like bullion all these years, and now I'm sittin' on a case, just like that. And the new duds. Why the heck they think a condemned man needs new duds is beyond me. All I care about's not windin' up on that Hill. They say it's like Purgatory, only worse, 'cause it ain't temporary, you're stuck there for all eternity, sufferin' in ways you ain't never suffered in your worst nightmares.

When we reached the Lake, the man told us to pull in and stop the car. Then he told us to get out and start walking. He followed us with the gun held to our backs. He joked and laughed a lot, and kept

213

promising that he wouldn't hurt us. He said he just
wanted the car and that we'd be free to go. We
believed him, and kept walking.

> "Recreation" was equally abusive
> and traumatic. The subject's
> father's idea of Hide-and-Seek
> was to give the subject and his
> eight siblings a half hour to
> hide outside the house, before
> hunting them down with a loaded
> shotgun, threatening to shoot
> anyone who was found.

Just after three, new duds on, stomach full of grease, lungs full of nicotine, they come get me. Strap me in, release the dogs. Ready to roll, even tell 'em so. Look around, see 'em all here watchin', every one of 'em I wronged. No more get outta jail free cards, my number's up, it'd take a goddamn miracle to save me now. Got no choice but to suck it up and take it like a man.

"PULL IT."

I heard a loud popping sound. Then I felt a hot
burning sensation in my back. A few seconds later, I
heard another loud popping sound. Then I felt
another hot burning sensation, but in my head. I fell
down. I couldn't see or move. But I could hear. I
could hear the man laughing.

A few months prior to the subject's tenth birthday, the family relocated to a farm labor camp in the San Joaquin Valley. It was there that the subject's eldest sister was arrested for theft and sent to juvenile hall, where she revealed yet another form of abuse in the Harris home.

The subject's father habitually molested the subject's sisters, often forcing the subject to watch. The subject described one incident in particular, when his father tried to force the subject to take part in the assault. When the subject was unable to achieve an erection, presumably due to the atrocious nature of the situation, he was castigated and beaten unconscious, then locked in a closet for several hours.

In early 1963, the subject's father was deemed a sex offender and sent to Atascadero State Hospital for a year and a half. Upon his release, the habitual molestation resumed, until the end of 1964, when he was caught in the act by police officers who had gone out to the house on

215

a domestic violence call.
Shortly thereafter, the
subject's father was convicted
and incarcerated for the crimes.

Ten minutes into it, another no go. They cut me loose, and here I am, back in that cell, eatin' jelly beans, smokin' Camels, waitin' to die. Reckon it might never happen, but scared to let my guard down, 'cause in the backa my mind, that Hill's still bellowin' at me, like a lion at feedin' time.

I heard my best friend scream. It sounded like he was running away. Then I heard two more popping sounds. The man started laughing again. I was never more scared in my life. I felt the man standing over me. I could hear him breathing. I wanted to get up and run, but I still couldn't see or move. He pushed my body with his foot and asked me if I was dead yet. I wished my dad was there. He would have killed the man and rescued us, I know it.

With the subject's father in
prison, the Harris family
migrated up and down the valley
for two years. Then the
subject's mother moved the
subject and five of his siblings
to Sacramento, where she took up
with a new mate. By now, the
subject had already embarked on
a life of crime, and before
long, was sent to juvenile hall

216

for stealing a car. In 1967, the
subject's mother abandoned him
altogether, claiming he was too
difficult to rear any longer.
The subject, now fourteen, was
left to fend for himself.

They say it's a pitch-dark wasteland, can't see a
goddamn thing, can't move neither. Like that
picture, *Johnny Got His Gun*, 'cept worse, 'cause your
smellin' and hearin's stronger than a hound dog's.
The stench of death, your own flesh rottin' away,
swallows you whole, and every sound cuts through
your ears and into your brain, like an ice pick bein'
drove through your head. Worst part of all's what's
happenin' inside your head turns into a big ol' TV,
'cept the only programmin' is your worst pains and
traumas. Ain't no off switch neither, it just keeps on
goin' and goin' and goin', playin' over and over
again.

*The man walked away. I heard the car start and burn
rubber. The laughing stopped. It was quiet, so quiet
it hurt my ears. I was going to die. I thought about
my Mom and what it would do to her. And my sister
and my brother. I wished I'd stayed home that day. I
wished I stayed home. I. Wished. I'd. Stayed. Home.*

The subject made his way to
Oklahoma, where one of his
brothers and one of his sisters
resided. After several more run-
ins with the law, the subject

217

spent the next four years as a ward of various federal reformatories, where he was diagnosed as schizophrenic with suicidal and homicidal tendencies.

When the subject reached adulthood, he was released from custody. With fifty dollars in his pocket and a one-way bus ticket, he headed back to Southern California, where his father now resided. The subject soon found work and started a family, but within three years, had fallen back on his old ways.

Coupla hours later, batter up, home run. 'Cept I ain't ready to go no more, and it ain't just the thought of that Hill waitin' for me. Last thing I seen was that boy's father glarin' at me, hatin' me for what I done to his boy, wishin' me dead ten times over.

"I'm sorry."

The police came later that night. I wondered how they found us. They left us lying there for a long time while they walked around doing their work. They talked about how tragic it was. Tragic. That was the word they kept using. I kept hoping it was a nightmare. I tried and tried and tried to wake up, but I couldn't. I just lay there, memories spilling out of my head, like the blood I'd felt trickling down my neck. My little brother's birth. School. Learning how to ride a bike. Learning how to drive. My friends. The girl I wanted to ask out. I thought about the future that would never be. I would never have a job, go to college, marry, have children, grandchildren. It felt like forever before the police put us in those bags and loaded our bodies into the van.

It is believed that the subject's intense anger and hostility toward other living things – humans and animals alike – can be attributed to the relentless cycle of terror and abuse, which began while the subject was still in his mother's womb. The subject exhibited violent tendencies at an uncommonly young age. As an adolescent, the subject took great pleasure in torturing and killing neighborhood cats, a crime which led to his first arrest. It was not long before the subject had moved on to humans.

Could feel my body thrashin' around as the poison seeped in, but my mind was sufferin' more. Them stories y'hear 'bout folks' lives flashin' before their eyes when they're dyin', like a picture show? All true, 'cept there weren't no happy scenes in my picture. Thought about Pa stickin' that shotgun in his mouth, takin' the easy way out. Weren't no easy way for me. Hung on for seventeen minutes. They said sixteen, but that last was the killer, felt like a thousand. Before I know it, they got me stuffed in that giant Ziploc. And I'm gone from this life, for good, just like that, headed for that Hill.

In 1975, the subject was convicted and incarcerated for the voluntary manslaughter of his next-door neighbor, who was also the roommate of the subject's brother. The victim was beaten to death, allegedly without provocation, while the subject cruelly mocked him for being unmanly. The subject then cut off the victim's hair, before dousing him with lighter fluid and throwing matches on him. At the scene, the subject claimed he was acting in self-defense on behalf of the victim's wife, alleging that the victim had threatened her with a knife. The subject later retracted his statement, shifting the blame onto his brother, claiming he had only confessed to protect him – a maneuver that would be repeated, with a different brother, three years down the road. The subject was paroled in January of 1978.

Five months and 26 days later,
he would kill again.

But I wasn't dead. Not inside.

ECCE HOMO
David Gionfriddo

Monday was always a slow day at the Carlyle Collection. The staff arrived in a lazy trickle; coffee and pleasantries, two necessities for the white-collar gentry, kept much of anything from happening before noon. But June 4, 2007 was a different kind of Monday. The offices and cubicles of the administrative wing were filled before 10:00 with nervous conversation and restless energy. And when the Director strode eagerly past the sea-green Gerhard Richter abstract that scandalized the Kossoff Room's west wall, and convened the weekly all-hands meeting at 11:30 sharp, everyone anxiously anticipated the "major bombshell" they had been told would be forthcoming.

G. Dane Lassiter was the very picture of urban curatorial splendor. His gray hair was immaculately trimmed and pomaded, his collar starched, his Louis of Boston suit flawlessly draped across his body, taut and lean from a regimen of vihta massage, racquetball and triathalons. Lassiter's wristwatch, a Vacheron Constantin Traditionelle tourbillon with an ostrich-skin strap, so the joke went, could ransom a stolen Stella or Pissarro. And the black calfskin loafers, hand-stitched by a reclusive Spanish octogenarian of international reputation, simply defied casual comment. For the interns and junior staff, he was the ultimate aspirational figure. He made the typical Fortune 500 executive look as striving and common as a cold-calling timeshare yokel.

"Ladies and gentlemen, I promised you big news, and big news you shall have." With subtle aplomb, Lassiter gestured to his assistant Sarita, and, leaning gracefully across the ebony Empire conference table (revealing a tantalizing slice of cleavage), she handed those assembled a series of exhibition announcements, beautifully rendered in full-color on glossy cardstock. Carson James, a curatorial assistant in Prints and Drawings, carefully fingered his copy, picking out the raised words rendered in majestic script – Charlesworth, he guessed:

THE CARLYLE COLLECTION AND CARTIER PRESENT:

FEDERICO SANGIOVESE

THREE WORKS

July 16-September 9, 2007

Carson could hardly believe his eyes. They all knew, of course, that no Sangiovese had ever left Italy, and the upcoming touring exhibition had been the talk of the art world for more than a year. Friends of his at the Steele in Miami told him calls had been coming in months in advance from congressmen, businessmen, pop singers and porn stars, all looking for private tours of the big must-see.

The show was supposed to open at the Babbage in Cambridge, move to the Steele in autumn, and close with a Christmas gala at UC Berkeley. It had been quite a scandal that the exhibition was to bypass New York, but everyone chalked it up to lingering bitterness among the Italians over the City's store of dubiously-sourced Roman antiquities. Clearly, no one had expected this.

"Quiet down, quiet down...The Babbage has regrettably suffered some recent storm damage to its physical plant that will render it unable to host. And the Steele can not be ready until, at earliest, mid-August. And so, with some help from our friends at Cartier, we have offered to step in." Lassiter could see that the gallery of faces – excepting Sarita, whose wonderful eggshell features betrayed only boredom and impatience – wore looks of high nervous excitement. This was an opportunity for the ages, but would require the sort of full-court pressure more suited to accountants at tax time than art historians who measured time in centuries, not hours. For the first time Carson could recall, he had no idea how things would turn out. Failure was not simply an option; it was the *default* option.

Carson and Etta Macalester from Textiles traded nonplussed glances, and his Montblanc hastily scribbled a note on the back of his flyer, a note he subtly slid toward Eddy Krulik, shifting nervously in his powerchair. *Yikes*, it read. *I didn't go to Choate to work this hard.* Eddy smiled, tapping nervous breakbeats with a #2 pencil.

"Now, we're all going to get a little refresher on Sangiovese," Lassiter said.

"Even the Euro staff?" asked Bart Paternoster. *Pompous prick*, Carson thought. Bart, a fiftysomething Iowan scarecrow perpetually leaking straw, was the kind of guy who always spelled "color" with a "u" and complained about the "chockablock" traffic. For some reason, Lassiter and Rand Cleaves, Bart's immediate boss in Euro, loved the guy, and kept him supplied with a steady stream of pretty, attentive Columbia and NYU interns to be crushed by his pregnant silences and to clean up his sloppy paperwork. *Lest he break a nail*, Carson groused silently.

"*Especially* the European staff," Lassiter crowed. "We will, after all, be relying on you to make this work."

He went on with a not uninteresting sketch of Sangiovese's life and work -- something, Carson mused, that the average person would find worthwhile, but whose merits were lost on this overeducated mob. The Director gave detailed briefings on the works that would be exhibited. Earliest was Sangiovese's first major commission, an "eye-popping, if cluttered and emotionally facile," marble grouping of *The Flaying of Marsyas*, executed for a prosperous Sienese merchant with a love of classical themes and a taste for the macabre; next came his only portrait, a bronze relief of one of the Borgia cardinals, a likeness just diplomatic enough to prop open the Vatican treasure-house doors. Lastly, was the star of the show, a massive unfinished *Pieta*, immensely well-loved among the Italians and never before exhibited outside of the Boot, if you didn't count 18 months in a Swiss castle during World War II hiding from Hermann Goering and his minions.

"The *Pieta*, it goes without saying, has enormous significance. Anyone not familiar with its execution and history is urged – no, *ordered* – to bone up. The library has some good sources. I've asked Arlette to Xerox some of the better pieces." Carson knew there was some internal eye-rolling going on. Every first-year Art History dabbler could identify the *Pieta Cremisi* and spit back some of the lore. For a museum professional, being handed Cliff Notes on a work so well-known bordered on a professional pimp-slap. But he would play the game and pick up some material on the way out the door. It might make a good icebreaker if he ran into some of the artsier chicks from the Café Kino. He loved watching them twist and squeeze their way into those conversational openings, wringing all they could out of their memories of H.W. Janson, until they were thoroughly ensnared and exposed. It made for good sport.

"Yes. I'm a prick," Carson whispered, to no one in particular.

"Let's all think in terms of works in the collection that will complement, but not upstage, our guests." Lassiter was well satisfied. He and Sarita would never resort to overt courtship, but Carson could see that she, a conspiratorial smirk on her lips, had released some of the tension in her body, slipping down in her chair and letting the noonday sun spotlight her exquisitely Hamptons-tanned throat, guarded by an angry jade dragon on a silver chain. She seemed to be subtly suggesting a posture of conjugal surrender to the leader of the pride, the kingly cat who had sauntered off into the veldt and returned with the choicest kill.

The alphas, Carson thought with an inward grimace. *And everybody must see it. At least Kleimans must have noticed.* Denis Kleimans was his good lacrosse buddy from Williams: weekend brothel creeper, roller coaster historian, one-time amateur tenor and easily the single brightest researcher in European Sculpture. He did not reflect Carson's gallows humor, but wore an expression equal parts thrill and terror. He was, after all, the understudy who would be playing Macbeth, even if only for the Sunday matinee hags. Carson lifted an imaginary glass to his lips and Kleimans nodded in calm submission. They were both going to need it.

****

The Bindery, the nearest watering hole to the Carlyle as the crow flew, was one of those places whose folkways were hatched in Grand Junction, Colorado, memorialized in a three-ring binder brailled with frozen-drink rings. It was the kind of place where no man, regardless of the size of his tab or his eloquence, was better than any other, and patrons' goodwill was always wasted on a series of interchangeable service drones. The photos and paintings were halfhearted reproductions, sepia mosaic tiles reflecting some never-lived consensus past. Any ambience it had was owed not to history and happenstance, but to elaborate consultation and focus group research. But it was cheap, and stagger-distance from the subway, and that was usually good enough, Carson thought.

At the bar, a couple of well-worn, but not unattractive, professional women – lawyers, he guessed, from their rehearsed indifference – snuck guilty peeks over their shoulders at him as he skimmed the papers Arlette had prepared. He was only half-interested in the old clippings, but until one of these women came over, this sheaf of bourbon-stained copies would hold the secret of the Nine Gates, the location of the Philosopher's Stone. Carson squinted in concentration and silently let his lips move over the too-familiar passages from Baldessari's *Sangiovese and the Mannerist Impulse* (Stanford University Press, Palo Alto, 1968):

> The so-called "Crimson Pieta" of 1557 was the sculpture Sangiovese was working on at the time of his death. According to Vasari, one evening while he was hammering away at the giant block, his rival della Scala charged into Federico's cramped studio on the Via Condottiere "filled with rage and bile" over the loss of the commission for the

Bembo tomb. The two men struggled violently and Sangiovese fell back into his work "with a terrible and ghastly force," smashing his head and collapsing. He died from his wounds on the scene, leaving the telltale blood stain that named the work, but not before uttering curses against the dumbstruck della Scala, who, along with two of his sons, succumbed to cholera several months later. Since that date, the *Pieta*, a great imposing work whose rough-hewn state -- intimations of divine solace on the Virgin's barely-sketched *bas relief* face; thin, haggard arms pushing out from the stone to embrace a seemingly-weightless, snowy volume of marble that had only begun to be shaped into the body of Christ; a wildly-gesturing high relief of the Magdelene, somehow being pulled back into the earth by some strange gravity of grief – only heightened its elemental power. It was clear why sculptors like Rodin, who knew the evocative power of uncut stone to suggest mystical forces or supernatural worlds, repeatedly cited the *Pieta* as a towering influence. The Rodin Museum at Meudon contains hundreds of obsessive ink-and-wash studies of the piece.

Almost equally as telling a measure of its influence is its enduring hold on the Italian popular imagination. From the time of

Sangiovese's death until 1618, the *Pieta* was exhibited outside the studio, which became a makeshift museum of Sangiovese's work. In 1603, a Swiss tourist was killed by a loose piece of stone – since restored – that fell from above the face of the Virgin. Four years later, a pair of homeless children who had crawled onto the unfinished body of Christ during a nighttime Tiber flood, were found dead, their bodies showing no signs of struggle or forcible restraint. Shortly thereafter, the work was moved to the Capitoline Museums, where in 1903, a guard was accidentally crushed while attempting to move the statue to an upper floor. A peasant legend grew up around the 1607 incident, claiming that anyone who desecrated the work by climbing into the Virgin's arms would be victimized by the wrathful Sangiovese's curse. For the last 70 years, a special guard has always been assigned to prevent the disrespectful from testing this grisly legend. At any rate, this persistent public fascination with the *Crimson Pieta* is best seen as a measure of the emotive power the work retains nearly five centuries after the artist's untimely death.

Carson didn't know about the Meudon drawings. He would have to file away that bit of ephemera. In the reflection of an artificially-antiqued mirror, he noticed that his dowdy duo had shifted their attentions to the bartender and his effeminate friend, a gaudily-dressed mesomorph who feigned interest in a signed Dan Brown novel and made sounds like a flooded piston engine climbing a grade. *Just as well*, he thought. From the entryway, he thought he heard the faint whirring of gears, and turned to see Krulik rolling toward him, Kleimans a measured, respectful two paces behind.

"The ruling triumvirate," he crowed, brandishing his Maker's and ginger, "is back in session!" With exaggerated jauntiness, he rose and moved to a roomier oxblood banquette. "Your thrones await! Except for those of you who travel with your own."

Eddy winced as he pulled up to the table. "Your humor is only as good as the booze you're sucking down. Let me guess. Are they stocking something more vile than S.S. Pierce on the rail these days?"

"The family fortunes," Carson said, feigning an emotional wound, "could never fall so low."

Kleimans, always the too-grave sort who never participated in ritual jackassery, slid into his seat and wearily hefted a stack of papers onto the table. From its midst peeked out a photograph of the *Pieta*, before which stood a bespectacled couple in sixties *dolce vita* drag.

"We have to pull together a bulletin," Kleimans moaned. "It should have been to the printer a week ago already. Good times."

Carson picked up the photo. "This looks like it was taken before unification. Are you telling me that the country that gave us the *paparazzo* can't come up with a more recent snap?"

Kleimans and Krulik shared a sad, knowing glance. "That was the first thing we asked on the conference call," Kleimans said. "We needed a cover shot. Here's the freaky thing. The Romans said they couldn't get one."

"Couldn't get one? What do you mean?"

"Couldn't get one. They tried. Wouldn't photograph. It always came out blurry. Like in *The Ring*."

Carson moved his glass and leaned in, with meaning. "What is this? Some kind of Barnum crap to get more suckers through the turnstiles?"

Without a sound, Kleimans pushed forward five faxes, four photos of the hulking stone, festooned with streaks and swirls, the last a contact sheet with a series of twenty shots shrouded in what appeared to be dirty campfire smoke.

"Say what you will," Kleimans said, "*kitsch* beats crap. Every time."

****

It had just struck midnight, that time of night when a man's special qualities were liable to end up in a urinal drain and Carson, his workpapers pored over multiple times, was four drinks into a Sharpie doodle-from-memory of the *Marsyas* group, the unfortunate hero replaced by a heel-suspended Dane Lassiter, the satyr leading the execution wearing a long, goateed face based on Carson's own. Kleimans and Krulik had long since decamped, Eddy to a *bon voyage* party at a Chelsea gay bar, Denis to his sister's loft in Tribeca. As he stippled a dramatic shadow he couldn't help but admire, his reverie was pierced by the clinking of empty glasses.

"Almost time for last call, Picasso," spat a glass-eyed waitron, her corporate-issue shirt stained with *ersatz* remoulade, her frizzing hair misted with a long nights' perspiration. "One more?" For just a few seconds, he considered the merits of a quick lecture on Picasso and how his own neo-pontillist approach drew more heavily on Seurat and Signac, but then thought better of wasting his breath on a chick too worn down to merit the James *duende*.

"Why not? *'The road of excess,'* and all that good shit..."

She examined him with the same cheerless scorn with which a midwife might view an absentee parent. Carson felt a temporary urge to hang that contemptuous head on the 10th Century Frankish broadsword over the door of the Driessen Armor Hall, but suddenly, there, through the crook of his wench's arm, he caught sight of her, the One and Only, tapping blankly on her Trio, looking like she had just missed the last bus on earth.

"May I?" he cooed.

"May you what?" She had not even deigned to glance up from her texting.

"May I join?"

She smiled, as you might at an ant carrying a branch many times his length, and gestured toward an empty chair. "You know, if you had six or seven more degrees on your wall, you might be as smart as you try to act all the time."

Not the warmest welcome, but he had made contact. "That's no way to talk to a Williams man."

She returned to her messaging. "Am I not slurring my words enough?"

Ah, Sarita. Sarita Heloise Gottschalk. Executive Assistant to the Director. Employee #118. Fourth door on the left from the main lobby. Muse to few, siren to all. Like most office succubi, SHG almost never discussed herself with the staff, and those few morsels she let spill were nearly always fictitious. The Carlyle's premier Saritologists doubted that she had spent three months nursing William Burroughs in Lawrence, Kansas, had burned off all her hair accidentally on the closing night of Burning Man, or been Gus Van Sant's inspiration for a character in *Elephant*. Ditto the month allegedly spent touring the American Southeast as a midway carny. The Portland strip stint was credible, but Carson doubted Sarita was capable of creating even the sort of sham rapport that the job required. During one of her frequent vacations, Dugdale from Development had answered her phone, to find on the other end a frail-sounding woman's voice with a faint drawl asking for "Sara Louise." Carson considered it ironclad proof that their fair lady had unilaterally exoticized her name, without resort to the instrumentalities of the state. It made her seem somehow bone-sad and a little desperate, like an angrier Holly Golightly.

234

Audrey Hepburn with priors.

But, as Carson well knew, fortune favored the bold, and in the minutes before the house lights came up, he coaxed out a couple of smiles with jabs at Lassiter's peacock-pride and Kleimans' problems with the *Pieta*'s photos.

"He said it was like *The Ring*, but I forgot to ask him if he meant Wagner or Nat Fleischer."

She laughed a little under her breath. "I think he meant Naomi Watts. The horror flick, stupid."

"Not familiar with too many of those *genre* films. All I know is when they tried to take pictures of it, the film looked like it had gotten caught in the rain."

"Creepy," she intoned without emotion. "Maybe there's something to the old superstitions after all." At that, an idea, brilliant and simple and audacious, began to unfurl in Carson's mind, an idea that, for now, he would keep to himself. With mock gallantry, he swooped up Sarita's tab and motioned for the waitress.

"A fine gesture," she said.

"Hey, first of the year, my trust reverts, and I can grab *all manner* of checks. And the Carlyle is history." Weary Edison James had made a pile trading commodities futures at Lansky Brothers. Some of Carson's co-workers made jokes about the "pork-belly patricians," but his eight-figure safety net had kept him from having to give a fuck for as long as he could remember. Money talked, and the sniping bullshit of overleveraged museum gofers most definitely walked.

"So, that's your come-on? You going to make me one of the idle rich?"

"Idle? Don't you worry now! I can find some ways to keep you busy." Carson knew the A+ babes liked their guys to have just a touch of the asshole in them. It gave them something they could convincingly loathe when the need for distance arose. As he made his way to the register, he reflected on what had been a successful outing. His work would be there in the morning, but he had finally reached out. That was the main thing. He was several steps closer to taking down the only game that mattered.

****

With the eyes of the world upon them, the Carlyle staff felt the weeks fly by. There were interviews for the trades (who would want to monitor progress more carefully than the civilian *Parade* readers), conferences regarding exhibition space and the selection of companion works. Scholarly essays had to be written, fact-checked and copy-edited. Ticketing arrangements had to be made and priority access arranged, or gingerly withheld. It was decided that the Arthur and Mabel Kessler Gallery – a large airy space with a generous skylight, added in a 1962 expansion – would house the exhibition, and care had to be taken to document and pack the Kessler's collection of ancient Judaica, and to quietly move it to storage, as the original bequest of Ottway Carlyle,

Scottish Rites Freemason and anti-Semite, had prohibited the exhibition of Jewish art anywhere in the original family residence. Carson had been inexorably drawn into the Sangiovese maelstrom because Lassiter and Paternoster chose a series of rather crude and undistinguished 19th century engravings of Sangiovese's works to accompany the exhibition, "to flesh out the growth of the *Pieta* cult." *Little better than picture postcards,* Carson thought, but nobody had asked his opinion. And besides, it was just the kind of simple-minded historical accompaniment that the PBS- and NPR-tote bag crowd, essential to a profitable show, would devour. Carson had used this *entreé* to justify almost daily visits to Sarita's desk, his amorous aims cloaked in a variety of professional pretexts. This day, he had been seeking sign-off on the exact pieces the exhibit would require.

"Such hackwork," he said, leaning close enough to Sarita's beautifully freckled shoulder to detect a pronounced ridge of scapula and inhale the fragrance of sandalwood and spice. "Looks like it could have been finger-painted."

"But we must explore the cult!" Sarita chimed. So artful had he been, that now she even clandestinely jabbed at her benefactor for Carson's entertainment.

"And not even the *real* cult," Carson appended. Kleimans had dug up some genuinely interesting 1921 French newspaper articles about a splinter group from Aleister Crowley's Abbey of Thelema that had petitioned the Italian government to use the

Pieta in one of its rituals, but Paternoster had denied them wall space. Though Kleimans had forcefully argued the mass appeal of Buffy and Harry Potter, the stories had been deemed too upsetting for the younger patrons. Things would stay blissfully bland, at all costs.

Sarita sighed. "That hunk of rock sure brings the crazies out in force."

Carson blotted some stray vinaigrette from Sarita's desk with a dunning letter, stamped "Final Notice," from a commercial painting contractor. "We can only hope," he said.

****

The morning of the 12th was the busiest anyone could remember. Signs outside the museum announced its closure until Monday morning, when the grand spectacle would open to the public. The marble floors were covered in plywood, the walls with cardboard and dropcloths, as in-house carpenters and masons put finishing touches on pedestals and supports, and movers wheeled the precious crates into position at the sculptures' planned locations. Once the works were painstakingly maneuvered into place, track lighting could be adjusted, paint touched up, the Italian marble floors rebuffed to a high sheen. Carson had to confess he was impressed. The turbulent *Marsyas* grouping struck the viewer as he entered from the Annex's public foyer. Surrounding it on three sides were wonderful paintings showing the lingering importance of classical themes in late Renaissance Italy: a fresco of *Hercules and the Hydra* from a villa in Cremona, Del Sarto's *Judgment of Paris*, and a fine Rosso Fiorentino *Rape of Europa* rescued at the 11th hour from a Belgian conservator's *atelier*. It was quite stunning. Cardinal Borgia sat is a virtual rogue's gallery of painted clerics. But most impressive was the *Pieta*, basking in natural sunlight, rimmed by the best of the Carlyle's religious works: the Master of St. Helena's gilded *Maesta*, with its famous side panels of the *Stoning of St. Stephen* and the *Martyrdom of St. Lawrence*, Andolino's moody *Scourging of Christ*, Bronzino's magnificent tondo of the beheading of St. Cecilia.

"A symphony of suffering," Carson sighed to Eddy.

Eddy grimaced at the thought of the work to come. "Theirs or ours?" he asked.

The following days were full of the kind of "big-boy babysitting" that Carson hated most of all. A series of blonde news reporters from cable and local outlets, bereft of any background in art, were shuffled in with their lights and cameras, to run through the perfunctory "Around Town" segments riddled with basic errors. An Italian cultural attaché hosted some local merchants and museum donors at a *prosecco* reception. A special salon was readied for the use of the Cartier bigwigs, who had rechristened one of their tank watches "the Maestro," and were flying in the delicate wrist of Spanish film star

Marisol de Dios for a photo shoot and a carnival of promotional events. A steady caravan of VIPs, in groups of three or four, were led through the exhibit on "private" tours. No one was exempt; everyone had to pitch in for docent duty. "Is that really the original one?" a bumptious housewife whose husband had been famously killed by a runaway subway train asked Carson, pointing at the *Pieta* while the Honorable Simon Levine (D-17th Dist.) looked on approvingly. Carson decided to reserve his Rodin insights until a more appropriate opportunity presented itself.

The final Saturday group, attended by a half-dozen staff, consisted of Archbishop Heathcliff Deegan, a small, carbuncular man with a voice like a January wind through a drafty window, his aide Monsignor Ross Dichau, and a cluster of visiting Italian priests from a Bayside parish. Deegan, a noted *prima donna*, soaked up the staff's attention, making pointedly long, meaningful stops in front of the religious works and showily grimacing at the various painted atrocities. The three foreign visitors stood transfixed before the *Pieta*, chattering away like soccer fans in excited Italian. The smallest, a bald-headed man with a wino's relief-map nose straight out of a Ghirlandaio portrait, pulled a delicate glass bottle from a velvet sack in his satchel.

"Father Guglielmo would like to know if he may bless the work," Deegan wheezed to Lassiter, who seemed taken aback for a moment at the thought of this man flinging strange liquids at the masterwork in his keeping. "Now, now," Deegan cajoled, "it's only holy water. What harm?" Candace from Public Relations subtly nodded, and Lassiter passed along his effusive consent. The priest unscrewed the bottle top, recited a Latin blessing, and gently sprinkled the statue in the sign of the cross. For a second, nothing happened, but then, the spots the water touched – the Virgin's face and arm, the unfinished horizontal torso of Jesus – began to bubble like fat on the surface of a hot griddle, and, with a soft, insistent hiss, sent small feathers of smoke fluttering toward the ceiling. At first, no one knew how to react; none of them had ever seen such a thing. But after a tense instant, Lassiter gestured to Kleimans, relaxing at a card table with a glass of Evian, and, with a display of exaggerated nonchalance, ushered the priests toward his waiting office. As soon as they had gone, Kleimans ducked under the thick velvet rope, armed with an oilskin cloth, and inspected the marble.

"Nothing hurt," he told the pack of curious staff that had elbowed in for a look. "No sign that it was even touched."

Rosenzweig, a maintenance man enjoying his double-time duty, had the last word. "Fucking screwy," he moaned.

One by one, the crew filtered out to attend to odd last-minute jobs, until only Carson and a lithe shadow in the corner of the room remained. He spoke quietly, just above a whisper.

"The game is afoot," he said. In the shadows, Sarita, uninvited to the sherry toast in Lassiter's

241

inner sanctum, crossed her arms on her chest in an interrogatory posture.

"You're not really going to do this, you freak? Still time to back out."

Carson stole a glance back at the *Pieta*. "Nonsense. I fully intend to execute my part of the bargain. And I expect you to fulfill yours. A brave man dies but once..." He watched Sarita stifle a full-on giggle, wrapping and unwrapping her purse strap around her matchless, tapered fingers. Bad girl, or *faux*-bad, it made no difference. There was no quicker or surer way to mutate disdain into mischief than an invitation to gamble on a potentially-dangerous, life-damaging dare. If the adventurer succeeded, his quarry could brag about the price at which her favors had been bought. If he failed – even better – she could enjoy the spectacle of his humiliation and feign disbelief he had ever done anything sofoolish. After all, who would believe a man in Carson's position would test the Sangiovese curse? Or that the office Venus would offer mankind's oldest prize as his reward?

"Pretty soon, I won't need this job or any job. What a man in my position needs are stories. Tall tales, that can be told and retold. And they definitely will." He had grabbed her can of Sprite and took a swig in anticipatory celebration.

"Pig." She laughed quietly. "How are you going to even do this?"

Carson had for years listened to Gary the security guard's secret bile for the rich white bosses, and for the relatively modest price of $300 and some downloaded Internet porn, he had bought his complicity and silence. He could not think of a better way to exit this stage than to flout the sanctity of Lassiter's proudest moment and defile the boss' midlife trophy in the bargain. And getting off wouldn't be too hard to take either. It had been a long, dry spring.

"The less you know, my exquisite fawn, the better," he said. "Just be thinking about the hotel where you're going to pay off." He could practically taste the room service ceviche, the savory broth of carnal surrender. It made him a little hard just imagining it.

"Someplace," she smiled, wheeling away, "ridiculously expensive. And dark."

Flush with daydreams of his impending coup, watching the metronomic sway of his lady love's perfectly-modeled bottom, Carson barely noticed how a leftover television light cast the shadow of Giambologna's silver crucifix onto the gallery floor inches from the *Pieta*'s feet, or the telltale scratches on the marble floor, where it had only recently rested.

****

In his darkened office, Carson grabbed a pack of French cigarettes from his top desk drawer, and watched the reflected image of the director's office door in the glass of a framed Tanguy exhibition poster. Halfway through a Gitane, he caught sight of the tipsy priests emerging, followed by a glad-handing Lassiter. When their footsteps had long died away, Carson slung a leather bag of provisions over his shoulder and, humming a Bowie tune he had recently heard promoting a shaky discount brokerage (*"Nothing's gonna touch you/In these golden years..."*), he began to make his way back to the Annex, all the while checking for any lingering signs of life in the Carlyle's halls and rooms. All was still, the only sound Gary, ears wrapped in headphones, drumming his fingers on a marble bench as he browsed the pages of a recent *Maxim.* Carson waved a hand before his face to draw his attention from Megan Fox's elaborately-tattooed torso.

"Hey hey, there he is," Gary growled. "Don't be sneaking up on me like that, man. Scared the shit out of me." With his phones pulled down around his neck, Carson could hear he was listening to the Brothers Johnson singing "Strawberry Letter 23." Gary was one of those guys who was convinced he had missed something by not living in the 1970s. Ask him about the Hughes Brothers or Usher and he would give you a dumb stare, but he could retrace Fred Williamson's career like he had lived it himself. Like all men out of time, he would be perpetually snakebitten and dissatisfied. Though he strained to effect a sort of heartless lassitude, you could tell in the tautness of his neck, the point of his shoes, that he harbored a lingering tension. He was like an undercover narc, whose façade of blessed-out disinterest could explode in a moment into violent action.

"So, all quiet on the western front?" Carson asked. "It's just about that time, time for me to ascend the catbird seat."

"Man, half the time I don't know what the fuck you talking about. Why you wanna do this shit anyhow? Ain't you worried you're gonna get whiteboy assprints on this expensive piece of *high art*? G.D. finds out he'll fry both our asses." Gary always referred to Garland Dane Lassiter as "G.D.," as in "got-damn boy cut back my hours again!" Carson had to give him style points, if nothing else.

Carson took a quick inventory of his provisions. "He's not going to find out, 'cause you're not going to tell him. And as for me, I couldn't give a fuck if he does. I'm out of here in six months anyway." He threw a nervous glance at his watch. "Just Hennessy, 'hos and hotel suites after that. If everything goes smooth, maybe I'll throw in a bottle for you."

"Best make it VSOP, if you so flush," Gary countered. Carson smiled and walked away, reflecting that the fastest way to win the contempt of a man like Gary was a display of reckless generosity. He'd have to be more careful in the future. The Annex lay at the end of a long hallway floored in warm, blonde oak, through a small sea-green gallery that had held a loaned collection of Giacometti's bronze stickmen. In anticipation of the Big Event, it had been transformed into a makeshift gallery shop, two glass cases filled with every kind of *tchotchke*, cheap and intricate, enriching and crass. It amused him that the creators of the culture's most durable and resonant art were celebrated with the basest commercial crap. Van Gogh vodka. Monet perfume. Rembrandt toothpaste. Sangiovese had some catching up to do, but this show would really help put him on the branding map. In addition to three new monographs and reprints of some nice old scholarly works, the Carlyle was offering note paper, pens, paperweights in the shape of the *Pieta*, video tours of sites relevant to the artist's life and career (hosted by Rupert Everett!), commemorative coins, scarves, neckties and coffee mugs emblazoned with his craggy, hawk-eyed visage, and the boldest masterstroke, a Monopoly game using the streets and piazzas of 17th-century Rome in place of Atlantic City. As he admired the hand-tooled leather case, he made a mental note to pick one up to amuse Sarita during their post-coital languor. Carson reached behind the counter for a stepstool he had secreted there, and crossed the threshold into the exhibit galleries, pulling closed the door behind him. Nothing would disturb him now.

It didn't matter how many nights he had spent here after-hours, there was always something eerie about a dark, empty gallery. Carson felt his stomach tighten a bit as he brushed the red velvet curtain that surrounded *Marsyas*. Maybe it was the mostly-unfounded awe with which society addressed the Old Masters; deep in the unreachable circuits of his mind, there was the crackle of dread, as though the works were endowed with mysterious energies to which they could only give play in the absence of spectators. He imagined Fragonard *mademoiselles* soaring on upholstered swings, Breughel peasants gamboling over an imaginary countryside. The Pearl Gallery, home of the Carlyle's sole Bosch, was given a particularly wide berth afterhours. Christ only knew what went on in there. So it was with a lighthearted caution that he moved aside the velvet rope, placed his stool, and prepared to climb into Mother Mary's arms.

The unfinished body of Christ, his bed for the evening, was cool to the touch and unexpectedly smooth, only the beginnings of his form sketched out in the rough strokes of the claw chisel, an indentation that would be his emaciated belly, the faint grillwork of ribs, two breast-hillocks that framed a small gully of throat. He had been worried that Mary's arms might not hold his weight, since he was, after all, better fed than a Roman urchin, but he was comforted to find that his perch was solid and steady. He dug into his satchel and pulled out his digital camera, which he turned on himself while he smiled, holding up his Tag Heuer to show date and time (11:46 p.m., although he always set his timepieces five minutes fast). The flash was like lightning in the darkened chamber, and Carson maneuvered his butt around the marble platform, seeking a comfortable position in which to recline. It was going to be a long night. There might be some time for sleep, but he wanted to be awake at the appointed moment – 5:00 a.m. – so he could be safely away before Hudson – an older, more loyal, humorless and risk-averse employee -- came to relieve Gary on the day watch.

By 1:15, he had finished a bunch of seedless green grapes, listened his way through the first disc of *The Many Sides of Fred Neil*, and grazed the first pages of an Elaine Pagels work his book group had assigned. The bumps and ridges of his marble couch had begun to raise sores and he feared that he would run out of diversions before his vigil had concluded. What could he count to coax a few moments of sleep? Surely not sheep, not in this setting. He thought that lambs might be more appropriate, and, closing his eyes, he watched one, then another, of the darling little creatures hop a rail fence in a peaceful Constable pasture.

Carson was just giving in to sleep when he became aware of a gentle whine, not the bleat of lambs, but something more mechanical and familiar. As he pulled his lids apart, he could feel a blade of light forming in his vision, a sliver filling a widening crack in the gallery door he had only recently shut. In his palms and the soles of his feet he felt the beginnings of a dry chill. Carson knew that marble was always a few degrees cooler than the air that surrounded it, but this had the feel of a coward's shiver, like the one that accompanies a deadening fear.

"Gary, is that you?" he called.

A familiar voice echoed from down the hall.

"Checking to see you're OK," Gary said. "Don't want you falling out of bed."

"It's all good," Carson said, relieved. "But close that door. You scared the hell out of me."

Gary looked puzzled. "Hey, I didn't open shit. I was down making sure none of them suits of armor walked away."

Just like Gary to try and fuck with my head. Carson supposed it would be rattling chains next. Best to pop the earbuds back in and drown out his crazy-making thoughts. *Everybody's talkin' at me/I can't hear a word they're saying...* Out of nervous habit, he rechecked the glowing face of his watch, and was shocked to find it reset to 11:46. On the north wall, the Sonnenschein Clock, a 16th-century gilt bronze Baldewein from the home of a Marburg salt merchant, which Lassiter obsessively insisted on maintaining in working order, also seemed frozen at the same hour and minute. Pulling out a bud, Carson shook his wrist feebly and raised his watch to his ear.

In the hallway, Gary closed the door, and mumbled words under his breath.

"That's what he gets for buying that damn Swiss shit. Needs a nice American Timex." With quiet satisfaction, he checked the scratched face of his own watch, and saw it read 2:23. *Time for a smoke break,* he thought. *A long one.*

Carson breathed in and out and tried to relax. The dark and the setting and situation had no doubt tricked him into some kind of a waking dream, whose tone was set by those last pages of Pagels.

How could one imagine the Demiurge, hack deity, creator of the debased material world, sullen, sequestered in his lonely cloud throne, without believing that locks couldn't hold, that clockworks lost their precision? Yet even as he assayed the deepening of his breaths, he could feel the inexplicably frosty air that surrounded him, the barely noticeable plume of mist into which his breath had condensed.

Still, he was not afraid, even as these improbabilities closed around him. He sifted through thoughts of all the things he had ever disbelieved: God, the afterlife, spirits, natural justice and order, the essential goodness of Man. The enduring possibility of love: real love that conquered pleasure-seeking cruelty. In the twist of a fresh breath-wisp, he now saw that all of these could indeed be real, and that this thesis implied some deeply unfortunate things. The size of these thoughts pressed down on him, and forced him into a joyless drowse, the manufactured music in his ears dying, succumbing to a faint, crystal dappling of dulcimer notes and a keening *castrato* voice so pretty he could barely stand to hear it. Fatigue and a general uncooperativeness of muscles left him still and quiet on his perch, while the scene all around him seemed to swell with the frame-by-frame inevitability of the strange and imminent.

In this place of frozen time, suddenly lifetimes removed from the world of paperweights and whiskey and appointments beyond the gallery wall,

Carson was ready to see and accept. First, he was aware of a general misting, a zone of ambiguity, rising around the nearby paintings. Then, a sort of rustling and turbulence. His tongue too dry and leaden now to articulate a proper phoneme, he watched as that mist, itself like some kind of living breath, sculpted itself into pools of light and shade, giving shape, then depth, to what tired eyes might call the spectral figures of men.

The first stone hit high on his right shoulder, then seemed to evaporate as he waited for a final impact that never came. Its signature of pain was joined by a second, then a third, which Carson could now see came from the wan, hateful scowls crouched before the *St. Stephen* panel. He wanted to cry out, but his capacity for panicked action was suddenly flooded with lashings of nerve-fire from a shaft that pierced his thigh, sending a small geyser of blood rippling across the almost-translucent stone. Across the room, a window appeared to open into the depths of Luini's *St. Sebastian*, a nameless assassin admiring the flight of his arrow toward a second, stranger kill. *I believe, I believe*, Carson thought, draped on his sacrificial altar, even as the pale-violet shape of a Roman soldier lifted from *The Scourging of Christ* brought a *flagrum* down across his chest, tips of jagged calf's bone tearing away streamers of Briggs & Carmody shirt, along with corresponding bits of skin and meat. He felt the comfort of knowing there was little room for additional pain. Through the underwater vision of a teary eye, he saw glints in the shape of a sword and spear from Reggiano's *Massacre of Innocents* and thought he would never enjoy the warmth of Sarita's breath on his neck, and would be forever entombed in the footnotes to a legend he had always derided, perhaps the ultimate grisly drawing card for an unforgettable exhibition. The face of the Virgin looked into the distance, unmoved, unchanged, but now Carson thought her expression less placid than pitiless. These inert human limbs were no longer his. *How hard and cruel and lovely were the ghostly Judith's eyes*, he thought, staring up and into and through them, into a sky of laughably tangible stars. *The old man Jennetti, with his failing sight and palsied fingers, had scarcely done them justice...*

The Monday tabloids were as indelicate as one would imagine ("*MONSTER-PIECE*," the *Post* trumpeted), the blending of murder, misadventure and high society proving too intoxicating to resist. The museum had closed for 48 hours for the police to comb the crime scene, and when the Carlyle reopened, with the Italians' grudging assent, the crowds were legendary, the expected art lovers mingling with Goths, murder junkies, and the merely curious. The deluge of publicity made the place a required stop, alongside The Dakota and The Sparks Steak House, on the itineraries of visiting collegiate ghouls, and put the institution solidly in the black for the first time since the 1970s. Gary was fired, and although labeled a "person of interest" by the NYPD, was never charged with a crime. Sarita never again showed her face, her whereabouts unknown until a year later, when Candace received a postcard from a Midwestern girls' school, where she was teaching art and folk guitar. Carson James' office was taken over by a Marketing officer from Beatrice Foods, who turned a fleet of Americruisers into "mobile museums," bringing the Carlyle name, along with some B-grade reproductions, to schoolyards, shopping malls and state fairs across the mid-Atlantic. And as he had predicted, Carson was featured in news clippings handed out in Miami and Berkeley, and a footnote to an updated, 40th anniversary edition of Baldessari. Across the sea, the directorate of the Capitoline Museums had erected a plexiglass case – ostensibly for the marble's protection – from which Mary's affectless visage peered out at an ever-grander river of pilgrims seeking to touch, and be touched by, the *Pieta*'s inexhaustible power. And from time to time, a nervous guard would shoo away a wizened elder who pressed too close to see the almost invisible arrowhead scratches, and to wonder at the magic of Sangiovese's secret oath.

THE EMPTY PLACE
Gary J. Shipley

We are born dead, and moreover we have long ceased to be the sons of living fathers; and we become more and more contented with our condition. We are acquiring a taste for it. Soon we shall invent a method of being born from an idea.

> – Fyodor Dostoevsky, Notes From Underground

Long live the ghosts.

> – Jacques Derrida

1. THE TASTE OF TEETH

The Creature arrived a day late, missing his mother's funeral. They sunk her down into the freshly dug soil without him. There was snow on the ground and the mourner's black shoes marked semi-colons with their treads – symbols of continuity that slowly erased one another. He arrived the following morning in a dilapidated blue saloon churning smoke out its rear end, his head ensnared with regrets and excuses he was doing his utmost to shrug off. Gull was back and soon to make his dead mother's house his own.

Gull, as it seems I am to be known, switches off the engine and removes his keys from the ignition.

He finishes his cigarette, opens the door and lunges free of the car, my feet crunching into the crushed-bone snow.

An old man is sitting on a porch staring through the descending sky. He sits hunched over his swollen stomach like a vulture.

A spinal-cord town this one: a single road, nine houses, a shop, a graveyard soft in the middle just now, with a spiral of stone tongues mocking the sky. And there beside her rattled land a flaw in the honeycombed earth, space for one more skull in the dirt, a place for someone or some thing – an empty place.

A murder of crows dresses the fence with its flailed wings – the welcome of Gestapo leather coats – their black beaks hooked for death like scythe blades. The snow falls on their black bodies, doggedly braiding their feathers, as if desperately trying to erase them from view.

As I close the gate behind me and walk up to the front door I feel watchers pre-empting my every snow-bound step. I scan the street, the windows of the houses, but the only eyes I see are those of the pot-bellied old man next door, still held enraptured by the frozen haze. I put my key in the door and pause a moment before entering, as if to acknowledge those who would anticipate my movements, those for whom my stillness is a sign, a map of empty places waiting to be filled. I hear snow slump to the ground as I shut the door behind me. I light a cigarette and take a seat in the window, running my fingertips along the fractured paths of its cracked sill.

I'm born here now, in from the cold, out from a rotting mother, born as if only to reminisce on a past yet to be divulged. But I refuse to make myself old with the laboured footsteps of what might have been, or be force-fed time through the barrel of a gun. Turning my back on this scripted progeria, I'll live with the foreshortened promise of my breaths and nothing more.

I look out at the houses across the street, at the snow-bitten mesh of their chicken wire fences, their dark, curtain-less windows hovering in the air like spectral voids. I'm about to look away, to turn my attention to the room behind me, when I see a light come on in the house opposite. I strain to see beyond the glare, but the light goes out after a few seconds and, in the ten or so minutes I remain there watching, does not come on again.

The house is sparsely furnished and contains virtually nothing in the way of my mother's personal belongings. She'd been expecting to die for some time and had been whittling away at her possessions over the last months, slowly discarding anything she thought to be of no use. Unlike many old people approaching the end, the objects from her past pained her. She found no gratification in pouring over old photographs and home videos, in seeing her children frantically displacing water in their paddling pool, or riding high on her dead husband's shoulders. All her many trinkets eventually found their way into thick black sacks, which she buried at the bottom of the garden. She saw out her days free of clutter, rid of the depressing memorabilia of her fading existence.

Every wall in the house has been painted white. The carpets and what furnishings remain are similarly uniform: all an unimposing tope. The house does not appear to have been lived in: the kitchen is without stain or food, the beds crisp and flat, the bespoke shelves in the main living area unadorned but for dust. What am I to make of this disrobing in the face of death? It's as if she chose to shed the tiresome accoutrements of her life rather than leave them behind to ornament her absence, as if trying to undermine her eventual demise by removing its architecture, its scars. As I walk about the house, in and out of its six almost clinically vacant rooms, I notice that even its smell gives the impression as of something scoured, almost as if something vital has been sucked out of the air. I light a cigarette in the vain hope that its smoke might give substance to the space beyond my own vitrified presence, that its pale grey tentacles might infuse my surroundings with some semblance of tangibility, and with it some capacity for response.

2. THEY COME CALLING

I move through the house like an interloper, a thwarted and bewildered burglar who, in the absence of anything to steal, finds himself locked in a cycle of impotent meanderings. I try to settle myself, to decide upon a room and somehow make it my own. I have no luggage, so the mark I'm forced to make on this blank space must, at least for now, be confined to thought alone. The upstairs rooms make me uneasy: I can't stomach the tidy dreamlessness of the beds, nor can I bring myself to unmake their tight cotton skins; and the white box of cold ceramic sheen at the top of the stairs is no place for what it is I have to do.

By a process of elimination, I decide to colonise the large living area on the ground floor. I return to the chair by the window and stare over at the bare shelves, trying my best not to adorn them with imagined objects.

Clarity of purpose must be maintained. I must try and live unflinching in this infertile present. I must never return to the uncertain influence of what passes for humanity, to the company of those who claim to share space and time with me. They will come with ploys to spare, with well-meaning grins and vigorous handshakes, all in the hope that I might mistake the cold formula in their veins for blood. I look out at the darkening sky looming above the house across the street. I shift in my chair, reaffirming my mass as the first of them approach my gate.

They pick their way up my path hand in hand, the stooping vulture and his blind wife, her cane prodding the snow like a long bony finger, the rictus of their smiles belying the scheming intent burrowing through the makeshift substance behind their eyes. I sit and watch them as they scale the three frosted steps leading up to my porch. He guides her by the hand and she follows, digging her feet into the steps, mistrustful of their initial response. Once at the top, she lifts her cane in the air and taps it against the glass panel of my front door. I ignore the resulting noise as one would the sporadic ticking of an old clock out of step with time.

She is about to tap again when he places a hand on her wrist. He says something to her that I can't hear – asking her to wait where she is for a moment, or so he would have me think – and makes his way over to my window. He squints into the glass and sees me sitting on the other side looking straight back at him. He smiles, pretends to be taken aback, and points to the front door, where his wife is still standing, a wind-up windbag with loose coils. I look through him as if he is nothing but a fleeting form depicted, quite by chance, in shadows and snowflakes. His brow concertinas and flattens his eyes. He pushes this confusion of skin up to the glass and cautiously knocks on the pane with his fat knuckles, flashing another grin at me by way of cajolement. I drop my gaze to prevent my eyes from engaging with his, and plough my vision through his distended gut, through the wiry pink snake of his intestines and his compacted spine, and out the other side, over to the black windows of the house across the street.

I relax just in time to catch him shrug his

shoulders, turn and walk away. I watch as they carefully make their way back down the path and out onto the pavement, his head turning back at intervals, mouth springing open like a mantrap in a series of ghoulish yawns. I imagine the distain in her unblinking eyes, and immediately reproach myself for indulging in such needless invention. There's no point in playing into their hands at this early stage. If I'd wanted to partake in their façade I should have welcomed them in, subjected myself to their neighbourly goodwill and had done with it.

They'll be back, and others will come. For I've disturbed the sleep of this town, jarred it with the false weight of my footsteps. My arrival was an infective shot in the arm, the resulting scabs of which will, in time, draw scratching fingers from all quarters.

3. GARDENS FRONT AND BACK

The morning sun is lost in bottomless cloud, its last dying rays sinking into the open depths of my weary eyes. I didn't move from my chair all night. I spent those dark hours fortifying my scepticism, pushing my surroundings into the background, and opening myself up to a future free of the leash that strains behind me. I cannot be guided by my memories, and unless I learn to act in isolation from them I will never be able to befriend the beliefs and motivations that would have me as their source. I'm better placed to see the lies now than I was before. A fish cannot be caught once it has learnt, by heart, the drifting taste of steel. But what, someone somewhere asks, if the tang of the hook should purge all other flavours from its mouth? What then? ... I open the window a couple of inches and sink my fingertips into the night's cold deposit.

I have no aches and pains as a result of spending last night seated in this chair, leaving it only to brew myself more coffee. And despite having had no sleep I find myself not in the least bit tired. Nor do I hanker after food of any sort. So far coffee and smoke appear to be all the sustenance I need.

A young boy, aged about ten, is playing in the garden to the left of me. He wears bright red Wellington boots with chocolate brown cords tucked down inside of them. His blue parka is zipped up as far as it will go, so that his flushed face is barely visible within the tight confines of its fur-trimmed hood. I watch him intently as he digs at the snow with his gloved hands, throwing balls of it up into the pale grey sky and catching their withered remains. He is busy digging along the edge of the fence when I hear a woman call out: Not too deep, darling! We don't want you damaging mummy's plants.

He turns his head, periscope-like, in her direction, collects up his small pile of excavated snow, and stumbles off to the other side of the garden with it cradled to his chest. I don't know exactly why, but, as he disappears from view, I start thinking that he could be someone whom I could possibly trust. I

261

wonder whether or not I have always been a sucker for the mask of innocence; this and other forbidden reveries interrupt my quiet solitude, sending me off into the kitchen to prepare more coffee.

As the kettle boils I hear what sounds like a latch snapping back into its keep. I go and investigate, my nerve slipping at the very prospect of violent confrontation. I stalk the ground floor, peering into improbable hiding places, doors flat against walls and tiny cupboards, and find my courage lurking in their vacant spaces. Satisfied that I have nothing to worry about, that the noise had been just another one of those noises whose causes remain forever unknown, I return to the kitchen and pour out my drink.

I'm about to go back to my chair when I catch a glimpse of the back garden through the partially separated slats on the kitchen window. I look out. A wasteland of white swell lays bound on either side by the hollow diamonds of yet more chicken wire. The foot of the garden is unfenced, inclining steeply into a wall of snow-choked earth, the top of which is scarcely visible. Apart from the rusty remains of a child's swing in the garden to my right, there is virtually nothing to differentiate my garden from those of my neighbours': all lay dead beneath the suffocating, untrodden fabric of the sky.

4. THE CRIMSON-EYED DETECTIVE

Sitting at my chair in the window, I can just make

out what looks like a smudge on the horizon, a series of fat grimy chimneys throwing clouds of white ash up into the sky: a city in the distance, a black chunk of industrial fervour grinding away at itself behind high walls. I wonder what a place like that is doing stuck out here in the middle of nowhere, isolated, almost hidden by its own belching vapours. What is its purpose, and the purpose of those who inhabit it? What am I supposed to make of such an obvious lure?

I hear a floorboard creak above me and then, moments later, cushioned footsteps on the stairs. I stay seated, sucking in pearl-diver breaths. The walls deform and warp around me as I watch a pair of black brogues grow pinstriped legs, and those legs grow the rest of a tired suit, and the suit a head in its turn. His face, as grey and as creased as his shirt, turns towards me, his blood infested eyes lighting up like bulbs in a slaughterhouse.

Who the fuck are you? How did you get in? I say, trying to disguise the wobble in my voice by increasing its volume.

I have keys to every one of these houses: I let myself in. I'm investigating your mother's death.

What's to investigate? She was an old woman – she died.

All death is suspicious.

That doesn't explain what you're doing here.

Doesn't it?

You can't suspect me: she was already dead when I arrived.

How convenient.

Not if I'm her killer it isn't.

I'll be going now; I've seen what I came to see.

And what's that?

An empty house.

Except us.

Except you, perhaps.

Perhaps?

Maybe. In part.

His eyes lost somewhere in a crimson fog, he walks out the door, gently closing it behind him, and makes his way down the road, as sure-footed as anyone can be on that rutted surface.

His impudence had startled me. I wasn't prepared for any of them to make a move with quite that level of confidence. Those eyes had me hooked from the instant I saw them: I believed that some kind of life had made them what they were, that they couldn't have been that way – like looking into a pair of intestinal kaleidoscopes – without some genuine nocturnal horror having left its mark. His face looked as if it had been broken at some time and clumsily put back together, with little or no care put into obscuring the resulting joins. But then, on the other hand, he wore his suit as if every one of its seams were stitched into his skin, and as for the blind conviction of his stride and the tinny resonance of his voice, well, they were the attributes of an automaton, a cherry-eyed spook, a lie dressed up in life's blood and filth. Weren't they? I need more time to reassemble my instincts.

I go over to the front door and fasten the security chain. It was careless of me not to have done it sooner. I grab a chair from the kitchen and jam it in tight under the middle rail. I mock myself. I was a fool to think I could keep them out of here, that I could somehow segregate myself from the desperate exercises of sanity. There's always something to keep you handcuffed to the wheel. Even psychosis won't free you: it'll just break your teeth on the links. I wasn't in pursuit of lunacy. (Who would do such a thing?) No. All I wanted was a respite from the bland horror of fake smiles. I never had a solid plan, just a list of things I wanted to avoid. I guess I thought some alternative would come along to fill the empty space, an automatic substitute for the glossed-over fear I saw everywhere I looked: in the wide eyes of infants already narrowing at the edges, in the hard calloused hands of endlessly busy men, in the pinched faces of mothers suckling hope from their young, in the restless doom of alcoholics, compulsive eaters, drug addicts and artists, in every single person who measures time by any other means than the beat of their heart.

My hands hang alongside my thighs, unwilling accomplices trying to distance themselves from my pointless reveries. They make a grab for cigarettes, stuff one in place and light me up, reuniting me with their corrupt mechanics. I can't help thinking that paralysis would put me on the run from thought, that without the blessed inconvenience of my body, I'd bite fucking great chunks out of my mind and spit it as far from my limp frame as possible. My thoughts are such that were it not for my physical reaction to them they'd surely succeed in turning everything inside out, and the world around me, like those wretched progenies of modern science, would wear its shit and guts for all to see.

I spend the next few hours obsessively checking and rechecking the locks on both external doors, and every window, upstairs and down. I wander about the house submerged in the pleasant daydream of home security. I discover a metal toolbox and a carton of old screws in the cellar, and set about screwing down every window latch I can get my hand to, even going so far as to screw the sashes together on the ground floor. I can't help feeling the absurdity of my actions, but in spite of this sense of my own idiocy I keep it up and dread ever finishing.

5. THE BLANK ENVELOPE

Back in my chair, I watch as my car is slowly devoured. I close my eyes momentarily: a few seconds, a minute at most. When I open them again the old man from next-door is climbing the stairs to my porch with a white envelope in his hand. He wastes no time in posting it through my letterbox and making his way back home. When he is safely out of sight, I crush out my cigarette on the windowsill and go and fetch the thin white offering from the mat. I walk back to my chair, the letter sandwiched between my forefinger and thumb, as if

I suspect its contents to be contaminated with some fearsome contagion.

I don't open it immediately. I sit with it lying across my knees for a while, cursing the importance that I feel compelled to bestow upon it. Its flap has been stuck down, and there is nothing written on the envelope.

Returning to the letter, I read aloud:

"My husband and I called on you yesterday evening, but for some reason, known only to yourself, you didn't feel inclined to answer the door to us. We were, of course, disappointed, not to mention a little confused, but nevertheless respect your decision to act in whatever way you like at this troubling time. So as not to disturb you again, I have decided to write this letter.

Where to start?

It's been so long now that, were it not for my father's gravestone, we might well have forgotten quite why it was we ended up here. (This will probably sound quite absurd to you at this early stage, but you will almost certainly understand one day. Though part of me prays you never do.) Many have come and gone in that time, or so my husband informs me, for, as you no doubt noticed, I'm completely blind. Quite why we have remained here so long, while others have been permitted to leave, is something of a mystery to us. We can only suppose that there must be a reason for it, though we have no way of knowing what that reason might be. To say that we are held captive here would be to express our emotions at the expense of the truth. For we have not once attempted to leave, and so cannot know. But we feel trapped, and each passing day sticks to our bones like a thick glue, weighing us down, restricting our tomorrows to snow and half-forgotten dreams.

Before coming here we worked together as morgue attendants, or dieners. Not an edifying existence by any stretch of the imagination. I don't know why I stuck at it so long. I'd wanted for better things but, as often happens with long unfulfilled aspirations, they transformed themselves into the trappings of cynicism and self-mockery without my even noticing.

All my work colleagues were male. I didn't mind that one bit. I'd worked with women before and, without wishing to slight my gender, found the interplay more tiring than the work itself. I enjoyed the relative simplicity of working with men, even took some pleasure from the endless repertoire of foul jokes and the graphic depictions of their sexual encounters, many of which I suspected of being imaginary. We were a close-knit bunch and the fact that I was a woman, and an educated one at that – a fact that I thought insulting to disguise – never seemed to be an issue. There was some curiosity and a little goading at first, but that soon petered out. My work attire, at any rate – consisting of a scrub suit, rubber gloves, plastic gown, shoe covers, and face shields – served to play down any femininity that at best my less than buxom figure could have only hinted at.

Everyone asks about the smell. When they find out where you work it's the first thing they feel needs answering, as if the smell of the dead has been a source of consternation and intrigue their whole lives. I must say, it was always the sights that were most vivid for me: there were the gleaming grids of the refrigeration units and the bright lights illuminating every recess, almost obliterating your pupils – blurring your periphery vision so that it felt as if you were living in a dream state, or cutting up the dead somewhere in the bowels of heaven – and the striking hues of dead tissue, and the rigid poses of death, contorted limbs locked in the sculpted snapshots of their passing. But I told them what they wanted to hear. I told them as best I could of the smell, the blend of rancid lamb fat, sour milk, formaldehyde, old urine, fried food, and disinfectants. I told them and sometimes the list changed, but their reactions never did: they turned their noses up, as if they'd expected the aroma to be pleasant, and looked somewhat disapproving as if they could, now that I'd brought it to their attention, smell all these things on me.

You never forget the smell. It's something we all used to say to those who didn't already know. It stays with you; that is right enough. But it's not like, say, a visual memory. You can't recall it at will. Not its essence at any rate. You can recall all the things you once believed it to resemble, but not the smell itself. That exists outside of your control, and will return without prompt or warning. So it might be more accurate to say that the smell never forgets you.

The job could be rather dull. It was not all blood and guts by any means. A lot of time was spent either cleaning or performing clerical duties. Everywhere had to be spotless, not just the autopsy suites and storage units, but the break room, the night quarters, and the vending area as well. Meticulous records had to be kept, filed, and logged into the computer; the mail needed seeing to; supplies needed ordering; bodies needed lugging about, weighing and measuring. We were little more than lackeys for the most part. So much so that many of us actually came to enjoy the diversion that assisting at an autopsy provided.

Another thing that people always wanted to know was whether or not you ever get used to handling dead bodies. I used to say that you turn yourself into a carpenter and the cadavers into your wood, and that if you manage it, and some never do, then something strange happens. What? They would ask. And I'd pause, for effect I guess, for I knew what I was going to say. I'd said it before and envisaged saying it again. You guard against splinters, was the answer I gave. And sometimes I'd smile and even laugh, and sometimes I wouldn't.

One wet winter morning, the last full day I recall before arriving here, I admitted a Jane Doe. Two young police officers brought her in. They'd dragged her out of a ditch by the side of a road. A hitchhiker had happened upon her after climbing down out of sight of any passing cars to urinate. He was still in a bit of a state when they arrived at the scene, sitting by the side of the road like a man-sized tic, or so they said. They warned me that she was quite a sight. But I just shrugged my shoulders and began logging her in, unconvinced that death still had resource enough to carve a victim in any way that I'd consider novel.

A few minutes later I cut her free from the bag. Her right hand was clutching her stomach. Her left hand was clasping her temples as if in deep thought. Her jaws were still being yanked apart by muscles starved of ATP (I can still remember its formula ($C10H16N5O13P3$), for I had dreams of being more than just a diener) that took her scream beyond its music. A big yawn for the big sleep, joked one of the officers as he signed his name on the release form. His colleague snickered under his breath, more through duty than amusement as I remember. The instrument had outlived its player, as is often the case – a fact that anyone who has ever worked in a nursing home, as I have, will testify. But she was not old. No. No more than mid-twenties.

When I finally managed to wrench her hand away from her face and prepare her for autopsy, there, reflected in her bulging black eyes, was my reflection, my face haloed by the white ceiling and the crude glare of artificial light, my eyes in her eyes, looking back at me, into my eyes, from the darkness.

With the body block in place beneath her back, and her other arm out of the way, I opened her up with two deep scalpel incisions. After exposing her chest wall and folding one of the resulting flaps of skin up over her eyes, I chopped through the front of her ribcage with a bone cutter. What we found in there or failed to find, the pathologist and I, belied the former uncut purity of her skin. My husband called it a sick joke, and even now he still adheres to that opinion, considering it the most likely of all the possible explanations. I do not. I saw her. There wasn't a single laceration on her, sutured or otherwise. And it didn't end with her torso. For when I came to Stryker open the top of her skull, there was nothing inside. The brain was missing. Her cranium was completely empty.

The next day I woke up blind, a curse that served to fix the idea that the possibility of seeing and being seen is not all there is to being present."

The letter ends and I'm left filling in blanks on pages that aren't even there – another voice echoing in my ears. And then with a jolt I remember, my head nodding in acceptance of all that's missing.

RACHEL, KATE, AND CLAIRE
Tony Rauch

One night I hear a rumble. Though it's the middle of the night, I pay it no mind. I figure it's just somebody up and around to the bathroom or getting a drink. There is a storm which is making a distant hum of a racket, and I've been listening to that for a long while. The storm subsides and I roll over and everything goes quiet again. Later on I get up to fetch a sip of cider. And what do I find but the furniture in the living room completely re-arranged. Let me tell you, I am way too tired to deal with this kind of thing at this hour. So I get my drink and make my way back to bed. I figure my parents are just trying out a new layout or something. Those darn parents of mine, they're always up to something, let me tell you.

I get up in the morning and walk into the living room and there are my parents, standing there as surprised as I am. "Marcy, why did you rearrange the living room in the middle of the night?" They accuse, more astonished than upset.

"I didn't," I shrug.

"Now don't give us that, little lady. We heard you up and around last night," my mother places her hands on her hips and tilts her head down at me.

"I was up to get a drink, but went right back to bed," I nod to my room down the hall. "I just walked into the kitchen and then right back into my room. I was only up for, like, thirty seconds. Maybe less.

When I walked through here the living room was already like this. I didn't touch a thing. I figured you all rearranged the furniture."

"Marcy, why did you do all this in the middle of the night?" asks my dad, an admiration for my efforts shining through his displeasure and confusion.

"I didn't," I insist. But they don't believe me. And we end up spending the next hour changing the new furniture layout back to how everything was the day before. Even the pictures on the walls were all changed around. Even the rugs were repositioned.

Gradually, during the day, I end up forgetting about this odd incident, the strange feeling associated with it eventually dissolves until about a week later. Again a slight rumple startles me awake in the middle of the night. I roll over to listen carefully.

It is a rumble similar to the one the week before. This one seems to be rattling from a distant part of the house. Perhaps it is a ghost rearranging the furniture again. Maybe it's a real meanie of a ghost pulling a prank to try and aggravate my family to no end, and to try and get me into trouble in particular. Or maybe it's a helpful ghost, just trying to lend a hand in redecorating. Perhaps it's a ghost with extensive decorating experience. Maybe it's a strange house guest - a forest gnome or bridge troll living here among us unannounced. Or might it be my parents? Might they be playing another trick on me? Huh? Those clever pranksters.

I throw the covers aside and leap from my bed, hit the cold wood floor and burst from my room, sprinting down the hall as if the place were ablaze. I tool around the corner to reveal the culprit - the prankster of the noises and mysterious rearranging.

I huff to a slow stop, only to discover that no one is in the living room at all. I stop and listen carefully. I stand alone and concentrate. Sure enough, there is a slight rattle from upstairs in the attic. I turn and slowly make my way over to the stair. Slowly I open the door and climb, one quiet, deliberate footstep at a time. As I near the top, the noises grow ever so louder and more defined. I near the top and tilt my head in the darkness to listen. I try to gauge the sort of action taking place upstairs. It only sounds like a single person up there, only a wee little one moving stuff around. We keep old boxes and trunks up there with my mother's sewing equipment and other odd belongings of seldom use.

Although I'm afraid of the attic and its universe of darkness and musty smells, my curiosity gets the better of me. I decide to investigate further because I'm still upset, confused, and curious about last week's mysterious and celebrated redecorating event.

Slowly and ever so carefully I creep up the last of the steep old steps. There is a slight creek under my weight. It feels like it takes forever to get to the top, but once I'm there I peek through the keyhole of the door. My eye circles the room until it settles on a shadowy figure crouched beside an open trunk. A candle is lit on the floor, providing a small haze of golden light in the quiet darkness.

Gradually my eyes adjust to the dim, grainy light. The figure is digging through the trunk, pulling items out and holding them up for inspection. Eventually the figure leans in close enough to the light for me to see who it is. Why it's my mother!

Not realizing she may just want a tiny little moment alone to herself, I open the door slowly so as not to startle her, so as not to wake my father. "Hello mother. Whatever are you doing up so late?" I whisper.

My mother looks over to me, only her face crinkles into a confused expression. She opens her mouth, holding it open for a moment as I step through the darkness. Finally my mother says, "Who are you, little girl? Where did you come from?" Her voice has changed somehow. She has a strange accent, as if from another land, with a higher pitch and timbre, as if she has suddenly turned into a young adult.

"I'm your daughter, Marcy," I slowly utter.

"Oh, quit your funning, silly girl, for I have no daughter," she tilts her head and smiles. She shakes her head and looks down and resumes digging through the old trunk as if looking for something in particular.

"Are you a ghost?" I ask carefully, standing before her, watching the glow of candle throb on the sloped walls of the ceiling.

"I certainly am not. I'm a girl just like you and just

as real as you are. What would make you think such a thing, silly one?"

"What is your name?" I step forward, closer to the small glow in the cold darkness.

"My name is Rachel. What's your name, silly girl?"

"I'm Marcy. . . . Where did you come from? Are you a spirit?"

"Of course not. . . Could you help me please? I'm looking for an old photo album," she moves things around, lifts several small boxes and sets them aside. "I put it up here in one of these trunks," she lifts her head and looks around. She is down on her knees with old clothes from the trunk scattered around.

I bend to help. I ask her more about herself, wondering if my mother was dreaming, or sleepwalking, or if a spirit or ghost has inhabited her body. Maybe my mother has a split personality she's not even aware of. Maybe this is just another person living inside of her that only comes out in the middle of the night while I'm sleeping. Perhaps someone is accidentally seeping in from another part of the world and inhabiting my mother momentarily. Maybe, at the same time, my mother somehow inhabits that other person as well; maybe by accident. Maybe she doesn't even realize it.

As we get to talking, she tells me of her life. It seems she is not a ghost or another personality my mother may have hidden deep within herself. This Rachel girl seems as though she has seeped in from another time or another dimension somehow. It's as if we are each a similar, but different person in other dimensions or planes of existence. And that each dimension is very similar, but also slightly different from our own. For example, in Rachel's world, she is a young painter who goes over to people's houses and decorates people's stairs, trim, and rooms. She seems to be from another time entirely - like the 1890's or something. She earns extra money as a seamstress. She hopes to marry a boy named Brixton. He lives just down the cobblestone street from her family's tall townhouse, and isn't aware of her feelings for him.

And I recount my crippling crush on Nigel, a fine and well behaved boy from down the block.

After looking through several of our old trunks, she finally finds what she needs. It was in a trunk that had been left here when we moved in. I ask her about the furniture and she admits to changing it around to match the layout in her house. "Did you like it?" she asks.

"Well, yes. I guess so," I respond. I'm trying to be positive, yet still look over my mother, thinking now that she may be ill with a high fever or something. "I thought it was different and interesting. But my parents didn't care for it, so they moved things back to how things were arranged before."

"Oh," she looks down, "I was hoping you'd like it."

"Well, I did, but you know how parents can be. They get stuck in their ways and get used to things one way. But thanks for helping."

"Are your parents nice? Do you get along?"

"Yeah, mostly. I wish we'd get new drapes for our front windows because they're looking rather shabby and out of date. And I wouldn't want Nigel to think we were out of date or sloppy or unfashionable or anything."

"I should go now," she stands, holding the little photo album close to her chest. She turns and walks into the darkness and disappears through a back door that leads down to the back stair. And that is that. She's gone.

The next day, I don't mention any of this to my parents, only asking how my mother slept the night before. She wonders why I would ask such a question, then tells me that she did sleep well through the entire night without incident, and that she awoke feeling quite rested and ready for the day. Then she mentions that she is going to go shopping for some modern new drapes for the big picture window in order to spruce up the living room.

I forget about the whole attic thing, thinking maybe mom was just sleepwalking or dreaming or playing a gag or something. Until a week later. Again late at night, I hear someone in the kitchen. I get up and go in there to see who it is, thinking someone is up getting a glass of water and that I'd like some water too. Maybe I can sit down for a snack or something. And who do I find standing there but my mom again.

My mom looks down on me and says, "Hello,

Marcy. It's so good to see you again."

I stand in the doorway, "Rachel?" I ask, confused.

"Why yes, of course it's me. Have a seat, silly one. We can talk some more. I'm so excited to tell you all about Brixton. He finally asked me out and we went for a walk along the creek, all the way up to the old mill. Oh, I was so excited. On the way back he even held my hand. His hand was so warm and smooth . . ."

Rachel and I end up eating a snack together in the kitchen and chatting for over an hour. Even though this Rachel person has a different voice than my mother's, different facial expressions, mannerisms, and hand gestures, even a different laugh and way of tilting her head and smiling, I still feel very comfortable with her. I share with her some of my thoughts and feelings about things, and about events that are going on in my life.

After awhile she has to leave. She ups and walks into the darkness of the back room. She turns in the doorway and says goodbye. And I assure her that she is welcome here anytime, and that I hope she will come back soon. She turns into the darkness and is gone again, and I go back to bed.

About a month later I catch my mother up really late in the kitchen again. It is impossibly, hysterically dark out and here she is in the kitchen peeling carrots. Just standing there in the dim of candlelight, peeling away.

"Rachel?" I lean in from the doorway.

"Oh, hello again," she sings, and we end up staying up and talking again. I tell her about how my parents are so very very busy with work and taking care of the house that they aren't around much at all. I tell her about the fashions and trends of the day and about how my clothes do not quite measure up, a situation similar to our living room drapes. My clothes are getting frayed. My pants and skirts are just a tad too long, that girls my age are wearing them shorter now. I fear I am somehow falling behind, and that I may lose favor with the other kids if I fall too far back.

Rachel and I get to talking about other things too - about how yucky boys are, about how impossibly smelly and gross they can be. All that stuff. She tells me about one yucky boy who cornered her in the music room at school and tried to kiss her one time.

"Oh my," I gasp, my hands jumping to cover my mouth. "Whatever did you do?"

She explains how this boy is so tremendously yucky and mean to everyone, and especially mean to her. So she goes on to tell a series of simple, but effective submission moves created to momentarily disable a mean boy. She relates her experiences, and I find them to be useful and instructive. Many of her moves are secrets that I can not pass on, but they mainly involve stiff jabbing of hands to the eyes, throat, and groin; various kicks to the sides of the knee, scratching, biting, screaming, telling bigger boys and girls, and the like. I don't see Rachel again for a few weeks. The next time she's around we clean some radishes and talk about all the changes young women can go through when they get older. It's all very informative. I listen intently while helping peel, all the while wondering if and when Rachel will magically return back to her place in time. I expect my mother to come to at any moment and snap out of the trance she is in. But she never does. Not until Rachel leaves and I go back to bed and wake up the next morning.

A week later, another girl appears in the middle of the night inhabiting my mother's body. This new girl says her name is Kate. She appears in the form of my mother in the hallway. She is sitting on the floor rehemming a skirt. Again, I hear something and come out of my room and sit with her and we get to talking. She claims to be only several years older than myself, and tells me about all manner of bad influences out there that try to divert you and others from their true paths in life. And boy, she sure can think of a lot of them - liars and cheats and people who steal. They never change, she says, so be sure to stay away from them.

Basically, she works on my skirts, showing me how to hem them. We talk, then she says she has to get a drink of water. She gets up and walks to the dark kitchen and never comes back. And that's the end of Kate for a few weeks.

The next one I meet is Claire. It feels like she has seeped in from another place in time too. I catch her sewing up my jacket for some reason. I help her out, and this one shows me how to sew other things, you know, like how to make nice skirts and neat hand bags and such. Back where she's from she wants to be a writer, which is a nice thing to want to be. She tells me about how she is trying to do something positive. And talks to me of all sorts of different situations a person can find herself in. She also reports on how it's good to have a high set of standards in this world. But yet to cut people some slack sometimes as people can be imperfect, or can be going through all sorts of trying circumstances that you wouldn't even believe, and how these situations can affect someone's behaviour. To her, life just seems to be a matter of not making the same mistakes over and over. To her, life is about moving forward and progressing.

We stay up hemming and she shows me how to do some other things too. And then Claire is gone. So that makes three of them: Rachel, Kate, and Claire. And I find them here and there in the house late at night sometimes. They come back to do things around the house and tell me of their experiences with boys and self defense and life and everything. Rachel tells of secret rooms inside of secret rooms hidden all over town. Kate tells of all the ways in which boys are like goats, only with pants. Claire explains how important it is to remain positive and always move forward and keep things in perspective and count your blessings. She says that everything is an opportunity, that everything is a stepping stone, so don't get too down about things. Nobody likes a mope, she says, so always be in good cheer. And I believe her. And it gets to where I feel close to each of them. It's nice to have some older people to talk too, but yet not old enough as to not listen to me or not be able to understand what I'm thinking and feeling and going through.

After a few weeks of this, I get to looking forward to seeing them, my new friends seeping in from who-knows-where to inhabit my mother for a while, as if they were broadcasts on the radio waves in the air and my mother was the radio receiving their transmissions. It's nice they drop in to talk with me about things. And man, they sure know about a lot of things that I don't think I'd feel comfortable talking about with my actual mother. Maybe the fates feel sorry for me and have dispatched Rachel, Kate, and Clair to assist me through life. I don't rightly know. Either way, here they are.

I've thought about this a lot over the months now – about who these three girls are and how they get here. I don't know if my mother is faking being someone else to try and spend more time with me - just pretending to be someone closer to my age so I'll be more comfortable and open up and all, so she can get to know me better and show and teach me things; or if Rachel, Kate, and Claire are some kind of ghosts or people from other dimensions or something. But then I think about it some more and I wonder if it really matters. I get to talk with people who are slightly older than me, and I get to see their perspective on matters. Over the months I get to know Rachel to the point where we become very close. And to my surprise, Kate starts showing up more and more too. Kate and I also grow to become good pals. Eventually she teaches me more about boys and girls and mean, lying tricks people play on one another and how to spot them, and things like that. And then Claire will show up, and man does she really know a lot about boys. It's nice to have some friends to talk to. And it's sort of a relief that they don't live around here in that I don't have to share them with anyone else, worry about losing them to others, or have to be afraid that they might betray my trust or tell all my secrets to everyone else. Also, I don't have to worry about them moving away, like people tend to do in my life.

Yeah, I think about it a lot over the months, about what is really happening, what is really going on. And in the end I decide that it doesn't matter. I don't care one way or another. The way I figure it, explanations are for teachers and scientists. They only take the fun and wonder out of things. In thinking of it, I guess I'm just glad to have some more friends, some more people to talk to and share things with, that's all. And in the end, that's all that's really important.

Over the ensuing years, one of them would appear from time to time. Sometimes in the garden out back, sometimes in the garage, but mostly late at night. And it seemed each time they would show me how to do something – hem a pair of pants, cook something, plant something, fix something, shave my legs. Until gradually, over the years, they appeared less and less frequently. Maybe they felt they had shown me all they could, or maybe they needed to move on and aid someone else. I don't know why they stopped showing up. Maybe they couldn't get back here for some reason. Maybe it was just my mother acting the entire time, trying to teach me something, trying to get me to open up more, trying to get to know me better. Or maybe after awhile I just didn't need them any longer. Maybe I was the great radio who was tuning them into me. Maybe I was really the one bringing them to me all along. Maybe it was really me all along and not my mother at all.

Over the years I find myself stopping and thinking about them and I wonder why they stopped visiting. I wonder what each of them ended up doing with their lives – where they live, how things ended up for them, what they've learned in all their adventures, and if they're happy or not. You know, even to this day I miss them. Even when you get older, it's still nice to have someone you trust to talk too. And in thinking of it, I miss them as much now as I did back then.

CLOSE TO THE EYES
Hero MacKenzie

One evening in 1967, whilst travelling through the Guajira region of the Colombian peninsula as a young man, I experienced a most extraordinary event, one that at the time left me quite dumbfounded and which only now in retrospect, almost 45 years later, can I possibly explain, even to myself. The evening was the first of the year's rainy season – the 'Iwa', locals called it - in which sheets of cold rain descended ruthlessly from silver clouds, merged with the emerald rivers and flooded the arid plains so that sky could not be distinguished from land, creating the impression of two vast mirrors, as if an eternal passageway had been created. Guajira became a sparkling wonderland that evening – but so incredibly difficult was it to pass through that Harry, my close school friend and I resorted to clambering up viciously rocky mountain sides to avoid the fast and rising waters, when finally, and rather miraculously, since there had been no one around and our clothes as well as flesh had become torn in the process, we came across a small rancheria. Harry knocked nervously on the door.

I interrupt myself here to point out two things, first, we had only arrived in South America a few days before but already we had journeyed along the country's coast with the plan – as much as there is ever plan for two boys travelling around – to venture through the plains towards the National Park of

Macuira, and second, more important, that the region, Guajira, is known for its indigenous community, the Wayuu, a large Amerindian tribe which speaks an Arawak dialect called Wayuunaiki and who have existed in the region since the pre-Colombian times. Of course I know all these specificities now, I even speak some Wayuunaiki. Back then, however, I knew only what I had heard of these peoples in those few days since my arrival.

A young man opened the door. He scowled at us and uttered words that sounded more like bird song than any human phonetic. What was most peculiar about the boy, however, was that despite all the facial piercings and the beaded jewellery that fitted perfectly with our preconceptions of a tribal member, he, rather bizarrely, wore a long tie-dye dress of bright reds and yellows that was not so dissimilar to the ones I possessed and that sat in my drawers in Kent. A short, plump woman pushed the boy to one side, she greeted us in a strong harsh accent but nonetheless recognisably Spanish, and beckoned us inside, 'Entrad, entrad!' The piichi was a small damp space of semi circular shape. The walls were made with clay and straw and the roof thatched with, what I now realise must have been, yotojoro, the heart of cacti. Some ten Wayuu men sat by the fire talking quietly but stopped as we entered. Eventually one came over and exchanged words with the lady. He had long dark hair and wore black beads tight around his neck. The only attribute that might have distinguished him from the other men – despite his apparent authority – was a long thin scar right the way across his forehead. He smiled gratefully at the woman who gave a gentle bow before walking off. The Wayuu breathed in deeply, he placed his palm on his heart, 'Yambo', he said, 'me llamo Yambo'. Despite our nerves we managed to introduce and deliver our thanks without shame. 'Te duele?' He pointed at Harry's torn shoulder that continued to bleed profusely. 'Pasad...pasad!' Yambo led us to a dimly lit room. In one corner there was a hammock. He walked quietly over and firmly shook the bundle. A person, a young girl appeared. She sat up as Yambo whispered something sternly to her. He signalled for us to come further into the room. 'Esmeralda', he said pointing at the child, 'mi hija'. The girl, who was petite with long jet hair, slid down carefully onto the floor and crossed her legs. She spoke softly to her father who nodded repeatedly in abeyance at his daughter's words. Clasping Harry's arm, he pointed at the open wound on his shoulder.

The girl drew him down onto the floor next her. Beside them I made out an array of small wooden pots. She took one and opened it. Harry looked up at me hesitantly but said nothing. The girl dabbed at the cut with the white substance and then with her fingers she began to prod gently around the edges. 'Gosh', Harry responded almost immediately, touching at his wound in amazement. 'What?' I asked. 'The pain', he said, still looking curiously at his shoulder. 'What about it?' I said edging towards him to get a better look. 'Well....it's...' he looked at me and I could make out his expression of disbelief, 'it's gone...completely, I mean...and the bleeding...it's stopped.' Harry looked at the girl in astonishment. He gave a small bow with head at which point Yambo gave a light laugh. Smiling with pride at his daughter's work, he signalled for me to sit down too. 'She's a healer', Harry said, rising, 'Go on, Pete, let her see to your wound too, she has a magic touch...Never...', he beamed in awe, 'Never have I seen anything like this...' Yambo took my hands bound in the now blood soaked handkerchiefs and presented them to his daughter.

I crouched down on the cold mud floor. An ambiguous look of fear and wonder conquered her dark eyes that caused me to I looked away. She began to unravel one my hands, her cold fingers trembling. I sensed her gaze, a gaze filled with awe. My wound began to sting but still I kept focusing on the clay walls, their swirling patterns in red ink. I listened to the soft tinkling of bells hanging from the doorway decorations. I could feel my hand fully exposed to the air now and I could sense her scrutiny. A liquid touched my burning palm. It had an agonising sensation and I thought for a moment it might be some sort of ointment, but then as I turned to look, I realised the moisture was not any balm or medicine, but quite the opposite.

Tears, fierce tears, were rolling down from Esmeralda's cheeks and falling into my palm trickling along the deep lines and into my wound. Entranced, the child began to rock slowly back and forth, her eyes were bulging wide, and her small mouth muttering. I withdrew my hand quickly. I could hear her father's cries behind us but I remained motionless, my whole body petrified with fear as our eyes locked in mutual horror. I could feel Harry trying to hoist me up but my limbs were too limp. Esmeralda's words became louder but I could not understand them nor could I really hear them, for there were screams all around us. The girl's body was convulsing and her mouth foaming. Her glazed eyes looked up as if to the heavens. She began coughing and choking and people...people were throwing themselves at her, patting and stroking her, and wiping her brow. Her yell, a final yell of astonishment that I couldn't understand was the last thing I recall for, at that point, I fainted.

The following days became fused and confused. Both Harry and I became physically sick, too unwell to go anywhere and too fatigued even to talk to one another. Although the Wayuus looked after for these few days during the worst of the Iwa, there was no sign nor even any mention of Esmeralda and what had happened. Harry and I decided to cut short our trip and left to go back to England some days later. Neither of us have ever referred to the events of that evening. In retrospect though, I realise the moment with this intriguing, enigmatic creature prompted in me two seemingly paradoxical sensations; an irrepressible curiosity combined with an inexplicable fear. As if fate were sealed by this very experience I realised two things about myself; one that I wanted to learn all I could about this child, and two that I would never return to the continent again in my lifetime. I have achieved the former and more so, I believe. I am Peter Lockeman, the Emeritus Professor of Amerindian tribes in the Department of Anthropology at the University of Exeter. I have reached such status – rather incredibly perhaps – without disclosing the latter. Until now. Until now when I am forced to confront that experience with Esmeralda and her terrifying prophecy.

Eight weeks ago a vast and formidable haul of gold artefacts was found buried in El Rincón, Guajira. With as many as 1,500 gold and silver items, it is said to be one of the largest hauls of pre-Colombian treasures ever to be found. In my specialist opinion, the Wayuus knew all along what was there but due to the region's history and the new 'Indian reserves' – partly funded by the Colombian government – some scholars (indeed colleagues of mine) were permitted entrance to research the area and tribal community. According to the news, it was one such scholar who, with only a metal detector to hand, realised there must be such treasures buried beneath ground. A large team of experts of archaeologists and geologists was organised immediately. Due to the nature of these expeditions, anthropologists are expected to attend in order to communicate with the community at hand – for moral and ethical purposes. Since I am one of the few people in the world who has studied the Wayuu culture and language – and in such detail – I was approached by Madrid's Museo de América to 'mediate' – to use their word – between the Wayuus and archaeologists. I refused. Instead I sent my assistant, Dr. Juan González Iglesias, a bright young enthusiast from Granada, Spain, a junior specialist of the Wayuu culture, on my behalf. Six weeks ago the team – all twenty two members including Dr. González Iglesias – went missing. I knew even before they did that they were in trouble because by then the voices had begun...by then she had come to me...

The first day of the Guajira expedition, I sat in my study – a large room with oak panelled walls that overlook the lush and misty fields that surround our Devonshire home – researching a paper on Cunhadismo of the Brazilian Tupi people when I heard a loud knock at the study door. I remember thinking it odd since Hazel, my wife, had already left for work but I nonetheless shouted at whoever it was to come in. When after several attempts there was no response I rose from my chair, rather irritated I do admit, and walked the way across the room to open the door. Now I am not one to exaggerate and the circumstances I am about to relate are ludicrous, I do realise this, but I put my hand on my heart that what I say is true, Father.

-I understand. What of these circumstances?

-No one was there, Father. No one was at the door. But I felt a cold rush of air pass me by as if someone had walked into the room. I closed the door shut believing it to be a draft and walked back to my desk. I sat down. There was silence and I was ready to believe that I had imagined the whole thing, the knocking and the cold sensations, when I looked down on my work to find a piece of paper upon which the word Patsuarui had been scrawled in large black ink.

-Which means?

-I had no idea at the time. Not even any idea of which linguistic family it might be from. I went through several of my dictionaries before I came to learn that the word Patsuarui is from the Wayuunaiki language. It means frightened. I sat still for a moment staring at the word on the page and the word in the dictionary. I closed it shut and as I did so I looked up at the room. On my wall hangs a map, a seventeenth century map, not a real one of course, but a colonial map, one that shows the empires of the past, and I could see, even from where I was standing that the map – it was bleeding. I walked over to it, not believing my eyes. But there it was. There were trickles of blood running down the wall, like deep red tears, and the source, the source of blood on the map, it came from Guajira. At that point I would have picked up the phoned to anyone, my wife, anyone to witness the moment but I noticed that blood was dripping from my fisted hands. I opened my palms and the scars, the wounds had reopened, and all the lines cut, exposed, stinging in agony, just as they were all those years ago in Guajira. I fell to the floor and I cried. Perhaps I stayed there for a few minutes before I decided to recompose myself. I washed my hands, bandaged them up, took two sleeping pills and went to bed in the hope that I would reawaken to Hazel's soothing voice and that I could forget all that had happened that day.

I did awake to a voice – but not to Hazel's nor to any soothing one. A low whimper, a child's whimper is what I heard. I sat up. It stopped. The bedroom glowed an evening blue, casting various shadows, but there was no one there, and I thought it must be part of the nightmare I was having. The clock read half past five. Hazel would not be back for another hour. I climbed out and walked over to the lights. They would not turn on. I pulled at the door. It would not open. I kept trying. It was locked. My heart began to race but I had to keep my mind straight. I knew that I had taken these pills and I thought perhaps in fear I might have locked the door and misremembered. I turned to our mantel piece and took down an old candelabrum which I lit. The room flickered with the light. There was someone there; a person's body in the corner. Although I could not see a face I could make out that it was a young girl's body, and that her legs were drawn up close to her, and she was murmuring something, as though in pain. I ran to the door and began to frantically rattle at the handle, banging and yelling, in the chance that I might be heard, by whom I have no idea, but I was desperate, you see. The child's words became louder and louder, Tuikii. Tuikii. Tuikii. Wane. Akarachi. Aippirua. Mekietsat. I looked behind me. The creature was approaching me now. I continued banging at the door. Matuwolu'u. Matuwolu'u. She hissed. Still she was faceless but I could feel her. Close to the eyes. Matuwolu'u. I began to sob but still her I heard the soft whimpering, Poloo. Poloo. Piama. The candles went as if suddenly blown out. The room was dark and still. There was silence. 'Please', I whispered, 'please, tell me, tell me what I can do.' At that point I heard the bedroom door unlock by itself. I walked over and threw it open. The landing lights flooded the space around me. There was no one there but I felt the same cold air brush past me as earlier and I could hear footsteps, all along the landing. A door across the way, the door to my library, opened. I stood there puzzled and as I did so there came loud crashing noise. I ran over to the room. My books, all my books, they were falling - no, they being thrown, thrown off the shelves and onto the floor. They showered down so much so that I could not enter the room. Instead, I stood there in the doorway watching, powerless, as the cascade continued. Finally, it came to an end.

-And all your books had been thrown to the floor, you say?

-All but one.

-Did you see what the remaining book was called?

-Yes. I realised too that she was giving me signs of sorts. I gently climbed across the pile to the book on the shelf. It was thick and leather bound with a gold embossed title, Los Mitos y Leyendas de los Wayuus Vol. I. I thought about the words she had spoken to me before. Wane akarchi aippirua mekiestat. It's a date, a year, the year 1769. I jumped straight forward to the chapter of that year. It told of the enslavement, torture and mass execution of the natives, the Wayuus by the Spaniards under Jose Antonio de Sierra's command in El Rincón, Guajira. But what drew my attention was a story – The tale of May 2nd, 1769 – when on one occasion, as Sierra and his men took captive twenty two natives, enchained them, and forced them into labour work in Cartagena, there was a most unexpected reaction. With a strong and fearless leader named, Polujalii, the Wayuus rebelled, setting fire to their village and killing the Spanish soldiers. News of the successful fight against Spanish oppression travelled and other Wayuus in the region joined forces. According to Messiah at the peak there were 20, 000 Wayuus waging war...They've maintained this land, still to this day. Present there are some 150, 000 Wayuus, 48% of Guajira...

  -But what has-

  -The myth goes that Polujalii was caught by Sierra's men. They nailed his hands to the wall – like a crucifixion – and starved him to death – but Polujalii warned he would return.

  -I see...

  -The Wayuus believe that his body died that night, but his spirit stayed alive. Don't you see! --The evening I was in Guajira it was May 2nd! And my palms, my torn palms, were the sign. She saw! Esmeralda knew! I didn't understand it at the time, but she saw!

-What, Peter, what did she see?

-She saw that I had returned, Father. That Polujalii had returned. It is not me who should be afraid but you, you all here. I have nothing to fear for I am I am the phantom of the past. My whole life, my very being, has been constructed to bridge the past with the future, to bring their message, our message...That it has begun...

-What has begun?

-The rebellion, Father. The destruction of the West, the destruction of imperialism has begun. Instead, there is a new order – the new power of indigenism – The Wayuu power.

Sekuolu'u! Sekuolu'u! Sekuolu'u!

MEMORY'S NEST
Paul A. Toth

Charley opened the door to his dead wife Julia's house. Exhausted from the 400 miles of driving that day, he sat on the couch, a small one with just enough room for a big man like himself. The shades were drawn, but there were no neighbors, only a town 20 miles away that as yet had no idea the house had suddenly been possessed by Julia's widower. To them it remained unoccupied, just as it had in all the years since her father died. They thought about the house only occasionally, perhaps when driving by on the way to the interstate, when they might say, "I wonder if she's ever coming home?" until the last few months, when they said, "Looks like she's never coming home now... thank God."

Then he saw what he called Julia's ghost in the darkness at the edges of his vision. He preferred thinking this way. To feel differently about a thing, he called it by a different name, so that a ghost was preferable to his memory of Julia--the ghost, unlike his wife, was quite friendly, taking pleasure in the way he felt better now, encouraging him to relax and enjoy the remaining years. In fact, earlier that day the ghost had actually thanked him for the time he had spent with her. "I regret my black moods," the ghost said, "which you endured and eased for me." She would never have said such a thing in real life. Nor would she have ever placed ice cubes in his drink or returned some portion of the bed covers (which she routinely gathered about her head, trying to forget his presence).

"Yes, well," he said to himself, and then he located the barely used briefcase he had purchased so many years ago, took it around the back of the house, found a large rock and began hammering the leather. He continued for 15 minutes. By that time it could be called a battered old briefcase. "You are my companion of many years," he lied to it, "and you have stayed with me since my first days in practice. You've faithfully carried my prescription pads and my coffee-stained notes and about 1,203,002 pencils and for that I thank you by never, never parting with you, no matter how soiled your appearance, despite your holes and creases and the embarrassment you have often caused me in the presence of others."

He went inside to the bathroom. There was no electricity, so he leaned close to the mirror. He studied his hair, pulling the bangs back against the top of his head, stroking his newly regrown beard. He saw that his glasses were much too straight. He removed them, bent the frame a little to the right, then pushed the nose rests apart so that when he put the glasses back on, they slid down his nose. His old face emerged. He remembered who he had been before he met Julia: A doctor.

"I'm afraid," he said, looking at his reflection, pretending to talk to a patient, "this is not the news we had hoped for. He shook his head, pretending to hold an X-ray toward the outside light. "It could be worse, however," he added. "We have to learn to balance things, to see them in perspective. We can't think only of the good or only the bad."

He returned to the living room, picked up the phone and ordered the electricity, gas and telephone service restored. Then he gathered his briefcase and left for town, hoping to find a patient or two.

It was a pleasant enough drive, but as Charley approached town he noticed nothing remained of his memories. Perhaps it was the drained colors in the scrapbook photos, but now the town seemed brighter, with chain stores and restaurants having replaced the small-town businesses his wife hated. "That ridiculous place?" she'd reply whenever he mentioned taking a trip back to visit her father. "You have to be retarded to live there. If my father wants to see me, he can take a plane ride here. It won't kill him."

The town now reminded him of certain parts of Los Angeles, as though two blocks had been cut out of that sunny city and dropped into the middle of Virginia. It disconcerted Charley to see the exact same chain restaurants and drugstores in such a pastoral setting. He had, after all, decided to return because it was almost as far as one could get from Los Angeles (the reverse motive of his wife's having them move to L.A.).

"This is a gigantic city, Los Angeles," Julia used to tell him. "We have the money, we have the ability to travel any where we want and eat anything we want, and yet here you stay in the same little corner, this same box, as though you're on 24 hour guard duty."

"You've got your friends," he'd tell her, knowing she preferred to socialize without him.

"It's true, I do have friends. And why? I'm a gregarious woman. I can't live like a redneck's wife, going to your patients' funeral receptions, sitting at card tables in some church cafeteria, picking over friend chicken. It makes me sick just thinking about it."

"That's how you see it."

"How I see it? Charley, do you know what a doctor is? A glorified janitor. I won't live with a janitor. A doctor is worse than a freeloader like you."

"But I'm not the man you want. Why don't you accept it and let me go back to being a doctor?"

"First of all, that's ridiculous. How are you going to start practicing 30 years later? How will you treat your patients, with castor oil? Why can't enjoy what I've made of you, rather than thinking you have to achieve something?"

"The terrible things I used to say," the ghost butted in. "I realize now how I must have hurt you, and what incredible patience you had not to strangle me."

"That's all right," Charley said. "There's no need to apologize. If you knew what I was thinking whenever I held a fork or passed a knife."

"Bullshit," Julia said.

Arriving in town, he scanned the strip malls for a local hangout, but even the bars were recognizable from other places. There was not one place called

Ray's or Lucky's where he might have sat down, eased his way into a conversation and said, "You may remember my name: Dr. Charles Galuszka. I'm back in practice, so if you ever need a check-up..." But he also knew that even if such a place existed, it would never happen; he never started conversations with strangers, and because he radiated discomfort, only rarely and by necessity did strangers begin conversations with him. So he kept driving.

"Well, Dr. Galuszka," he imagined (then forgot he was imagining) a stranger beside him to say. "You don't remember me, but I remember you. I had an appointment with you long ago, but you and your wife moved first. How long did you practice, three months? You must have really fallen for her. Me? I never moved. I never travelled. What's the point? Things trail after you, residue and scrapbooks, dust mites. My name's Harold Wicker. I'm a plumber, retired. With a profession like that, I never had a chance. Don't call me Harold, call me Harry, Charley. Unless you prefer Charles. I bet she called you Charles.

"Yes, I knew Julia. It's easy to know everybody here. I knew all about you too and you were only here three months. You've come back into that cave you call yourself see what's left. Strip-mined, plumbed of natural resources. You should see my house: House of the Strip-mined, nothing but ghosts. I hear a thousand voices, all the time, every single minute. There's ghosts in my mind too. I've got comedians, kings, pickpockets, any kind of bastard you can think of. I can't get any sleep.

"Did she ever talk about me, compare me to you? I bet that pissed you off, didn't it? Happened to me too. Never a good comparison. I bet her first boyfriend, some little shit three feet tall, had it up to here with her talking about fairy tale princes. Any goddamned thing she can think of to cut your nuts off, she'd do it. 'A plumber!' she used to say to me. 'A toilet cleaner!' 'That's right, a necessary and important career,' I'd say, and she'd shake like she was having an earthquake. But with all her promises, I started thinking about it. Why not? My dad worked hard enough for 10 men. That left nine more after me who wouldn't have to work. I tried it for a summer, the one before you first came to town. I lived like a king. She had it worked out that we'd move together, New York City in my case. All I had to do was not eat dinner with the goddamned salad fork. But then, every time I ate that summer, staring across the table at her with that salad fork in my hand--you know. Her spidery nature couldn't help but emerge."

Charley watched the rows and rows of corn stream past, splitting moonlight, and remembering, said, "The day before we left, a plague of caterpillars covered the house."

"That happened every year," Julia said. "It had nothing to do with you."

"Well, now I'm lost," Charley said, and though the moon was swelled full with light he did not know how to navigate by the celestial. "I'll be goddamned if I know which way to go." An untrained captain, piloting a ship lost in a sea of corn, he said, "So then tell me what to do. I'm listening."

"If I were you I'd drink myself to death," Julia said.

"Fall in love, and forget about me--her--us," the ghost said.

"No, no, no," the stranger said. "I'll tell you what I'd do. Actually, I'll tell you what I've done. I mean what I did all those years ago, between when I told her to get lost and when she made you get lost? I retired from that part of life is what I did. I told myself, Harry, Harold, Wicker, that part of life is gone for you now. Most people need something to recover from--a hangover, sickness, anything--before they get to dusk, to music. But I tell you, say goodnight to that spidery bitch. Tell him, ghost. You're just playing with time, thinking about her the way you do. Playing tricks with your mind."

"Yes," the ghost said.

Harry said: "Would you like us all to come together, now, your little Greek chorus? Even Julia, for we need her wasp-filled throat to sing this tune."

"We all agree on this?" Charley asked.

Julia sighed. "Harry's right this time: I have to sing with these fuckers if that's what you want."

They sang a terrible sounding song, arrhythmic, full of grunts and moans. It was a song that would give anyone a headache. Charley's head did indeed begin to ache, fiercer and fiercer until he could hardly see. Then the car shot into a cornfield, straight across the rows. Ears of corn splayed off the windshield into the black. The tires caught mud ruts, choked, spun, slamming over row after row.

Then the car seemed to find its way onto a road--certainly Charley had nothing to do with its sudden success. "Here I am," he said, realizing he was in control of the car and, even more surprisingly, alone, hearing no voices. He began to diagnose himself. He saw his symptoms clearly now. They made sense, like a once impossibly complicated math problem. "There's nothing wrong at you at all," he said. "All of these things have been in your head and if you scratch your ass and see, you'll see it turns red, as any ass should when scratched." To speak to ghosts, to have conversations with ex-lovers of his wife, to hear Julia's recriminations still, all of these things were as funny to look at as an ancient security blanker or set of training wheels.

That night he put them all away in the attic, where no one but spiders would visit them again, and he dreamed of new strangers, who had never heard his name, or the name of anyone he knew, and despite feeling quite strange and not a little frightened, he was glad at the mystery he found outside himself. He was glad at the time he found there, which passed so naturally that eventually it disappeared, like the painted yellow lines of a parking lot.

TOMB OF THE LOST VAMPIRE
Ron Garmon

Boyd Caddington stood before the barred gate, feeling his stomach clench a large, jagged rock. It was one of those impossibly sunny Friday afternoons for which the San Fernando Valley is noted, but Boyd, reared in the haze of Hackensack, could do little better than squint moronically down the cracked and weedy sidewalk, only now discovering he'd left his sunglasses in the car.

The upper windows of the large ramshackle house behind the gate were visible from the street. Boyd could've sworn he saw a light flick off behind one of shutters. A bleached-out note laboriously stapled to the wooden door read DELIVERIES IN BACK in neat block letters. There was, as he already knew, no mailbox.

The fading sun was prickling Boyd's hairless scalp. He saw no obvious ingress into the alleyway GPS assured him was behind the house. Given the keyed-up state of his nerves, Boyd couldn't have known how long he'd been standing there twitching before a passing skatekid slid to a wobbly halt next to him, opining in confidential tones how the old dude never went anywhere anymore.

"Wait," squawked Boyd, "You mean you've *seen* him?"

"Oh, I've *seen* him," the kid snorted, "Me and my brothers did yardwork for him last Fall."

That means he'd been inside that wall. Maybe

even in the house. Boyd was dumbfounded and it showed.

"What does he look like?" Boyd asked.

"Gimme five dolla," the kid demanded. He was eleven and had seen 'em come and go on this street.

Boyd blinked and scarcely felt the note leave his hand.

"He's old. Badass. Walks with a stick," The kid popped off his board nimbly and began to circle Boyd, eyeing him while miming the famous drag-footed walk. "My dad say he got all the wimmen back in the day, but he is one *fugly* bootch now," the kid laughed, "My brother, he rent that dude's janky-ass old vampire movie an' even the bitches he was chewin' on must be at least a hundred by now." The little dreadlocked imp cackled merrily at the thought of dry dead old bitches glazing in the sun somewhere.

"Is he alive?" Boyd blurted, but his head was swimming too badly to feel foolish.

The kid just started at him, blinking and smiling. "He was when he paid us last September or so." He gestured vaguely toward the roof where a palm frond lay curled in advanced decay. "You see lights go on and off upstairs at night and shadows though the slats sometimes. He got a *big* sweet-ass old Bugatti in the garage, but I ain't never seen it on the street. Probably don't run no more"

Boyd's heart was racing. The other three addresses were washouts. The first led to a heavily barred warehouse downtown on Mateo Street. Rusty

signage on an iron door read "LPK Properties, Inc."
The second turned out to be a battered apartment
building in Lincoln Heights where nobody spoke
English and residents set dogs on him. The third
Boyd had already Yelped out as a thriving residential
hotel situated at the corner of Normandie and 87th.
Boyd dutifully drove past it anyway, this time
staying in the rental car. No way would *his* guy live
there.

This decaying Spanish-style house some distance
from the NoHo arts district was paydirt.

At once he thought of his investment.

"Has anyone *else* been by here looking for Mister,
er..., um..."

The kid laughed, thanked him for the money,
bitch, and skated away, wheels clacking *dip-shit, dip-
shit, dip-shit* in two-syllable commentary.

Boyd's specialty in life was ignoring the obvious
and it had brought him this far by an ill-traveled
route. As founding publisher-editor of horror film
monthly *Gore Graphix*, he'd eked out a hole-in-the-
corner living since the early Nineties, writing about
the scary movies which were the only thing that held
his attention as obsessively as the money he never
got out of it. Authorship of five out-of-print books
added surprisingly little to fandom's stock of lore on
that curious, oft-maligned art form, and quite a lot of
that little came out of his fannish obsession with the
screen image of the man who was almost certainly
inside that house.

Retracing his steps, the writer found the alleyway

entrance hidden behind the low-hanging purple mop of a jacaranda tree; another one of those stupid things you find only in LaLa, he snorted. Boyd brought a penlight, pepper spray, heavy gloves, and a tape recorder along with his cellphone, and felt himself well-prepared. Boyd also carried a single sheet of cheap copyshop paper, folded into a compact square in an inside pocket. It was the text of a biographical essay on the Internet Movie Database authored by Boyd himself, the distillation of most of what was publicly known about the object of his queasy attentions:

BIO for LEON GREVILLE
(b. May, 1915, Indianapolis, IN, as Leon Pierce Kunze)

Tall and menacing, with broad shoulders and large, staring blue eyes, Leon Greville lumbered though fifty movies on the clubbed right foot that gave him his trademark limping gait. The future horror film star left Columbia U to join a road company of *The Petrified Forest*, understudying Humphrey Bogart in the role of Duke Mantee. Signed to Warner Bros. in '38, he played small parts in films directed by the likes of Raoul Walsh before moving on to Universal in the early forties, where he was groomed as rival to the studio's new horror star Lon Chaney, Jr. Greville's effective cameo as a lunatic villager in

The Ghost of Frankenstein (1940) led to higher profile parts. In *By Night Walk the Dead* (1941), he scored as a vengeful corpse stalking and slaying his ruined father's business partners, which included Claude Rains at his most hysterical. *Return of the Dead Man* (1944), a sequel of sorts, was the actor's last film for the studio.

Of Greville's eight Universal horrors, Joseph H. Lewis' *Bayou Beast* (1942) and *Sherlock Holmes vs. The Strangler* (1944) by Roy William Neill are notable cult films, but he also showed an unexpected flair for comedy in the 1944 farce *Ghost Catchers*. Arguably his best-known film is PRC's *Vampire City* (1946), a minor *noir* masterpiece directed by Frank Wisbar featuring Leon in a career-defining role as a psychopath (with a hinted penchant for blood-drinking) at large in fear-crazed backlot Manhattan. James Agee's tossed-off line about hunted psychopath Greville having the look of "a tender-eyed trunk murderer" stuck, and painters from Salvador Dali to Lucian Freud appropriated the actor's soulful and carnivorous eyes for some of their bleaker portrait effects.

Invalidated out of WW II service and increasingly idle as the horror boom began to fade, Greville inherited a small fortune in 1945 from sale of his late father's Indiana-based drugstore chain.

Though shrewd investment in L.A. county oil and real estate made him a millionaire by 1950, Greville continued to take occasional, often bizarre roles in films by directors as diverse as Michael Reeves, Jess Franco, and Lina Wertmuller. The actor's last appearance in a Hollywood movie was a small part in Sam Fuller's *The Big Red One* (1980) as a Nazi general, but he had a memorable bit in Lucio Fulci's *The New York Ripper* (1985) before retiring a semi-recluse, reportedly to Europe.

Fun Facts! Half of Greville's fifty films were made during his time at Warners and Universal, with most either gangster or horror outings. He avoided television, apart from interviews and a single 1965 episode of *The Addams Family*.

Like fellow Warners player Humphrey Bogart, Greville was an avid amateur chess player and the two maintained a friendly rivalry at the game, continuing to play by mail as Leon became more reclusive and Bogie's health worsened. Greville defeated Bobby Fischer in fifteen moves in a private 1960 match and is considered by many a leading endgame theorist.

His scene in Stanley Kramer's *It's a Mad, Mad, Mad, Mad World* (1963) as the bellowing redneck in a pickup truck who drives hitchhiker Don Knotts to a flaming death was deemed too violent and cut from general release, though the footage survives on DVD.

A specialist in thug and villain roles when not playing outright monsters, Greville, by one fan's count, committed in excess of one hundred onscreen murders.

A lifelong bachelor, Greville knew considerable success as a ladies' man, with his name romantically linked to a long string of actresses, including Evelyn Ankers, Malia Nurmi, and Angelique Pettyjohn. Sixties cover girl Donyale Luna was briefly his mistress.

His last public appearance was on a 1987 West German television programme, where he casually mentioned he'd fired his agent and would happily kill anyone who tried to hire him ever again.

Boyd had decided that the nearly $101,000 in securities, money orders, and uncashed checks were impractical to lug to either a first meeting or burglary, so these were left in the car he parked near the Red Line station. These weren't the only things the writer found when he kicked in the door of the tiny house trailer in Pahrump, Nevada early that morning, but they were the most valuable. Boyd had vaguely heard of things like "mail drops" on cop-show TV, but it wasn't until he was tearing open envelopes from a dizzying array of gilt-edged senders all bearing the magical name "Leon Pierce

Kunze" that he understood what they were for. Postmarks made it plain no one had been by to pick this shit up since late last year. Who knew a decade's worth of fitful effort to locate some screwloosed old actor would lead to *this*?

There was no one around for miles to hear Boyd's caws of unhinged delight at finding the hoard before he found the man who owned it.

After that, it was a simple matter of sleepless driving and address chasing. Boyd kept himself awake by mental calculations comparing the relative value of Leon Greville alive and talking or dead and forgotten. Twin vistas of profit and/or notoriety shimmered before him, each permutated potentiality more dazzling than the last.

The alleyway turned out to be broad and spacious; nothing like the death traps Boyd knew back in Jersey, so he relaxed somewhat. Some sprawling three-story apartment complex dominated most of the block and the air was heavy with jasmine and cooking. The few houses further down were surrounded by a series of tall fences, with the most forbidding by far being the stout redwood plank and razor-wire combination guarding the house of the reclusive movie monster.

The door sported a barred window taped over from the inside and no exterior handle, but Boyd was relieved to see the wall reach to only about eight feet or so, up to more razor wire. There wasn't even a "No Trespassing" sign on the garage door; nothing but a formidable padlock.

Boyd snorted and paced the alley, eventually lifting his eyes from his oversized Reeboked feet to spy a battered mattress propped upright against a fence two houses past Greville's. Wrestled from a dumpster the night before by a migrant hurting for sleep between jobs, the filthy collapsed thing was no great effort for Boyd to pull thirty yards, but still only half a solution. Sweat, unimpeded by hair, made a sodden mess of his collar and this didn't make for clear thinking.

Boyd was in the act of wheeling an ottoman salvaged some blocks away when he spied a child's small trampoline incautiously unattended in a well-manicured backyard. Dropping one burden, he took up this other, thinking – correctly, as it turned out – it better suited to his purpose. Little seemed to disturb the dense quiet of the neighborhood and the only other humans Boyd saw as he scuttled back with his find were fellow transients too worn with their own mumbled cares to notice him.

Once back, Boyd paused to take a few deep breaths, taking care to fish the muted cellphone from his pocket as a means of keeping his mind occupied lest he talk himself out of this ad-hoc breaking-and-entry. It was just then four twenty-seven p.m. PST and Boyd hadn't slept in over thirty hours.

In a lung-wrenching burst of effort, Boyd picked up and flung the smelly mattress over a spot on the razor wire well away from the door, lurching back to admire the way it draped over the coils. He was pleased with the progress of his rudimentary idea and noted happily that plenty of greenery and at least one parked car obscured the view from the nearest street. He dragged the trampoline over for a few giddy practice bounces before suddenly bounding rabbitlike over the wall, hitting the mattress with his ample middle.

The bounce from the coiled wire worked rather better than expected, taking Boyd ass-over-shoulders all the way over before he could take hold of the mattress to break his fall, as he'd hoped. The mattress flopped back into the alley, where a homeless wino spent the night on it. The stolen trampoline vanished many hours before, when Papa found it and dragged it home, cursing how the 'hood had gone truly to Hell if shit like this can happen.

***

The wino's snores were loud, but it was a spritz of icy water from the broken sprinkler slapping Boyd's face that finally woke him up. The moon hung hugely in the night-time sky and this very amateur cracksman stilled his nerves by focusing on its grinning face. Boyd found himself lying among wet weeds on some heavy discarded blanket with no more than overall stiffness for his folly.

He slowly made out a grey, weirdly forked shape massed a few yards away. Creaking to his feet, Boyd crept closer to take in the second of the night's many surprises- a large metal crossbow squatting lethally on the concrete walkway, with nylon cord rigged from the inside handle to the trigger. A sharp metal bolt was pointed squarely at the door. *Holy. Fucking. Shit.*, he gasped.

A sudden sharp pain in his foot made him yip and topple over on the patio stones. Carefully, Boyd removed a homemade caltrop from his shoe, stifling an urge to whimper as he spotted a half-dozen others left widely scattered on the grass and walkway. He gasped as a light came on from behind a shuttered upstairs window, holding his breath until it flicked off again.

The back door, to Boyd's surprise, was not only unlocked but ever so slightly ajar. This was worse news to the writer's hammering heart than the siege engine, never mind the activity inside the house. A nearby window was cracked and slightly open, showing every sign of forced entry, but thick dust and yard debris indicated no one had stood in this spot for months.

Boyd noted the faded 1960s-era red, white & blue stamp on the cracked glass reading HOUSE PROTECTED BY OWNER, but the new-blossoming green LED of the surveillance camera above his head failed to register, likely because of the black tape placed over it. The lens swerved to watch his progress across the lot from the moment he began moving across the yard.

Boyd gingerly inched the window open and limped inside the house.

To his left, he saw a crude wooden brace nailed into the bare floorboards, with another unfamiliar rope-and-pulley arrangement on the ceiling, only with the rope dangling cut. Padding on his bruised foot, Boyd began to feel his way around what seemed like a carefully bricked wall of cardboard boxes of various sizes, making a walkway barely four feet across and stacked to the ceiling as far as his fingers could reach. He could make out flickers from some distant reflected light and there were faint tinny murmurs from upstairs.

Suddenly the light snapped on overhead and Boyd gaped madly around in terror at nothing at all but stacks and crates of boxes, some open and overflowing with papers.

Nothing moved and Boyd held his breath, expecting his life to end any second. When the light winked back out thirty seconds later, he whimpered at the blackness, only to hear himself improbably alive within it.

A long, uncertain interval passed as first feeling, then movement, returned to Boyd's limbs. The faint noises in the distance definitely sounded prerecorded to him, some of it faintly familiar, which creeped him out as much as anything yet. He fumbled out his penlight, clicked it on, and began to scope out the ground floor.

Boyd recognized original posters for *Bayou Beast* and *Return of the Dead Man* moldering in frames on the walls behind heaps of bursting cardboard. Decades' worth of play-by-mail chess games littered the floor, along with bills bearing a half dozen addresses and heaps of yellowed hand-scrawled envelopes addressed to as many more. The kitchen was a horror of heaped dried plates and crusted cans. Boyd fumbled though an imposing assortment of vials and pill bottles arrayed on a dusty oak table-codeine, oxycodone, hydrocodone, Inderal, Hydergine, Selegiline, Warfarin, Lipitor, Xanax, and big inhalers of something called Salbutamol, which Boyd fancied as compensation for seventy years of baking inside the brown L.A. air.

The front door appeared unblocked, as did the other two doors in the front parlor, though the windows were taped-over and heavily draped. Sections of tape were cut out at eye level allowing a view of the padlocked front gate. Boyd could just make out three fat sticks of what Boyd took to be dynamite wired to the door just below the handle. Another light abruptly went on, this time in the kitchen Boyd just left. He stood unblinking and rigid with shock until it cut off ten seconds later.

Boyd flicked out the penlight and began to squeeze his nerves back in place. The dust, crust, and neglect of the house told him that, despite all appearances, it was Powerball odds Leon Greville was dead on the premises, most likely upstairs. Of the ancillary phenomena around him, he had no clue at all. The sudden hum of an air-conditioning system plunged the ambient temperature still further, but Boyd scarcely noticed as he limped into the dim light still flickering on the upper floor.

From the landing, Boyd could see a thin rectangle wedge of plasma screen. Dancing on its wide surface was the last reel of *Vampire City*, the scene where Greville finally spills his guts to unsympathetic Ann Savage-

FRANZ: This is how the common herd always treats genius!

SUE (spits): *Genius?* Yer nothin' but a gimpy freak they're gonna send to the Chair!

FRANZ: You don't understand. (Slumps toward her, cracking knuckles one by one) People like you are born, live a little while, then die. People like me are rare, irreplaceable, and *would* die if not for the life you temporarily possess.

(They struggle; SUE screams)

The stairs creaked, of course. Gingerly climbing up them, Boyd turned to see a long-settled avalanche of boxes and yellowing paper spilling from the nearest second floor room, blanching when he realized the nifty looking cufflink glittering at his feet was attached to a human hand. A broken shotgun lay on the hallway carpet nearby, its former wielder buried under the heap. A solution to the mysteries of the wrecked window and botched booby-trap would've suggested itself to someone less mind-blown than Boyd.

The programming on the screen smash-cut into the jitterbug sequence of *Ghost Catchers*, and Boyd's shaky knees bent until he lighted on the top step, well away from his grisly find. There was very little meat left on the bone and the fingers were like curled strips of bacon, but the sleeve of the suit attached looked new, if dusty. Boyd thought of digging into the spilled tons of bundled mail, 1950s-vintage paperbacks, back issues of *Playboy*, *Oui*, and *Psychotronic Video* for some equivalent to a formal introduction, but well-advanced squeamishness stayed him.

Instead, he settled in to watch the merry film. He knew this bit really well- a comic swing-dance sequence with pudgy comics Ole Olsen and Chic Johnson crammed into zoot-suits and cutting up with the rest of the cast, including Leon Greville popping in-and-out of closets with an outrageously oversized axe. Kirby Grant and his Orchestra were rocking the joint and Ella Mae Morse's brassy voice rang, *"Quoth the Raven, you have found me with my best foot in the groove."*

Boyd's eyes wandered the splendid corridor. Unlike the confusing heap downstairs, the hallway was neat and orderly, except for the catastrophe that buried Mister Cufflink. Dim light peeked through from one of the two open doors at the end of the hallway.

The number ended with another abrupt edit, this time to the start of Greville's unbearably slow-strangulation of blonde Judy Huxtable in the gory *Nazi on Blood Island*. This was one of Boyd's favorites among Leon's many kills, but curiosity inched him down the hall, where he peered into the wider-open of the two doors. By penlight's gleam, he took in the outlines of an impressive array of film-editing and telecine hardware; ancient personal video recorders, scanners, and reels of 16mm and Super-8 film, discarded beside the dead eyes of several cathode-ray tubes. Boyd counted among his few friends back in Jersey one DVD pirate with a lot of this same stuff.

Boyd went back into the hallway, where Ilona Massey was whimpering her last in *The Mummy's Grasp*, as insane cryptkeeper Leon shoved her half-naked into the scorpion pit. From this angle, the screen looked dimmer and more blurry, as if this show had been running many weeks for few customers. He paused before the other half-open door, expecting to find some kind of final answer to an increasingly obvious riddle inside.

Sure enough, there was a dead man in the room, but that small relief didn't help. Sitting as he was in a tall reclining chair before three laptops and a bank of TV screens giving closed-circuit views of various spots inside and out of the house, Leon Greville looked as deceased as five months or so inanition could make him. Ants had long since disposed of those famous eyes, but their sockets were almost as striking in their gnawed emptiness. The dressing gown the actor was wearing was filthy, but looked expensive when new. It was also open, revealing little save twin lengths of well-rotted thigh.

Boyd's mind heaved and squirmed, yet clung to the obvious fact there was nothing to fear. The master of the house was indisputably dead and he was unlikely to be disturbed again anytime soon.

The laptops were still on and Boyd tickled the middle one to life. The man paused in the middle of some really horrific doings onscreen was definitely Leon Greville, but the other two cast members were not-terribly charismatic unknowns. The face of the girl tied to the chair was out of focus and partially erased by duct tape, but the frame was dominated by the other, a redhead with pale skin heavily seamed with welts and a face purpling from strangulation. Greville was using a silk scarf, just like in *Return of the Dead Man*.

Boyd pressed PLAY.

The original film source must have been some sometime in the Fifties, an impression sustained by Greville's receding scalp and the brunette's battered bouffant hairdo. The camera, by some stroke of auteur genius, caught the light dying in the redhead's eyes better than any Hammer or Cinecitta cameraman ever could. The sound recording on the ambient screams and pleas as Greville cut the brunette loose and proceeded to rape her was a bit off, despite indications of post-production tinkering. Shot from above, in an unadorned bare room containing a mattress and three chairs, the angle allowed for about as much camera mobility as some of Lugosi's Monogram flicks, but the action on the screen was far more naturalistic, as befitted Greville's style as an actor. The drain in the middle of the concrete floor was prominently visible and efficient.

Greville hung the first corpse from a just-visible hook and proceeded to skin her on-camera, his naked chest gleaming with spilled blood.

Nauseated, Boyd fast-forwarded, skimming the scummy veneer of what looked like hundreds of hours of self-made torture film and video, captured by increasingly sophisticated equipment and displaying a surer hand over time. A half-minute's viewing of a file irresistibly titled *1979 Tranny Bitch* was enough to clearly indicate an older, more deliberate artist. The set was different and better designed and the actor also mastered audio well enough to give himself a few lines of ludicrous racist dialogue.

Boyd pressed PAUSE. He'd once crashed a showing of Pasolini's *Salo* somewhere in the East Village and left shamefacedly after his penis went erect. That was the only experience Boyd's addled wits could summon that even remotely compared and he clung to it fiercely. He'd heard of the guy who ran wild for twenty-five years, stuffing dead hookers into dumpsters all over South Central and that mook didn't have one-hundredth of Greville's resources.

Inquiry of the other two laptops revealed a giant cache of pain and trauma images and –far more to Boyd's liking – the power and security controls to the house. The lights that seemed to go on and off at eccentric random were precisely that. Greville had apparently wanted to give every sign of lively animation even as his wits and strength faded.

Now, Boyd was thinking about how this place was somebody else's goldmine.

Correctly assuming purpose would look every bit as random as purposelessness, Boyd switched on a few interior lights, starting with the room he was in, unlocking the back gate as an afterthought. Looking around for something easily fungible, his eyes lit upon Lucien Freud's sketch of the actor hanging above the dead man's desk. The fanzine editor only knew who the painter was at all because of the semi-famous study done of the actor now hanging at the Tate or someplace. Once the media shitbomb ticking all around him inevitably blew, this daub would be worth millions; perhaps tens of millions. Who was to know?

Boyd lifted it from the wall and practically skipped downstairs, pausing reverently before the last half-minute of *For a Price, Sartana Will Send Your Soul to Hell*, a 1973 Eurowestern in which father Leon Greville and son William Berger cheerfully gunned down twenty bounty hunters before putting as many squibbed bullet holes into each other. Boyd always liked that one too, and wondered idly how much a 35 mm print would cost. He was going to find out.

Despite fresh illumination in the kitchen and back patio, Boyd turned right instead of left at a crucial juncture in the box maze, stepping on a cartridge trap that sent a .44 caliber bullet messily through his right foot before proceeding upward through his soft palate. The top of Boyd's head exploded, shutting him off like a blown forty-watt bulb. Dense blocks of cardboard deadened the noise almost as well as the professional sound-proofing job Greville had done on the house back in the Fifties. From the street, there was no more sound than a trapped rat would make.

Tow trucks came for Boyd's rental car mid-morning on Monday, about twelve hours before a three-man burglary gang in a battered white van pulled up outside the alleyway fence he'd climbed. The lights had been burning the entire weekend and the old fuck inside had to be dead at last. A half-minute later, the van went roaring back to Pacoima minus diminutive ex-con Manny Escobar-Hinton, age 27 and just then shuddering his last on the public gravel with an eighteen-inch spike cracked through his face. News chopper footage of the house ran on the eleven o'clock news when police found the front gate of some unremarkable old house in NoHo wired with enough dynamite, announcers raved, to make a crater of this quiet residential street. Reporters ferreted out the magic name "Leon Greville" with far greater ease than the luckless Boyd, who provided a remarkably whole specimen among the parts of some fifty-seven human beings found in the house, most of them buried in the vast basement that also served as playroom, studio, and principal set.

Some individual human fragments were found to predate Greville's purchase of the house in 1943, a fact not widely commented upon in the press.

RALPHS MARKET AT MIDNIGHT
IN VAN NUYS, CALIFORNIA
Iris Berry

The lights are cruel
at the Ralphs Market
in Van Nuys
on Burbank
and Van Nuys Boulevard
at midnight
on the 1st of December.

It's the last month of the year
and apparently it's Christmas
according to the aisles at Ralphs market.
But if I had to guess by the customers
I'd say it was Halloween.

It's desperate here at Ralphs
In Van Nuys at midnight,
and the lights don't help any.
Florescent lights are never good for the complexion.
There's a young,
homeless couple
walking the aisles,
buying food
and looking happy,
at least they're in a relationship,
is what I say.
Freshly home from a trip
To "The Big Apple,"

I went with my boyfriend
and came home single.
We had to go 3,000 miles to do that?
It happened in bed
in the dark
in a dingy Times Square hotel room
or at least that's what they called it
I've stayed in crack motels that smelled better….
It was epic
and when that plane landed
20 hours later…
on California soil
I clicked my heels together
and quietly chanted;
there's no place like home,
there's no place like home,
there's no place like home.
And now
here I am
at home
in my neighborhood Ralphs market
feeling like an alien.

The thing about sunny California
is the only way to tell the seasons
is by what's selling on the shelves
at the markets.
I have a thing for the market
somehow it's a form of meditation for me
nothing in there
reminds me of my life.

I can do this...
I'm a spiritual giant
In the frozen food section
I'm Gandhi
In the greeting card section
and I'm Mother Teresa in the check-out line
forgiving all the tabloid sinners
and connecting with something
greater than all of this.

Credit or debit?
Paper or plastic?
Peace, please?
I'd like to give it a chance
after all
it is the Holidays.

Apophenia is an imprint of
www.paraphiliamagazine.com

For more information and to purchase other titles:
http://www.paraphiliamagazine.com/books.html